I0526038

The Stars Always Fall

Andi J. Feron

Copyright © 2024 by Unchained Imagination Publishing LLC

All rights reserved.

No portion of this book may be reproduced in any form without written permission from the publisher or author, except as permitted by U.S. copyright law.

Ebook ISBN: ISBN: 978-1-951802-26-4

Paperback ISBN: 978-1-951802-27-1

Contents

The Attic

Bryn

"You have to pee again?" Lachlan hollered from the bedroom.

"You don't have to stay up. Go back to sleep." I was miserable, huge, and exhausted.

He stood in the doorway, staring at me. "I'm worried is all. This has to be the tenth time tonight."

"It's normal. The doctor said so. The baby is low and constantly on my bladder. When will this baby come out?" I groaned and buried my face in my hands.

"You hit your due date three days ago. It can't be much longer."

"Tell *your* child that. Tell the baby they should be here already."

He walked over and bent down, rubbing his hands on my belly. "Come on, baby. Mommy is tired of you using her womb as a hideout. Make an appearance already." The baby kicked his hand, probably in protest. "Are you done yet? You've been sitting for a long time. You have a big day tomorrow."

"I'm done. I just don't think I can get up."

"My poor girl." He kissed my forehead then helped me to my feet. I washed my hands, and we climbed into bed. He rubbed my back until I drifted back to sleep.

Our alarm went off too early, and I groaned. "I need another hour."

Lachlan kissed me. "You're going to miss the interview."

"Oh no! I forgot. Help me up."

Lachlan chuckled, pulling me off the bed. He kissed my belly. "Morning, baby." He helped me put on my pants, socks, and shoes.

I glanced in the mirror. "I look insanely bloated."

"You look beautiful."

"Bloated is beautiful to you?"

"You having my baby is beautiful. You don't look bloated. You look nine months pregnant."

The doorbell rang, and I was glad they were coming to the house instead of me having to travel. My OB wouldn't have let me anyway. I'd been put on bed rest because of blood pressure issues. We were renting a house twenty minutes from our actual home because Lachlan didn't want me to be tempted to work.

We usually lived on-site of a home for human trafficking victims. I was the director, but for the last ten weeks, my sister and her fiancé had run it for us. I'd also hired some new people to help. My leave of absence would extend until my baby was four months. I couldn't wait to get back. I missed my girls too much.

Lachlan let the reporters in, and they set up. The reporter started right in with the broadcast. "We have Bryn West with us today, folks. She's talking about her organization that helps human trafficking victims recover. Bryn would you like to tell us a little bit about what inspired you to create the nonprofit?"

"My inspiration stemmed from my own personal story. When I was three, I was taken by my nanny and integrated into an underground community. The family who kidnapped me also took five other girls who I see as my sisters. All of us suffered immense abuse for years, and one of my sisters never made it out of the cave."

"I'm sorry to hear that. Can you tell us a little bit about your organization?"

"The organization is called Jada's House. I named it after my little sister who died in the cave. We take women rescued from traffickers and give them a safe place to stay for as long as they need. We also help them with education and personal goals. We set them up with on-site counseling and help them rebuild their lives."

"That is absolutely amazing."

The reporter asked me several more questions, including where everyone could donate. He and I thanked each other, and the interview concluded. When everyone left, I headed back to the bedroom for a nap. Lachlan stepped out of the room, startling me.

I screamed. "Are you trying to scare the baby out?"

"No, but we could try again if you think it will work." He pulled me as close as my giant belly would allow. "I'm so incredibly proud of you, Mrs. West."

"Are you trying to earn brownie points?"

"Did it work?"

"Yes, you naturally earn them just by being you."

"I have a bath waiting for you." He led me to the bathroom, where we climbed into the tub together. I leaned back against him in the water and dozed. In Lachlan's arms, I could sleep anywhere. I loved our wonderful life together.

I rubbed my belly, trying to make the cramping go away. It felt more intense than normal, but I didn't think it was contractions either. It started about ten hours ago, and I hadn't slept at all. It was now five days passed my due date, and the baby was still tucked in tight. Lachlan had an ER shift for the next twelve hours but promised to keep his phone close. I could always take a cab to the hospital, and since he worked there, he could walk right over to the maternity ward.

I stood back and looked at the gorgeous nursery my mother had designed. We wouldn't even be staying in this house long, and she'd still fixed it up. The theme was sun, moon, and stars. When the lights were shut off, constellations brought the ceiling to life. A beautiful mural with the planets, stars, and a colorful nebula painted the wall next to the large mahogany crib. Lachlan had struggled with that project, but he didn't give up. I had yet to tell him that the little crescent moons and stars should face the outside of the crib.

Ryo entered the nursery and held a brown paper bag, wiggling it in the air. "I got the goods."

I leaped at him and threw my arms around his neck, giving him a kiss on the check. "You are the best bestie ever!" I snatched the bag away and grabbed the first donut. It practically melted in my mouth, and I closed my eyes, savoring it. When I opened them again, I saw Ryo looking amused. "What?" I mumbled with my mouth still half full.

He held up his phone. "I just sent this to Lachlan."

I shrugged. "He sees me stuff my face hourly." I pushed past him and made my way up the stairs. I huffed and puffed all the way to the top. I tugged on the door to the attic. It was the most annoying door ever and often got stuck. You had to do this weird wiggly thing with the latch. I finally got it open, and a set of stairs descended. I started climbing.

"What are you doing?" Ryo stood on the bottom step.

"I'm getting all the things I stored in here for baby. When we moved in, I had the movers put them up here so my mom could design the nursery."

"Come back down. Your waddle is a little too unstable for such heights."

Ryo climbed the rest of the way while I buried my head in a cabinet, trying to remember where I'd left the crescent moon lamp. I heard a click and stopped.

Oh no! He didn't!

"Please tell me you didn't just close the attic." I didn't turn around because I didn't want to see.

"I can't really tell you that. Is that a problem?"

I walked over and tried to push on it. "Yeah, it's stupid and can only open from downstairs. "

"Who designed it that way?"

"Someone with little brains."

"Winnie the Pooh?"

I squinted. "What?"

"You know he's a bear of little brains. You need to know of all of this so you can acclimate the little bambino to necessary kid stuff."

"Right, but no, I'm pretty sure a bear didn't design this. Why did you shut it?"

"I didn't want you falling down it on my watch."

"You could have just waited at the bottom and caught me."

He thought for a minute. "Hmmm... You're probably right. I'll just kick it open." Ryo gave a good attempt, and it didn't budge. "I guess I shouldn't skip leg day after all."

"It's not a big deal. You have your phone, right?"

He pulled it from his pocket. "Yeah, I have it. You aren't going to like it, though."

"Why is that?" I looked at his screen and groaned. "No service. Seriously?"

"Sorry. We just have to stay in here until Lachlan gets home."

"Yeah, in twelve hours!" I rubbed the sharp pain in my back.

"Oh. We might as well make use of this time. Let's play charades."

"You're serious?"

"Yeah, I'll go first." He flapped his hands and ran in a circle.

"You look ridiculous."

"Wrong. You get two more guesses."

"I don't think that's how it works."

He kept flapping his arms. "You're just afraid to lose."

"Fine. I'll play your stupid game. You're a bird."

"Yes, but what kind of bird."

I scowled. "Seriously?"

"Loser."

I narrowed my eyes at him. "Did you seriously just call me a loser?"

"I did. Because that's what you are when you forfeit."

"Fine! You're a dodo bird." I plopped down in an old chair, trying to ease my aching back.

"Wrong again."

"I'm pretty sure I got it right."

"Nope. I'm an owl," he said.

"How was I supposed to know that?"

"By knowing my love of Harry Potter. Alright, your turn."

I bent over and clutched my stomach.

"You got in the swimming pool too soon after eating?"

I grimaced and shook my head.

"You are a robber that got punched in the stomach by the home owner."

"Ryo?"

"Yes?"

"Stop talking. Please."

"What's wrong?" His tone turned serious.

I gripped the side of the desk next to me and closed my eyes. "More cramps."

"What?! No, Bryn. You aren't allowed to have cramps in front of me. Not when you're forty weeks pregnant."

"You tell them to stop then!" I snapped, and he looked stricken.

He began jumping on the door. He threw a large weight on it and tried several other maneuvers to open it.

"Ow! Ow!"

He looked the palest I'd ever seen him. "This isn't happening. You're having the baby, aren't you?"

"I think I might be. It takes hours, though, so quit panicking."

"I'm going out the window."

I looked up at the small window the size of a basketball and almost laughed. I gripped the table. I couldn't be having this baby now. My mom and Lachlan were supposed to hold my hands while I pushed my baby out. It was going to be a magical experience. This couldn't happen in my attic with Ryo while he had a panic attack. I slid to the floor, still gripping the desk. Ryo tried for the next six hours to find a way out. I writhed in pain while my cramping more clearly became contractions. I heaved my breakfast into a drawer in an empty dresser. Ryo came over and held my hair out of the way.

He rubbed my back. "It's okay. Bryn, it's okay." He didn't sound convincing.

"Ryo?" I panted between contractions and shook uncontrollably. "You're going to have to deliver this baby."

"No! You said we have hours."

"It's been hours."

"Not enough."

"I think I've been in labor longer, but I thought they were bad cramps." I moaned as the sharpest contraction yet rolled across my abdomen. I felt a strange pop and water pooled underneath me.

Ryo's eyes grew big. "Oh, no!" He picked up a baseball and chucked it at the window. He typed into his phone and squeezed both arms out the window as far as he could reach them. "The message sent!"

I clawed at the floor, trying not to scream. "What message?"

"To your husband."

"Let's hope it's not in his locker." I huffed.

"There's no way his phone isn't attached to him with you this pregnant."

Time felt as foreign as it did the first time that I left the cave. I couldn't tell how long it had been since his message supposedly sent. Ryo sat behind me, and I leaned against him.

"Foo Foo hee hee foo foo hee hee foo." Odd sounds came out of Ryo.

"What are you doing? You sound like a dying train that smoked ten packs of cigarettes a day."

"I'm showing you how to breathe properly."

"That's not how you breathe properly," I snapped as another contraction rocked me.

"I guess I should have gone to Lamaze classes with you."

I elbowed him and gripped his leg hard, riding out the next contractions. "How long has it been since your message sent?"

"About an hour."

"I don't think he got it. Ouch. This hurts so bad. Ryo!" I squeezed his leg again.

"Man! I definitely feel your pain."

I had my eyes clenched tight when I felt a gush of air. I glanced up to see Lachlan with his head in the attic. I wanted to run to him but couldn't move. I gripped Ryo's legs again and let out a scream. Familiar arms wrapped around me.

"It's okay. I have you now. It's going to be okay." Lachlan scooped me up. "You're going to have to walk down the attic steps, and from there, I got you."

I shook my head. "I can't!" I cried.

"You have to."

"I have to push!"

"No, don't do that."

"I have to!"

Lachlan shoved at Ryo. "Go wait for the ambulance. They should be about here."

"I've decided the baby can just stay in. I won't complain any-more!" I screamed.

Lachlan smiled. "I think it's a little late for that."

I gripped his hand. "You need to catch the baby." I gave three almost on involuntary pushes.

Lachlan looked almost horrified. "Okay. I guess we're doing this. Bryn, sweetie, on your next contraction push."

I glared at him. "Like I have a choice."

He laughed and took off his jacket. I pushed and pushed. I didn't think I'd ever give birth. I fell back exhausted as our baby was born into Lachlan's arms. I glanced up to see tears streaming down his face. "She's beautiful," he said with awe in his voice.

"We have a girl?"

He nodded with a smile. "Luna Sky." Lachlan handed her to me and put his arms around us both. A few minutes later, the EMTs arrived and helped us down from the attic. Ryo peeked at our baby as they wheeled me to the ambulance.

"Yay! I'm an Uncle." He patted one of the EMTs on the shoulder. "I'm an uncle!"

"Congrats," the EMT said unenthusiastically.

"Hey Lachlan, I'm an Uncle!" Ryo beamed.

"Hey, Ryo, I'm a father!" Lachlan beamed back.

"Best day for both of us!" Ryo tried to climb in the ambulance with us, and the EMTs kicked him out. "I guess. I'll just meet all of you at the hospital." He pulled his keys from his pocket as the ambulance door shut.

Lullaby

Lachlan

I held Luna in my arms while Bryn slept in her hospital bed. She looked ghostly due to heavy bleeding after delivering Luna. Bryn had almost needed a blood transfusion. I offered to donate some for her just in case. My blood type was O negative, which is the universal donor. I felt better about using mine than a stranger's. Her doctors had shot my idea down.

I looked into the bright blue eyes of my daughter. Her little pink hat covered the piles of black hair on her head. I'd never seen a newborn with so much hair. She had to be the most gorgeous child to ever live. I was absolutely sure of it. I had my baby girl, and she was so much better than I'd imagined.

I let her wrap her little fist around my finger. "Do you remember me? I talked to you every day, telling you all the things we're going to do. I'm so glad you finally left your mother so we can get a start on them." She let out a little cry, and I bounced her. "Daddy's always going to fix this. He's never going to let you cry long. I'm going to protect you from everything." She cried again.

Bryn's eyes flew open. "My baby?" She looked around until her eyes landed on Luna and me.

I brought Luna and placed her in her mother's arms, and Bryn fed her. I climbed in the bed next to her. We'd made it to our family, and we were parents. Someone knocked on the door. I opened it to see Morely, Ryo, and Dahlia standing there with a pink teddy bear and balloons.

Dahlia ran for Bryn. "I want to see the baby!"

Morely quickly grabbed her and picked her up. "Slow down. You have to be gentle." Morely took Dahlia over to the sink and washed her hands.

Dahlia squirmed out of Morely's arms. "I want to see the baby!"

"It's okay. Let her sit next to me." Bryn patted the bed. When Dahlia came over, Bryn helped her hold Luna.

"I love her. She's my best friend. We're always friends. My mommy has a baby Luna in her tummy."

Bryn glanced up at Morely. "Did she just say you're..."

Morely glanced at Ryo. "Yeah, I'm pregnant. I didn't want to steal your thunder. I was going to wait for a few weeks."

Bryn held her arms out for Morely. "No, I'm so happy for you!" Bryn started crying. "This is the best news ever! My sister and best friend are having a baby." She grabbed the tissue box next to her and wept into it.

I smacked Ryo on the back. "Congrats, man!"

Ryo beamed. "Thanks!"

"You guys make me so happy." Bryn continued to carry on about Morely and Ryo's love story. "You're just the most adorable little family, and now there's going to be a miniature Ryo running around. The world needs so many more Ryos to make it random and happy." Bryn sobbed into her hand.

I elbowed him. "I think Bryn is happy for you."

He smiled at Bryn. "How can you tell?"

Morely climbed into bed next to Dahlia. The maternity beds were double the size of standard hospital beds. She took Luna from Bryn. "Look at those eyes. They're so blue."

Bryn dabbed her eyes. "If she keeps the color, they will be her daddy's eyes. You should see her hair." Bryn removed the pink hat.

"I didn't know a newborn could have so much hair. Dahlia was bald. Ryo, come look at all this hair."

Ryo came over, and Bryn looked at him. She started crying again, and he looked at her, concerned. "What is it, darling?" he asked.

"I just thought about how baby Ryo will probably come out with spiked, blue-tipped hair."

He raised an eyebrow. "And that made you cry?"

"No, the thought of there being more of you."

"Oh, I see how it is." He put his arms out. "I want to hold my niece." Morely handed him the baby, and he grinned at Luna. "She's pretty awesome. She's well made."

"Isn't she, though." I agreed with him. She was the greatest thing I'd ever done.

He held her out across his arm, carefully supporting her head. "Thank you for waiting for your daddy to show up. I owe you one, doll."

Byrn sat up. "Aww! She earned her Ryo nickname."

"Is that going to make you cry?"

"It might."

Anna, Bryn's mom, burst into the room. She ran over to the sink and washed her hands. "Where's my baby?"

Ryo handed her Luna, and Donovan, Bryn's dad, walked over and looked at Luna next to Anna. Ana, Donovan, and Ryo all gushed about Luna for the next fifteen minutes. My daughter would be well-loved her entire life. We were beyond blessed. Bryn fell asleep while everyone was still there. They all slipped out, and I held Luna. I couldn't put her down even for a second. It felt like I hadn't breathed for nine months, and finally, I'd found oxygen. My little girl had made it into the world.

"I will protect you with every ounce I have. No one will ever hurt you while I live," I whispered the promise and cradled her close.

"I'm a little worried. Is she supposed to be this tired?" I asked the doctor about Bryn when she came for morning rounds.

"Giving birth is exhausting. You add nursing every three to four hours, and it compounds it."

"She only wakes up when Luna cries."

"That's her mommy instinct. New mothers can hear their babies over anything."

I rubbed my chin, contemplating. I wasn't a doctor yet, but I felt Bryn should be awake more. "She checks out okay?"

"Yes, she's had a little more bleeding than we like, but nothing we can't manage."

"Are you watching her bleeding close?"

The doctor smiled at me. "Your wife is in excellent hands. I assure you she's doing well."

I nodded, hoping the experts were right. The doctor left, and I climbed into bed with Bryn. They'd taken Luna from me for newborn tests. I missed her. They promised she'd be back in twenty minutes and that felt too long. Bryn scooted closer to me, and I held her.

She opened her eyes and frantically looked around. "Where's Luna?"

"They took her to the nursery for tests."

"Was it a person with a purple badge?"

"Yes, I triple checked. I even took a picture of it."

She smiled. "Did you send it to Thane?"

"Maybe. Capri and Thane say congratulations, by the way. Capri hopes to get out here in a couple of weeks." Capri was Bryn's sister, and Thane was my best friend. They'd gotten married about a month before Bryn and me.

Bryn yawned. "They just need to have a baby, and the world will be perfect."

"I bet their baby comes out in a suit."

"I bet it never cries. It'll just lay in its crib until they come to feed it. It'll be the most docile baby ever."

"Wouldn't it be funny if it was an absolute firecracker?"

Bryn shook her head. "Don't curse them." She closed her eyes and nodded off.

"Bryn?"

"What?" She yawned again.

"Are you feeling okay?"

"No, I just had a baby. I'm pretty sure it's normal to feel bad." She fell back asleep.

The nurse wheeled Luna into the room. They had her in a clear cart wrapped like a baby enchilada. I had to get to her. I scooped her up and spent the rest of the morning telling her about how her mother and I fell in love. My supervisor called me.

"Hey, Rob, what's up?"

"I just got you the most amazing opportunity."

I looked at Luna, who scrunched her face. Why was she doing that? Was she having a bad dream, or was she in pain? She stopped scrunching her face and relief filled me.

Lachlan? Did you hear me? I got you an interview at Boston children's hospital. Could you imagine that for your residency? You won't have to uproot your family."

"That's awesome! That's a dream come true. When is it?"

"A week."

My heart sank. "I can't. Bryn just had our baby, Luna. I can barely put her down to go to the bathroom, let alone leave for an interview.

"This is a once in a lifetime. It's Boston children's hospital. You want to do pediatrics; it's top dog."

"Yeah, I know. I don't think I could. I couldn't leave my girls this soon."

"You're going to get your last pick. This is the rest of your life. It's only overnight. What could possibly happen with your family in one night?"

"A lot, actually." I thought back to Bryn being shot a few years ago. "Things can happen in seconds. Why do I have to stay overnight?"

"It's part of a special event with limited spots. They have a lot of interviews, and it's an elimination event. You'll pass. You have the charisma."

"I don't know."

"I'm going to leave your name on it for the next four hours. You call me if you change your mind." He hung up.

"What's a dream come true?" Bryn called from the bed with her eyes still closed.

"An interview with Boston children's hospital for my residency."

Her eyes snapped open. "You have to do it. All I've heard you say is you wish your residency could be there. It's your dream job, and we'll still be able to live at Jada's house."

It's in a week, and I'd be gone for a night. That's too soon to leave you. What if you try to do too much? There's no way I'm leaving you alone."

"You won't be. My mom lives across town. I'm sure she'll make me behave. She always does."

I looked at my perfect daughter. "I can't leave her."

"You have to leave for her. She needs her daddy happy. This is what you want."

"I want you and Luna way more."

"Will there be another chance for an interview?"

I hesitated. "No, the spots are filling up quickly."

She grabbed my hand. "If this really is your dream, you should go. It's only overnight, and I'll have my mom. Morely is a short drive away. I don't want you to miss this. You'll regret it when you spend months at a hospital that's not Boston children's." She was right. It was the opportunity of a lifetime.

I looked back and forth between her and Luna. It wasn't a long trip, and Bryn could call me for any issues. Any emergencies and I trusted her family to take care of her. I debated back and forth for two hours.

Bryn picked up my phone and handed it to me. "Call Rob and tell him you're going. Luna and I will be fine. I know the look in your eyes. You want this dream. You helped me for over a year to bring my dream to life. You help me every day with it. It's my turn to support you."

My finger hovered over the send button. "You're sure?"

"Yes."

I called Rob back and told him to put me on the list.

Just One Night

Bryn

"**A**re you feeling any better?" Lachlan felt my forehead. "You're still warm. Did you call the OB?"

"Yeah, she said if it gets to 101 to head into the emergency room. I'm fine, really. Mom is right across town, and she'll be over here a lot. She can't stand too long to pass without having her Luna time. You need to go to this interview. Boston is an amazing residency opportunity. Luna and I will be fine."

"What if she grows three inches while I'm gone? I might miss her rolling over or something big like that."

I found his worried expression cute. "You'll be back tomorrow. You're being silly."

"Babies grow a lot when they're first born."

"Seriously, Lachlan, you're going to be late."

He took Luna from my arms and cradled her close to him. "I'm going to miss you both too much to stand. Don't grow too big while I'm gone and let your mom get a little sleep. I can't put her down, Bryn. What kind of husband and father am I leaving when we have a newborn?"

"The kind of husband who wants to give his family immense opportunities. Seriously, babe, we'll be fine. I have family so close. You can't miss that interview."

He stared at Luna's face for another ten minutes before I finally took her from him. He kissed and hugged me for another five minutes. He grabbed my hand and held it as he stepped away. I smiled at him as he turned around three times before making it out the door. I fed Luna and turned on a documentary on Saturn. My phone beeped with a text message from Lachlan.

He sent: *I miss you.*

I smiled. *Luna and I miss you too.*

Him: *Should I walk back in?*

Me: *No! Luna is asleep. I'm going to catch some. You keep going.*

Him: *Fine, but I love you.*

Me: *I love you too. More than the stars.*

I reluctantly put Luna in the bassinet. I could hold her endlessly, but my body still needed sleep. I fell asleep almost immediately but woke after a short time to Luna's crying. I sat up, and my mom walked into the room.

She scooped up Luna and smiled lovingly at her. "How are you feeling?"

"Exhausted."

"You look flush." She walked around and touched my forehead. "You have a fever."

"Only a small one. The doctor said not to worry unless it gets to 101."

"Let's check it." She picked up the thermometer on my stand and put it under my tongue.

When it beeped, I held it out for her. "See 100.5. I'm fine."

"I still don't like it. You just gave birth, and a fever can mean a lot of things."

"If it gets worse, I promise I'll go in. Otherwise, I'd rather avoid it. I don't want Luna in an ER, and I can't leave her because she needs to eat. I don't want to introduce a bottle yet."

"Alright, but you better call me if it gets higher or you get any new symptoms."

"I promise."

Mom bounced Luna. "Bryn, she is the most beautiful baby I've ever seen. Look at all that black hair and those beautiful blue eyes."

"They're Lachlan's eyes. Like the ocean. That's what I thought the first time I ever saw his eyes."

Mom smiled. "I think you're right. They do look like Lachlan, but those full lips, button nose, and thick hair is all you."

"I had lots of hair?"

"Tons of it. Just like Luna. Why don't you get some more sleep? I have Luna for a while," she said.

"Are you sure you can stay?"

"Just try and tear me away from my grandbaby. I can stay with you for the rest of the day. I have to leave tonight for a New York trade show in the morning. I'd cancel, but it's an important one."

"No, don't cancel it. We'll be okay for one night, and yes, I'd love for you to stay with us all day."

My mom took Luna out of the room, and I fell back asleep. I woke up to cramps and took some Tylenol. Luna's bassinet was empty. I went to the nursery and found my mom singing and rocking her. I snapped a picture and planned on framing it.

"I think it's time for her to eat. That's what my chest is thinking anyway," I said.

"I bet you're right. She's the sweetest little thing."

"She's a really good baby. I expected her to be more demanding."

"That'll be the next one. She'll let you relax your guard and think babies are easy. The next one will come in like a tornado."

I laughed. "Are you speaking from experience?"

"Yep, have you met your brothers. Jace the calm and Cole the hurricane."

"What was I? The tsunami?"

"You had your own calm until you were mobile. After that, your bravery and curiosity were revealed."

Mom and I spent the rest of the day watching movies in bed, knitting blankets for Luna, and talking. My mom made a month's worth of freezer meals.

"You spoil me too much," I told her.

"You make that easy."

"Lachlan always says that."

"It's because it's true. Your heart makes you incredibly easy to love. I have to get going, but let's check your temp. You're looking pretty pale."

My temp was still 100.5, and Mom reluctantly left me. She looked worried, but I reassured her I'd be fine until Lachlan returned tomorrow. Luna was a little fussy, and my cramping felt worse. I tried the heating pad that my mom left by my bed and took more Tylenol. I fed Luna, and she became milk drunk. Her dopey eyes made me smile. I put her in her bed and climbed into mine. I was out in seconds.

A loud crash startled me awake. I tiptoed to the hall and heard voices. "You idiot! Do you want to alert her we're here?" They were coming down the hall. "A whole week wasted waiting for her to be alone. We can't mess this up."

If I bolted, they would see me. I had to get Luna and hide. I scooped her up and ran for the bathroom, locking us in.

My phone!

I carefully opened the door and grabbed it before pulling us back inside. I locked the door and typed to Lachlan that someone was in the house. Before I could hit send, Luna let out a cry. I hurried and started feeding her. I breathed a sigh of relief when she latched on and calmed. I went to grab my phone and send the text as well as call 911, but a loud thud hit the door, sending Luna shrieking. I tried to get her to latch back on, but now something was being rammed against the door. Luna screamed, and I bounced her, trying to calm her. The wooden door frame cracked like a tree split with an ax. What could I do? The window was too small to provide an escape. The door splintered and broke open. I screamed and reached for my phone. A tall man wearing a ski mask kicked it away from me then stepped on it hard.

"Grab the baby!" He yelled to the other man in the ski mask. I kicked at them, clutching Luna tighter. One of the men punched me in the side of the face, disorienting me long enough for them to snatch my baby. The other dragged me. I forced myself to sit up as I bit into his leg. He yelped and let me go. I found my bearings and ran after the man carrying Luna away. The other man recovered and shoved me hard into the dresser. He walked toward me, and I tipped the dresser on him and bolted from the room.

I ran after the man holding Luna. The other man caught up to me, and I grabbed the living room lamp, bashing it into his head. We struggled, and I fought back, sending the living room into chaos. He slammed another punch across my jaw.

Luna! was the last thing I thought as my attacker won, rendering me unconscious.

Losing Everything

♥

Lachlan

I wanted this trip to be over so I could get home to my girls. The interview had gone well, but I wasn't sure it was worth leaving Bryn and Luna so soon. Bryn hadn't been answering my messages since last night, which had me a little worried. Maybe it meant Luna had slept through the night, and she was getting some good rest.

The event concluded, and I checked my phone to see I still had no messages or missed calls. I decided to call Anna to see if maybe she was with Bryn.

"Lachlan! How did your interview go?" Anna sounded happy.

I must be paranoid.

"Really well. I think I nailed it."

"That's great to hear! I'm so proud of you, Lachlan."

"I was wondering if you've seen Bryn since last night?"

"No, I have a trade show all day. Is everything okay?" Her voice grew in concern.

"Probably. I just haven't heard from her since last night. She's not returning my messages."

"I'm hours away. Where are you?"

"I'm leaving Boston. Look, don't worry, Anna. She's probably busy with Luna or maybe finally getting some sleep. How was she when you saw her yesterday?"

"Feverish, but it was only 100.5 so she wouldn't go in. She hates hospitals. I was going to check on her after my show this evening. Let me know as soon as you talk to her."

"I will. Talk to you later." I hung up and tried calling Bryn again but got no answer.

I found my front door unlocked and felt uneasy. As soon as I stepped inside, my chest screamed. It looked like a war had taken place with the lamp shattered on the floor. A bookshelf was toppled over, papers covered the floor. I ran to Luna's room and found it undisturbed. Her crib was empty, but that was expected since Bryn wanted her close in the bassinet.

Chaos greeted me in the bedroom. The bassinet was tipped over, the mattress laid on the floor, and shoes were scattered everywhere. I picked up Bryn's cracked cell phone from the bathroom floor and stared at an open text message to me. It read *Lachlan someone is in the house*. It was unsent. I stepped back into my bedroom and caught red liquid dripping onto the hardwood. The words – they shall be purified – were written above the doorway. I dialed 911.

I paced my porch, waiting for the police to arrive. As soon as I saw the lights, I ran out to meet them. "My wife and newborn daughter. I left them for a trip and came back today. My house was ransacked. They're nowhere in sight."

Yellow crime tape went around the entrance to my house. I sat on the porch with my hands buried in my face. I didn't know who to call first. Calling Anna and Donovan and telling them their daughter had been kidnapped for the second time wasn't something I wanted to do. Instead, I called Ryo. He made it to my house in half the time he should've.

He stared at the crime tap. "Someone really took Bryn and Luna?"

"Did you think I made it up?"

"No, of course not. It just doesn't feel real."

I roughly ran my fingers through my hair. "It feels way too real to me. How could I leave them? I'm the worst husband and father in the entire world."

"Right, because you knew someone was going to steal your family while you were gone."

"What am I going to do? Ryo, my entire family!" I fell on my knees, hyperventilating.

"Bryn and Luna need you sane. You have to get it together."

I collapsed on my side and huddle into a little ball. I shut my eyes tight, breathing sporadically. My phone rang. "Can you answer that?" I managed to gasp out.

"Lachlan, it's Anna," Ryo said.

"I can't tell her."

"I will."

I hated my cowardice, but let him anyway. I doubted anything coherent would exit my mouth.

"Hey, Anna. It's Ryo." I couldn't hear Anna's side, but Ryo paused before continuing. "Yeah. Lachlan is right here. We have a problem. Bryn and Luna are missing." He went on to tell her everything we knew. He hung up. "She's on her way back. She's going to call Donovan."

A police officer speaking made me finally open my eyes. "Are you the owner of this house?"

I sat up on the grass. "Yes, it's my wife and daughter who are missing. *Please* find them!"

"We need to ask you some questions."

I followed him up to my porch swing, where he asked me all about the sequence of events to finding my ransacked house. He asked me the last time Luna and Bryn were seen.

"Is it possible she left with the baby?" he asked.

"She only gave birth a week ago. She's not supposed to drive. Our house looks like a tornado went through it. Someone wrote, they shall be purified, in something that looks horrifically like blood!"

"We need to cover all our bases."

Anna came running up. Police blocked most of the street, which meant she probably hadn't parked close. Her cheeks were tear-stained as she ran for me and hugged me. "Any word?"

"No, none."

The police asked Anna a series of questions since she was the last person to see my little family. The police told me to find accommodations for the night, and Anna insisted I stay at their house. Anna, Donovan, Ryo, and I all sat in the Hunt's living room, trying to make sense of things.

"I think the cult took them," Ryo said.

My head shot up. "Why?" It was a logical conclusion, but my mind hadn't gone there for some reason.

"The words written on the door jam. Rachel Slater had said something similar to Bryn and me when we went back into the cave."

"Neither of you ever said anything."

"It never seemed relevant, and things were crazy with all of us being injured. When you told me about it earlier, it sounded familiar."

Anna pulled out her phone. "I'll call Detective Lambert, and we better call Bryn's sisters."

"Yes, tell them that they can stay here. I'll hire extra security. We have plenty of room, and I can arrange all their plane tickets," Donovan said. He stared at the carpet and spoke too calmly as if he was trying too hard to keep in control.

We called all of Bryn's sisters, and everyone agreed it'd be best to go into hiding. I felt desperately sad that Bryn would miss this family reunion, and Luna would miss meeting our family. Over the next few hours, everyone trickled in. Despite the happiness of seeing everyone again, the atmosphere stayed solemn.

I stood on the Hunt's back deck, holding a Blue Moon beer with my two best friends on either side of me. Ryo sipped Umeshu, and Thane downed his Cognac whiskey shot. We stared out at the perfectly manicured, enormous fenced-in property. Green shrubs were perfectly trimmed. A fancy path, with colorful stones, winded around a flower garden that extended probably an acre on either side of the path.

The rest consisted of a vibrant green lawn that ran up against the fence to the massive pool. The pool had a waterfall, three diving boards, pirate ship, a lazy river, and two water slides. The Hunts basically had their own little water park. Next to that was the four-bedroom luxury guest house.

"I'm so sorry about Bryn and Luna, Lachlan," Thane said.

I took a swig from my bottle. "Thanks, brother. I'm glad we have the rest of the girls here safe."

"Me too. I'm grateful to Anna and Donovan for keeping my wife safe."

"How is Capri holding up?" I asked.

"She's a mess and can't sleep. She's terrified for Bryn. I think the cult returning is all of their worst nightmares."

"It's definitely Bryn's. Especially them getting their hands on Luna. I want to go rip apart the entire cave system." My phone rang, and I quickly answered. "This is Lachlan West."

"Mr. West, your neighbors have camera footage of Bryn and Luna being taken. I was wondering if you'd come down to the station. Just you and Bryn's parents, please."

"Yeah, we'll be right there."

I told everyone about the phone call, and the Hunts and I piled into their Rolls Royce. I moved my knee vigorously up and down all the way to the police station. Once we got out of the car, I had to remind myself to slow down for Anna and Donovan. We walked into together, and the detective led us back. My knee continued to tap as he showed us the footage.

Two men wearing black from head to toe got out of a navy SUV and messed with my front door. They got it open and disappeared inside. The detective fast-forwarded to the exiting of the house. One had Bryn flung over their shoulder, and the other carried something, probably Luna. I couldn't make Bryn out clearly, but it only made sense she was the person being carried out. I wanted to punch something.

"The good news is that the message was written in sheep's blood," the detective said. "Other than that, we have no leads. The cave system spans over 400 miles. We have thoroughly checked the cave that Bryn used to live in and have found it evacuated. There are remnants of people once living there, but no one has been found close. We're continuing the investigation and have alerted the media. Now that we have the make and model of the vehicle, we can issue an Amber alert for Luna."

We thanked the detective, and as we returned to the Hunt's. The wheels in my mind were spinning. I needed to be smart, but most of me felt tempted to hike all 400 miles of the Kentucky cave system. I needed to do something. I couldn't sit back while my wife and daughter were enduring who knows what at the hands of a psychotic cult.

Back at the house, I found sleep impossible. I flipped through pictures on my phone of my wife and daughter. Luna looked so much like Bryn. I flipped to one of Bryn holding Luna in the hospital. I had my arm around Bryn, and elation filled both our faces. We'd traveled a long road to that moment, and one dark night strangers had violated the sanctity of our home. They'd stolen my family when I wasn't there to protect them. Madness was all I found in the cold empty sheets surrounding me. I hopped out of bed and stuck my phone in my pocket. I found Anna in the kitchen, sipping something from a mug. Her eyes looked as heavy as mine felt.

She pulled out another mug from the cupboard. "I made some chamomile tea. Would you like some?"

"That'd be great. Thank you." I accepted the mug from her and poured myself some tea from the stove.

I hopped onto the barstool at the kitchen island while Anna leaned against the counter.

"I keep thinking this can't be real. There's no way my baby was stolen for the second time along with her baby."

"I know the feeling. I'm sorry I failed Bryn and Luna, Anna. I'm sorry I didn't protect your daughter and granddaughter."

Anna put her teacup down and took my hand. "Lachlan, take it out of your head that any of this is your fault. I get it. I really do. I'm struggling with the fact I went to the trade show. Maybe if I'd just stayed with her."

"You couldn't have stopped them. They might have taken or even killed you."

"I know. If they had taken me, at least I'd be with Bryn and Luna."

My phone rang, and I fumbled for it. "Hello, Lachlan West here."

"Mr. West, it's Detective Lambert. I'm afraid I don't have the best news. There's been a body found that fits the description of your wife. Police would like you to come down to the station to identify her."

My heart dropped six feet into the floor as my phone fell from my hands.

"Lachlan, what is it?" Anna must have known because tears were already rolling down her cheeks.

I looked at her slowly. "They think they found Bryn."

"That's great! Right?" Her voice shook.

I shook my head. "They want me to identify her body."

Anna screamed and slumped to the ground, grabbing her chest. I stared at her, terrified I'd just killed my mother-in-law. Donovan ran out and picked a dazed Anna off the ground.

Silent Pact

♥

Lachlan

T he police station had a chill that reached my bones. Detective Lambert led me back into his office. They were going to show me pictures of the body. Apparently, TV had it all wrong. I wouldn't be taken to my wife's body tonight.

Ryo had driven Bryn's parents and me over. They were all in a waiting room that had mounted TVs that displayed the news. Somehow, the world still carried on without Bryn and Luna. For me, that wouldn't be the case.

He held an envelope with contents powerful enough to destroy me. "I'm going to warn you, Mr. West. These pictures are disturbing."

"Please call me, Lachlan. Do you want me to identify her quickly? I'm wondering why you didn't use her fingerprints or another method."

His jaw went stiff. "The victim doesn't have fingerprints anymore."

I stared at him. "That bad?"

He nodded. "I mean, we're waiting on DNA evidence to confirm our suspicions, but we'd also like to know quickly if we're on the right track. If this is Bryn, we know to pursue the location and evidence to get to Luna. Your newborn daughter makes this more urgent. Normally, we'd wait for the DNA results."

"Okay. Show me the picture." I closed my eyes and didn't want to ever reopen them.

"You can open your eyes."

I did and stared. "How can I identify that?"

"The woman's clothes, her hair, and distinguishable markings."

"I don't recognize the clothes. It doesn't look like her. I don't think it's her."

"Are you sure?"

I raised an eyebrow at him. "How can I be sure?"

He nodded.

"I don't think it's her. The hair is off. I love her hair. I don't think that's her hair." I got up, trying to rid my mind of the pictures.

"Thank you for your time, Lachlan. We'll call you when the DNA comes back. We should have results sometime tomorrow."

Ryo and the Hunts looked at me expectantly.

I shrugged. "I couldn't tell. I don't think so, but I couldn't tell."

They all looked at me, horrified, and I turned around and walked out of the building. I found a bush and puked into it.

I stared at my phone, willing it to call, but it taunted me with its silence. Sleep wasn't happening anytime soon. I struggled to find it, and whenever I did, the pictures of the body drifted into my dreams turning into Bryn. It couldn't be her. There was no way.

Right? I yanked at my hair and stifled a scream. I didn't want to wake the entire house.

"I'm going to make you some coffee," Capri said. I hadn't noticed her walk into the kitchen. As the coffee brewed, she gave me a hug. "I'm so sorry about Bryn and Luna. It'd be dumb to ask how you are, but let me know if there's anything I can do to help."

"Thank you. How are you?"

"A mess. I keep thinking that if the cult has Bryn how extremely unfair it is. Out of all of us, she hated the cave most. I mean, it wasn't pleasant for any of us, but for Bryn, it always stole pieces of her soul."

"It stole her sky," I added. "I'm not going to sit around forever. If they don't find leads soon, I'm going to hike the entire cave system until I find her. They said it's 400 miles. I traveled triple that to make back to her when she got shot."

"Yeah, but the problem was this is unknown terrain. I'd hate for you to get lost in there."

I shrugged. "If we don't find Bryn and Luna, I really don't care what happens to me."

"We're going to find them. I don't think the cult will harm them. Especially not Luna."

"Right. Not Luna." The images of the unidentifiable body came into my head, and I shuddered.

"What is it?"

I snapped out of my trance. "Nothing."

"Lachlan, do you know something more about my sister. If you know something, please tell me."

I didn't want to tell her, but if they DNA came back as Bryn, I'd have no choice. Would it be better to prepare her or shock her?

I looked at her. "I have some information, but it may be nothing. I don't want to upset you if it turns out to be nothing."

"I'd rather be prepared for likely possibilities."

"It's not good news."

"Yeah, by the look on your face, I gathered that."

"Okay. You're right. You have a right to know as much as anyone. A few hours ago, the police called me in to look at a picture of a body they think might be Bryn."

Capri's eyes widened, and her hands started to shake. "Was it?"

"I couldn't tell. It wasn't good. We're waiting on DNA evidence."

"Oh!" she covered her mouth.

"I didn't want to get you upset without knowing for sure."

"No, I'm glad you told me. Please don't spare me in any of this, Lachlan. I need to prepare myself as much as you do."

"Okay. I'll keep you in the loop."

"Thanks." She poured me coffee, and as she handed me the mug, I could see her hand still shaking. "I'm going to head back to bed. Please, let me know if you need anything at all."

"Thank you, Capri."

She nodded, and I knew she needed Thane the way I needed Bryn. She'd helped me through the worst things in life. What would I do if the worst possible thing was losing her? How would I ever find reprieve from the suffering? I didn't think my misery ending would ever happen if I had to put my wife in the ground for eternal rest.

The rest of the day, I checked my phone much too often. The longer I waited for the DNA results, the more frantic I became. An ominous black cloud had settled around the Hunt's mansion. A movie played in the living room where everyone sat, not watching it. Almost everyone looked spaced off as we were waiting for our deepest fear to be confirmed.

I didn't want to picture a life without Bryn. Thoughts I didn't like surfaced. If we got Luna back, how would I raise my daughter without her mother? I didn't think I'd survive if I lost both of them. I'd be a shell where a man once lived. Ryo turned on the third movie that went unwatched like the previous two. The only noise came from Dahlia and Adely, who played with dolls in the corner. I watched them, praying my own daughter would one day play with dolls.

My phone ringing snapped me back into reality. All eyes were on me as I answered, "Detective Lambert?"

"Yeah, hey, Lachlan. We got the DNA results on the body back. It's not Bryn."

"Okay. Thank you."

"Yeah, we're still trying to find more leads. We don't have much to go one. The vehicle was stolen and has proven a dead end. We haven't been able to find any evidence in your house either. I'll update you as soon as we find anything out."

"Thank you. I appreciate it." I hung up and looked at all the fearful eyes on me. "It's not Bryn." I could hear everyone take a breath at once, and a few of them crying. I stood up. "I need some air. If you guys could give me some space for a bit. I'll be back soon." I hurried out the back door.

I bent forward, resting my hands on my knees. I couldn't breathe. The body wasn't Bryn. Thank God the body wasn't Bryn. I tried to force my breathing to slow as I repeated it over and over again. The body wasn't my wife. My beautiful firefly could still be alive. Two hands clasped my shoulders, and I looked to each side of me into the eyes of my brothers.

Thane swiftly pulled me into a hug. "We got you, brother. Whatever you need, we got you."

Ryo hugged us both, and it was as though a silent pact had been made. We were going after Bryn and Luna.

Fever and Chills

Bryn

I woke up to Luna crying, and I couldn't figure out why I couldn't see her or her bassinet. The dark room around me felt like a vehicle. Where was Luna? Her cry sounded both distant and close. What had happened? Everything started coming back to me, and as the fog of sleep cleared, I began to realize someone had placed me in the trunk of a car.

Luna must have been in the front. My hands were bound in front of me. I shivered, and sweat poured down my forehead. I shivered, and the pain in my stomach burned sharply. I needed to fight them when they opened the trunk, but I felt incredibly weak. The car drove a while longer, and I went in and out of consciousness.

The vehicle finally stopped, and I heard voices close. "She needs to feed the baby, Rick," one said.

"Yeah, yeah, that woman is feisty for a little thing. She gave me a goose egg and a sprained wrist."

"Nothing is more dangerous than a mother protecting her child. Don't you watch nature shows?"

"Yeah, but she's clearly ill. She shouldn't have had the strength to do that damage."

The trunk popped open to grey clouds masking the stars, which seemed appropriate for the setting. One of them yanked me from the trunk and shoved me to the ground. My bound hands made stopping the fall a failed attempt. The man grabbed my hair and pulled me to a sitting position. I yelped, and he gave me a kick.

"Shut up!" he barked. By his voice, I knew he was the one the other referred to as Rick.

They still wore ski masks, gloves, and black clothes. I couldn't make out any distinguishing features. I only knew they were men based on their voices. The second man brought out Luna and helped position her to eat. I held her the best I could with bound hands, and the man helped. I didn't like him so close when I feed my baby, but I wanted Luna secure.

They let her eat until she slept contently. I bit my lip to avoid the wail that wanted to escape as they took her from me. The first man picked me up and slammed me into the trunk. All the light around me evaporated.

We stopped five more times to feed Luna, and each time, I felt grateful to see her safe. My body ached from the rough handling that ensued every time they took me in and out of the trunk. I thought of the terror Lachlan must be enduring by now. He'd have arrived home from his business trip to find our house empty. My mother was probably beside herself, dealing with her daughter being kidnapped for the second time. I hurt for them.

On the sixth stop, forest surrounded us. The first man did his usual routine of throwing me to the ground, and the second man helped me feed Luna. After she finished eating, they didn't return me to the trunk. They made me walk with wobbly legs. Anytime I stumbled, the first man jerked me around and smacked me. I tried to stay steady, but having given birth the week before mixed with my rough treatment made smooth walking difficult.

They led me up a trail, and when we stopped, my heart froze. A black mouth in a rocky mountain greeted us. They were returning me to the cave. My knees buckled. I didn't want to enter my past. The cavern that hid in my nightmares stood twenty feet in front of me.

Rick pulled me to stand. "You better walk, or we'll take it out on the baby."

The second man's eyes widened. "We can't—"

"Shut up!"

"Please. I won't stumble. Please don't hurt my baby. She's only a week old." I mustered strength from somewhere.

"You shut up!" he snapped

The other one smiled at Luna in his arms. "I thought she was new. She's a sweet baby. Very pretty."

"I'm just going to call you buttercup from now on." Rick smacked his friend in the back of the head.

They pushed me into the cave, and my feet screamed as I obeyed my captors for Luna's sake. A chill seeped into my skin, and I shook.

Rick looked up at a tiny red, blinking light in the corner. "We brought them! Come get them and pay us!"

As we waited, I felt dizzy. I forced myself to stay upright, staring at my daughter for motivation. A glow caught my attention, and two men and a woman appeared.

The woman took Luna and smiled at her. "The Above One has brought us a blessing."

"Actually, Rick and Tony have. Now, pay up!" Rick snarled.

One of the new men handed him an envelope. Rick looked inside, and he and Tony left.

The woman placed her hand on my cheek. "Welcome home, Bryn Slater. We have missed our wayward daughter." Her smile faded as she moved her hand to my forehead. "You're burning up, child. We need to get her to my den. Bryn, my name is Brigid. This is Frodi and Ganesh."

Everything around me swirled as though I was water spiraling down a sink. I fell forward, and Frodi caught me.

"Carry her back. She is quite ill," Brigid ordered.

Ganesh picked me up, and my muscles weakened too much to protest. I must have fallen unconscious because I couldn't recall how I made it into a lit-up room. The walls, ceiling, and floor were created from the familiar rock landscape. They'd placed me in a bed with a cotton sheet over me. My pants and shirt were folded on the chair across from my bed, and a white fleece nightgown adorned me. Sweat poured from my forehead, but I shook from the frigid chill of the room.

"Will she live?" a deep voice asked.

"I'm not sure. I need to examine her. She gave birth a week ago. My best guess is a womb infection or a retained placenta. She has passed several large clots, so I'm going with the latter." I recognized Brigid's voice. "Damn pagans would have let her die. This is negligence. This should have been checked for."

"Examine her then. If she can't be saved, we will find a pure family for the child."

"The child is best with her natural mother."

"I know this, but the Above One may decide her too impure for motherhood."

Colorful, translucent orbs danced around my head, and I stared at them with wild eyes.

Brigid walked in with blue gloves on her hands. "Bryn, honey, I'm going to have to give you an exam. It's going to hurt pretty bad. I'm going to have Sadie and Laura hold you down." Two women came on either side of me, and each grabbed an arm and leg. As Brigid examined me, I screamed. My abdomen felt as though it was on fire. I blacked out and woke to Brigid's voice.

She gently rubbed my knee. "As I thought, you had a partially retained placenta. I've taken care of the problem. You should re-cover. We will give you a few days to rest before we proceed with your design."

"My baby," I croaked.

"Oh, yes, your baby. It's probably about time to feed her. Sadie, go fetch our little one."

Sadie went into the next room and brought Luna to my arms. Laura helped me sit up and positioned Luna better for me. I didn't want to release her to these people, but tendrils of sleep tugged at me, begging my body for surrender.

"You sleep, honey. I promise you. No harm will befall this child. She is of the utmost importance to us." Brigid took Luna from me. "What's her name?"

"Luna Sky."

"Luna Sky. She will be given a new name at her purification ceremony, but I will mark it in the book as her pagan name."

I couldn't even protest as my body forced me into slumber.

Brigid pointed toward the closet. "Put the white dress on over there. Hurry, we need to get you to your daughter's naming ceremony. After that, we will discuss your design."

"My design?"

"I forget you were much too little when the Slaters brought you from impurity. You don't remember your first design. The elders speak with the Above One, and he tells them the design for your life. You were led astray and taken from your original design. We are going to fix that, dear." She patted me gently.

"I want to go home."

She held my hand between hers. "You will have a home soon enough."

I put on the dress, as she suggested. It would be best for me to do what they said until I could figure the best way to escape. My legs trembled from fatigue, and the bed beckoned my return.

"You look extremely pale. I want you to take this." She handed me a pill.

"What is it?"

"None of your concern. It is safe to nurse your baby with. That's all you need to know. Take it, and we won't have to force it."

Reluctantly, I downed the pill. I couldn't afford them hurting me in a way that prevented my escape.

Brigid rubbed my arm. "Good girl. I see there is hope for your compliance. Your poor father's sacrifice cost him dearly."

"My father's sacrifice?"

"Yes, your father was our guardian. That's why your family lived close to the outside and didn't participate in the community."

"We went to church."

"Yes, everyone has to go to church. Let's get you to your daughter's naming ceremony. Directly after, you will be allotted time to feed your child. From there, you will receive your design."

I followed Brigid with wobbly legs. The room blurred, but I pushed myself forward to get to my daughter. The slimy brown walls that I despised mocked me as I walked through a continuous same. I would die before I let Luna stay in the hellish pit. My mind couldn't concentrate as though my body pressed me to sleep even while standing.

We made it a chapel. I could tell it was different from the one I'd visited weekly as a child. The shapes of the rocks weren't quite right. The ones here looked like jagged teeth, which created a fitting setting for how the cave community devoured its members' souls. This meant I had no clue how to escape. I'd have to learn the tunnels and the exits.

Brigid led me to the front where a priest placed Luna in my arms. I forced myself to stay conscious as to not drop my baby on the rough cave floor. The priest lifted his arms, and everyone chanted the sound that still crept into my memories. I glanced around at all the people and realized none were wearing the hoods. Growing up whenever we met with the other cult members, we'd worn colorful hoods to conceal our faces.

The chanting ended, and the priest took Luna from me. He lifted her in the air, and everything in me screamed to punch him in the gut. But he held my baby, and I didn't dare make a move.

"This child is a holy child. An oracle to lead us through triumphant times. She is set apart by the Above One for a special purpose. For this reason, she deserves a name of purity. We shall name her Abra Grace. Her old name shall henceforth fade away with her old life. We declare this little one pure." He pulled a knife from a podium, and I stiffened. He pricked Luna's finger, and she screamed. He placed her blood in a cup of water.

I launched at him, and Brigid held me back. "Shh! Dear, no harm will come to our baby."

"It already has! Give me my daughter!"

Brigid held me upright. Everything spun, and arms picked me up and carried me back to my room. I fought the sheets until I felt a pinch in my arm. I scanned the room deliriously. The walls melted like wax in the summer sun. The furniture warped and twisted, taking on odd formations that my mind couldn't decipher.

"Quit fighting it. Give in, and all will be well."

"My baby!" I didn't recognize my voice. It came out as distorted as my surroundings.

"Bryn, child. Quit fighting. Relax. Abra is completely fine. She's already stopped crying. Sleep."

I struggled, kicking and flailing my arms, but they were held to the bed. "Luna!"

My body surrendered as the drugs in my system forced me into unconsciousness.

When I next awoke, I heard a voice speaking close by. The first voice was a man's I didn't know, and the second belong to Brigid.

"She's still feverish. I thought you said you fixed the problem."

"Give time for the garlic and ginger to work. Her infection should improve soon," Brigid said.

"If she dies?" the man growled.

"Then the Above One did not wish her to raise our holy child. Abra will be given to those more worthy."

"She is the mother of a holy child. She is a vessel for which more holy children may be born."

"She is in the hands of the Above One," Brigid said. She stood over my bed. "Oh! Good, you are awake. You have slept for some time. Don't worry, Abra has fed while you slept. We would never let your milk supply dry up. We have plans for you today. It is your design ceremony. We usually require you to stand, but we will make an exception, given the hardship you have endured with your health. I will inform them you have awakened, and the ceremony will be carried out here.

My head still swam, and muscles extraordinarily weak. Four men and Brigid entered my room, and I recognized one of them as Ganesh. They gathered around my bed, and the priest spread oil across my forehead with his thumb.

"We anoint you and purify you in the name of the Above One. He has revealed your design as a vessel for holy children. You shall be wed to Ganesh. Your marriage to your old husband is seen as an impure match and has been severed. Once your fever has cured, your marriage ceremony will take place."

Fear gripped me. One of the biggest motivators for me leaving the first time was not being forced into an arranged marriage. I didn't even want to think about what this would mean for me. If I didn't have Luna, I'd have rather died than allow that to happen. My love for my daughter trumped everything.

Oracle

Bryn

Brigid brought me Luna to feed. My weak arms couldn't keep a firm hold, so Brigid positioned pillows to do most of the work. She stepped out of the room, and I took in my baby. She looked up at me as she nursed with her beautiful eyes. The eyes I saw her father in.

I wanted nothing more than to have Lachlan's comfort. He always pampered me when I was sick and held me even if it meant he could catch what I had. My cramps increased, and I squirmed. I needed him for more than relief from the physical pain. I needed his arms to destroy the fear inside of me and to feel his protection and security. I'd lost my safe space, and it unraveled me.

Brigid took Luna from my arms and handed her to another woman.

"I need to use the bathroom," I said.

She brought over a bucket and helped me. When I finished, she frowned. "Your bleeding has worsened. Have the cramps increased?"

I nodded.

"We may need to recheck you and see if there are more that I missed."

I winced as I remembered her last efforts. "I want my baby. Please."

"You may have her full time once you are married."

"I'm already married. I want to go home to my husband."

She whirled around with a furrowed brow. "You put foolish talk away. They will hurt you if they hear such words spoken. You were led away by temptation in the past and have found redemption. Do not squander it. The punishments of the Above One are plentiful."

I held up my scarred hands that my cave father had burned right before I'd escaped the first time. "I know. I experienced many."

"Yet you still ventured into a poisonous world."

"It's not poisonous there. I have lived there for years."

"I do not speak of a physical poison, daft girl. I speak of a poison of your soul. Out of discontentment and greed, you sacrificed your soul and left us. Your poor parents suffered greatly for you. You are lucky that you have proven yourself a vessel of holy children, or you would have been killed the minute you were brought to us."

"Why do you keep calling my daughter a holy child? Do you believe that of all children? My parents never called my sisters or me that."

Brigid shook her head as she looked through dresses hung on a metal rod. "No, you were not indoctrinated properly. The Above One has seen in your daughter's eyes that she is meant to be a guiding light for all our people. She will speak directly to him, which is a rare gift."

I stared at her in disbelief of her delusions. Luna's eyes were her father's. They'd see him as corrupt and impure. He was the kindest and most loving man I'd ever known. "How do we know what the Above One wants if speaking to him is rare?"

"There are holy ones among the elders. We haven't had a holy child for decades. We were worried we wouldn't find more. One of the elders saw your interview, and he knew within you would be born an oracle. He said we had to risk bringing you back into the fold." She pulled out an all-white dress and looked it over.

I hated white dresses because of how they reminded me of my childhood. I had rejected tradition and refused to wear one on my wedding day.

"How could they have seen my interview?" I had no idea there was TV in the cave community.

"The elders view boxes from the outside that tells them of the world around us. You have been followed since you left. It was thought to be too risky to retrieve you until the elders saw you had conceived a sacred baby. We have pondered bringing your sisters back, but we feel it would conjure too much attention. None of them have children for consideration."

I let out a relieved breath. They hadn't gone after my sisters, and I could only hope that they never would. I said nothing about Morely's baby or Dahlia. Besides, they had to know about Dahlia. Morely was heavily pregnant when I helped her escape the cave. They must not have seen Dahlia as an oracle. For that, I felt immense relief.

I looked at the dress set in front of me. "Am I supposed to put this on?"

"Not yet. You must have a bath of jasmine."

"I can't take a bath. My doctor said it could cause infection."

"You already have an infection. Your pagan doctors almost killed you. You showed all the signs, but no one noticed. Those around you were neglectful."

Lachlan had noticed. He'd asked my doctors so many times if they were sure I was fine.

Bridget interrupted my thoughts with more of her babble. "The treatment for your current infection should prevent more. You are to be wed today, and it is most important that you bathe in jasmine."

My lip quivered. "Please. I can't."

"You should be joy-filled. This is the most wondrous day of your life. You will have a husband pure of heart. Your old one will be lost to you, and you will no longer be bound to his corrupt ways."

"My husband is the purest of heart man to exist."

"That is absolute nonsense. Your old life is nonexistent. I warn you to forsake your old life. Abra cannot be killed, but that doesn't mean she can't suffer in ways that won't kill her."

I sat up too quickly, and dizziness ripped through my head. "What does that mean?"

"It means be cautious to follow what is expected of you or much worse things than a finger prick can be done to your baby."

"Why would you hurt a holy child?"

"Pain brings purification. Your parents tried to instill this in you, but you were a stupid girl. The road you walked was much more painful than necessary because you didn't learn. Abra will learn early if her mother is noncompliant."

"Why would you just not punish me?"

She put her face close to mine with eyes that burned through me. "Don't think that we won't. I know your type—the type who pulled her sisters with her. Your submission will be greater if someone you love is at risk rather than yourself alone. You destroy others with yourself. You have the worst type of rebellion."

Brigid helped me stand and led me to a room that smelled of perfumes and spices. The shelves held jars, bottles, and canisters of unmarked items. Along the wall were reclining chairs, and we stepped over a woven rug that scratched at my feet. She brought me to a room with a natural pool. The water was turquoise and clear. An abundance of white flowers with tiny yellow centers floated in the pool. It smelled of incense and something close to lilacs, and I guessed the flowers to be jasmine. Three women wearing blue dresses came from an entrance across the pool. They carefully stepped around the pool until they reached us. They removed my dress and undergarments.

"Blessed be you on your wedding day. May long life be granted to your marriage." Each of the women repeated the phrase as they helped me into the pool.

They scrubbed me with a peach soap that had tiny rough particles that scraped my skin. They piled vanilla shampoo in my hair and scrubbed my scalp until I felt it might bleed. They pushed me under the water, and I flailed. I held my breath, and they finally released me. I gasped for air, trying to regain control of my lungs.

They brought me out of the tub, dried me thoroughly, and ran warm brushes through my hair. One of the women wove my hair with a stream of tiny white flowers. The simple white dress went over my head, and my feet were left bear.

Brigid inspected me before roughly grabbing my chin. "You fulfill the ceremony, and you will get your new house with your daughter. You refuse your vows or cause problems, Abra will be given to another couple to raise. Am I clear?"

I nodded.

"See, we are generous, letting you keep your child. Do not forsake our gratitude or cause us to offer you no grace."

I followed behind the women with Brigid pushing into my back. We came to a station with white roses, and the woman in front handed me a bouquet of them. We continued our stroll back into the chapel where they'd changed Luna's name. Ganesh stood at the front with the priest who I wanted to pummel into the ground for cutting Luna.

Ganesh smiled at me, but I kept my lips pushed together. He wore a blue shirt and khaki pants. His dark hair rested neatly against his head. He appeared to be in his mid-twenties. Brigid shoved me next to him, and Ganesh clasped my hands. I flinched, and concern flashed through his eyes.

"We are gathered today to follow the design for Bryn and Ganesh. From this day forward, Bryn will no longer be a Slater but a Moretti."

I haven't been a Slater for years, asshole.

The priest reached into a bowl on the podium and rubbed his thumb through a dark red liquid. I prayed it wasn't blood. He smeared it across my forehead and did the same to Ganesh. "Your lives are no longer two. You will create children for the Above One's fold. You have one year to produce the first of your offspring. At which time this is not fulfilled, you will embark into the world and bring children of the corrupt world into the purification of our society. This is the will of the Above One."

"This is the will of the Above One," the twenty or so other people repeated his words.

The priest pulled out his knife again, and Ganesh offered his palm. The priest sliced across and held Ganesh's hand over a bowl until several drops of blood dripped into water. The priest yanked my hand forward and repeated the step. I felt woozy as I watched my blood blend with Ganesh's. Concentrating increased in difficulty the longer that I stood. The room spun.

"You are to seal your union with a kiss, and so shall it be official," the priest announced.

My heart pounded, and everything became blurry as my legs gave out. I saw nothing more.

I opened my eyes at the sound of a baby crying. *Luna?* I glanced around and saw Ganesh rocking her in a chair.

"Give me my daughter!" I snapped.

"You mean *our* daughter. I'm glad to see you're awake." He brought Luna over and placed her in my arms.

I backed into the corner as I fed her. Ganesh came over and stroked my cheek. I recoiled and pressed my back deeper into the cave wall. "Don't touch me."

He laughed but removed his hand. "It's my right to touch you. We're man and wife. I missed our wedding kiss. We can rectify that."

"I'm already married. My husband is Lachlan West. I can't be married to you. It's not legal."

He looked amused. "The Above One's laws overpower that of any government. I realize as the gatekeeper's daughter, you were not educated in our schools. I will teach you our laws. As your husband, that is my duty."

"You're not my husband!"

"I wouldn't say that. If they hear you, they'll take Abra from us."

Luna finished feeding, but I held her tightly. Ganesh looked at her and pried her from my arms. She stirred, and he bounced her until she settled. He laid her in her crib.

"Now, we can have some alone time." He took off his belt, and I looked at the exit.

"Don't touch me! I don't give you permission to touch me."

He laughed. "I don't need permission. We're married."

He came closer, and I jabbed my heel into his eye. He flew off the back of the bed. I crawled over the bed and ran for Luna's bassinet.

He caught me by the waist and slammed me on the bed. "I love your fire!"

"Please." Tears streamed down my cheeks. I expected him to pin me down; instead, he sat on the edge of the bed.

"You really don't want me to touch you?"

I shook my head and cowered in the corner.

"Okay. I won't touch you until you're ready."

I blinked in surprise as he left the room and didn't come back.

I fell asleep sitting up but woke with a blanket around me, and Ganesh was once again in the corner holding Luna.

He looked up at me. "She's a beautiful baby. I can see why the elders feel she's a holy child."

"They thought her a holy child when they saw me pregnant with her. Before they saw her."

"That's because she probably is one, and they are wise. Her looks definitely match."

"What do you mean?"

"Holy children have a unique beauty to them. It's been a while since one has been born, but I've seen pictures, and they have angelic faces. Abra has that. Her blue eyes are piercing with her mountain of black hair."

"They're her father's eyes," I said almost bitterly.

Ganesh smiled, looking amused. "Then, I am grateful to her father for his contribution."

I squinted at his odd words. "He loves her, and he won't stop fighting until he gets us back."

"He'll fight his entire life and never find you. If our people are good at anything, it's hiding." He placed Luna in the bassinet and turned to me. "How are you feeling?"

"I think my fever finally broke."

"I'm glad to hear it. I made some soup. Let me bring you some."

"Okay. Thank you." I needed to keep up my strength to heal and escape.

He brought back a bowl with a spoon, and I reached for it.

He shook his head. "Please. Conserve your strength and let me feed you." He scooped a bit of the soup and brought it to my mouth. He fed me all of it. "Rest. I will let you know if Abra wakes to feed."

I stared at him. "Why are you treating me nice?"

"Would you rather I am mean?"

"No, it's just not what I expected."

He placed the bowl on the nightstand and sat in his spot on the end of the bed. "You're my wife. I am to show you love, even when I don't feel like it. I don't know you well enough to love you, but I start with actions, and love will eventually follow. That's what my mother always told me anyway."

"What if I can never submit to the things you want from me?"

"I don't expect your submission without me proving my love. As I said, it's too soon for me to love you. I imagine eventually you will make a wonderful wife."

"Ganesh, you deserve someone who can love you back. I can't because I love another in a way that will never be removed."

He grinned. "I don't expect you to stop loving Abra's father. I expect you to find a place for me in your heart too." He didn't wait for me to respond. He grabbed the bowl and left the room.

This had to be a trick, but I couldn't figure out why. Even if it was deception, I felt grateful Ganesh hadn't gone through with things.

Distorted Time

Bryn

"**B**ryn, wake up. It's time to get ready for church. Brigid brought by your expected attire." Ganesh stood next to me, wearing a blue collared shirt and khakis.

"I'm not feeling the greatest. Can I skip it?"

He put his hand over my forehead. "You do feel warm again. I will have Brigid swing by after church to look at you. I must take Abra with me."

I sat up quickly. " No, what if she needs to eat."

"Feed her now, and she won't need to eat before I return from service."

"Why do you have to take her?"

"Because she is well. All who are well must attend."

He changed Luna and dressed her in a white garment. I was surprised when Ganesh put on a wide-brimmed hat and not a hood. When I was growing up, we had to wear hoods to church with no exceptions.

He peeked in on me as he cradled Luna. "Do you need anything before I leave?"

"Just my baby."

He smiled. "I promise I will bring her right back after the service. I will keep her safe with my life."

"Why aren't you wearing a hood?"

"The Above One has abolished that law."

"Why?"

"We don't question the Above One. Doing that made you corrupt. Be careful."

"If what I found in the world is corruption, then falling into impurity was the best thing to ever happen to me."

He glanced behind his back as if someone might be listening. "Don't say such things. It's one thing to cause damnation for yourself and another for you to grant it to Abra. I'll return with Brigid later. Please feel better, wife."

"Not your wife!"

He shook his head and left. I needed to tone it down to gain his trust for escape, but acknowledging our sham of a marriage made my skin crawl. I was Lachlan's and only Lachlan's until the day my lungs no longer breathed oxygen.

I napped, which seemed to be all my life entailed. I struggled to heal from my birth, and I figured it was because I needed antibiotics instead of these home remedies Brigid kept pushing. She woke me up from my nap and fussed over me.

She turned to Ganesh. "This could be a secondary infection from consummating your marriage. I know it was necessary no matter the circumstances, but I suggest you abstain until her fever has stayed gone for a week."

I stared at Ganesh in fear, and he met my eyes. "We definitely will hold off until she's better."

"You are a good husband to show her such grace. You would have every right to deny my suggestion." She patted him on the shoulder and smiled at Luna. "Our beautiful little one. The Above One has smiled on us by bringing you into our fold." She turned back to me. "Rest well, dear."

After Brigid left, I spoke to Ganesh. "Why didn't you tell her we hadn't? I'm grateful you didn't, but I'm surprised."

"Because it would have brought us both punishments. You more than me. I don't wish to see you harmed. It looks like we made a wise choice if it can make you sicker during this time." He handed me Luna to feed. "I will make you soup."

Luna looked up at me and smiled. I kissed her fingers. "Oh, sweet, Luna! Look at your beautiful smile." I started nursing her, and then it struck me. How long had I been here? Should Luna be smiling already? I sat for a while, contemplating how many days had passed.

Ganesh brought back the soup. "Is she finished?"

I looked at a sleepy Luna and nodded.

He took her from me and started feeding me the soup. "You look so pale. Are you bleeding more than normal?"

"I'm not sure. I've never had a baby before."

"What does Brigid say?"

"She is sometimes concerned but is doing all she can."

He spooned another bite. "I'm thinking about joining the next supply run and seeing if I can gather better medicines for you."

"Why are you so kind to me? I know you told me the whole love thing, but you aren't what I expected from the men here."

He looked thoughtful for a few seconds. "I want our marriage to work. It's the ultimate failure to the Above One to fail as a husband. I've seen the men be violent to their wives, and I've seen it make submissive wives. I've also seen it destroy the wives. I don't want obedience at the expense of destroying the person I'm going to spend my life with. I know you feel you can't love me. I feel in time you will as I will you."

"Ganesh, how long have I been down here? Things feel off, and I believe it's the fever. Luna seems older."

He sighed. "You must call her Abra. I know it's difficult with all these changes, but if they hear you, they will punish you. I can't protect you among many."

"I'll do better. Her name is important to me. I named her with purpose."

"Don't most parents? To answer your question, you have been here for four weeks."

"Four weeks! Are you certain?"

"Yes, quite certain. When you first arrived, you slept frequently, and you still do. I'm not surprised time is distorted for you."

I stared at him. Lachlan had missed out on an entire month in Luna's life. In some way, I had too. I wondered what my family thought by now, and my heart hurt for my husband. He had to feel he'd lost his entire family by now. I wished I could comfort him.

I swam in fire and thrashed, trying to escape. I couldn't reach Luna, and flames engulfed her bassinet. Her cries were tormented, and I screamed as she turned to ashes. An earthquake smothered the fire. I opened my eyes to see Ganesh standing over me

"Bryn! Wake up. My word you're burning up! The hottest I've felt. I'm going to get Brigid." He ran from the room.

The front door clicked shut. I pulled my blanket to my shoulders to stave off the iciness of the room. I stared at the little girl glowing in a white dress. She had blonde hair and bright blue eyes. Where had she come from? She smiled as sleep pulled me back.

"I'm going to get her real medicines. Antibiotics. She's going to die otherwise!" Ganesh's shouts woke me up.

Brigid spoke next. "You're going to wake her. Lower your voice. You have to seek approval from the elders, and the oracle has to say yes."

"I'm going to talk to them now. Can you stay with Bryn?"

"Yes, I will care for both of them."

The cramping had moved on from my stomach to nearly every muscle in my body. I couldn't understand why my body wouldn't heal. Brigid walked into the room and ran to my side.

She stuck her hand on my forehead. "You look terrible."

"I think I'm dying."

"If so, it's the Above One's will."

"Please. I want to go home."

"You are at home. You belong with your daughter and husband. I'll feed you your soup." She brought a bowl over and held out a spoon.

I shook my head. "Please. No, I can't."

"You have to eat, or you will lose all your strength."

My breasts felt empty, and I became alarmed. "How long has it been since I fed Luna?"

"I'm afraid you have proven yourself unworthy of feeding her. We let your milk dry up. We are feeding her condensed milk now."

"What? No!" I sobbed into my hands at how they'd stolen yet another thing from me.

Brigid pushed me until I took bites. I forced them down but promptly threw it all up. My entire body cramped, and I couldn't even move. I needed to hold my daughter. I needed Lachlan to hold me, but all I could do was sleep.

I woke up, finally feeling better, and sat up. I looked around and saw Luna's hands moving over the top of the bassinet. I slowly got out of bed, trying to rid the dizziness coursing through my head. I stood for the first time in what I guessed was days. I walked over to her, and she smiled as I looked in. She looked too old. How much time had I slept away this time? I didn't think I wanted the answer.

I picked her up and carried her back to my bed. I propped my knees up and rested her on them. She babbled and grabbed at my face.

"I love you. I'm so sorry I haven't gotten us out of here. I'm so sorry you've had to miss Daddy and me all this time." I ached to nurse her, but that ability had left some time ago, and I didn't think it would return.

She started to fuss and suck on her hands. I bounced her, and she continued to cry. Ganesh ran in, first looking in the bassinet and then at the bed.

He smiled. "You look more alert than I've seen you in a while."

"I feel better. Not completely but definitely an improvement."

"That's great. The medicine is working." He walked out of the room and returned with a bottle and handed it to me.

I gave it to her even though my heart sank. At least she'd be fed. That was all that mattered. I tried to convince myself it was. I didn't think anything was wrong with bottle feeding my baby, but having the choice ripped from me felt like a violation.

"Did you give me new medicine?" I asked.

"Yes, I pleaded your case to the elders. They almost didn't let me go, but I convinced them."

I smiled. "Thank you."

"Don't mention it. You're my wife. I care about you."

"How old is Luna now?"

"*Abra* is almost two months."

I shoved a tear away. "I'm grateful for your kindness, but I really miss my family."

"In time, that will lessen."

My heart knew it wouldn't.

Over the next week, I regained my strength almost entirely. I started to get out of bed more, and every morning Ganesh put my hair up into a bun to align with wife attire requirements. I attended my first Sunday service, and I felt grateful we no longer had to wear the hoods. Ganesh led me over to a log, and I held Luna. We chanted, and the priest droned on about the Above One's will.

When the service ended, a woman approached me. "You're Bryn Moretti, right?"

I opened my mouth to correct the last name then stopped. I needed to avoid trouble until I escaped. I nodded instead.

"A few of us women in the community get together for sewing and other activities every Monday afternoon. I have a fifteen-year-old daughter who would love to watch your little one while we visited."

"That sounds amazing. I'd love to come."

She squeezed my hand. "Wonderful! My name is Grace, by the way. I'll come pick you up tomorrow, a little after lunchtime."

Ganesh walked over and hooked arms with me. We walked home, and I cooked lunch. Ganesh had brought Luna back a little bouncy chair from his supply run. She sat in it happily batting at toys while we ate our stew. I told him about Grace's invitation.

He finished his bite of the stew. "This is delicious. You sure know how to cook."

"Thank you."

"I'm glad you're getting involved in the community. I know this was forced on you, but we'll have a good life here. I promise that I will take care of you and Luna well."

"I'm confused, though," I said.

"How's that?"

"I know you said they abolished the hoods, but when I was growing up, families stayed isolated. The community never had activities."

He took a sip of his water. "They did. Your father, as the guardian, had to stay separate. He couldn't grow partial in who he allowed to leave and enter the community."

"If he hadn't been a guardian, I would have gotten to make friends?"

He nodded. "Yeah, I guess thinking on all of it, I can see why you felt inclined to leave. Things will be different for us. You can make lots of friends here as can Abra."

Luna giggled and swatted at a dangling butterfly. I looked at her and back at Ganesh, catching him smiling at her. He had an attachment to her and cared for her during my illness. I cleared the table and brought them over to where Ganesh waited at the sink. He washed, and I dried.

After clean up, I played with Luna on the floor. I laid down a blanket and placed her on her tummy. She rolled over, and I clapped and cheered.

Ganesh ran over. "What did she do?"

"She rolled over." The words gripped me, reminding me of Lachlan's words the night he left. *I might miss her rolling over or something big like that.*

Ganesh studied me. "What is it?"

"Nothing. She's growing so fast is all."

Bedtime came around, and when I walked into the bedroom, I stared at Ganesh in the bed.

He looked up. "The couch is getting kind of rough. I was hoping you wouldn't mind if I slept in the bed. I won't touch you. I promise."

"Yeah, I can sleep on the couch."

"No. Please. I've been a perfect gentleman so far. Haven't I?"

"Yes, you have. I just don't think I'm comfortable with it."

"What about this? I sleep with my head at the foot of the bed. I'll be under my own blankets, and we'll keep a pillow barricade between us?"

I pondered it for a minute. I feared pushing my luck with him. If he wanted to take advantage of me, he'd had many opportunities. His strength far outweighed mine. "Okay. If we do all that, I'll be okay with it."

He set everything up, and I climbed in next to him. I kept my back to him and cried, wishing the warm body next to me was my Lachlan.

In the darkness, Ganesh whispered, "I'll never hurt you, Bryn."

You already have.

Brain Fog

Byn

Ganesh put my hair up in a bun. "You have fun with the ladies today. I'm happy they are accepting you into the community."

I stared in the mirror at my dead eyes and sheer skin. "I look terrible."

"You're recovering. Your beauty will return in time." He kissed my cheek, and I flinched. I picked up Luna and put her bag over my shoulder.

"I'll walk you on my way to the men's meeting." He grabbed the bag from my shoulder and opened the front door.

"I guess this is a change. You didn't have to have someone babysit me all morning."

"I only have someone with when I leave in case you fall ill again."

"It feels like they're guarding me," I said.

"Why would you need a guard? Are you thinking of leaving?"

"Of course not. I totally love it here."

He rolled his eyes at my sarcasm. "In time you will, this fun day with the women is a great start."

My head throbbed, but I tried to focus on the tunnels we traveled. I made a note of all the turns and tunnels we took. We walked through the chapel. My eyes stayed focused on the podium. Had the priest pulled out the book? I couldn't remember for some reason. Growing up, our priest had written everything in a book that he kept behind his podium. It also held a detailed map of the community. I decided that would be the first place I'd check. Grace lived in a section with closely spaced dens, and we knocked on the third door. On the ground in front of the door was a mat that said welcome. The door swung open, and Grace greeted me with a huge smile.

She hugged me, and I tried not to stiffen. "We're so thrilled to have you, Bryn. Come on in." She released me and moved aside.

I turned back to Ganesh, who gave me a nervous smile. "I'll be back at noon. If you feel sick, Grace knows where we live."

"She'll be fine, Ganesh. She's in good hands." Grace shut the door. "I never thought he was going to take a wife. I'm glad he's finally pleased the elders."

Grace had pictures on her walls, like in the above ground homes. A family picture with her, a man, and three children hung on a shelf. I wondered how she'd gotten anything to hang on the damp rock walls. Her royal blue couch looked shocking for the dullness of brown that surrounded us. A yellow rug covered the living room floor.

She pointed at each of the women. "This is Mallory, Lilly, and Felicity."

I tried not to stare at Lilly's bruised face, which was quite difficult due to the extent of the bruising.

"Deborah, Bryn has brought Abra," Grace called to the back.

A slender girl with coal hair and deep brown eyes walked out from a back room. She smiled warmly. "I'm so excited to play with Abra."

I handed her my baby and the bag. This went against my instinct, but Deborah seemed nice, and I needed to seem normal. Deborah bounced Luna, and Luna smiled and cooed. They went to the next room.

Grace handed me some knitting needles. "What colors would you like? Thank you for letting Deborah play with Abra. She's excited to gain experience. She's scheduled to marry in three months, and I'm sure little ones will follow shortly."

I paused my selection and glanced up. "I thought you said she was fifteen?"

"She is. The Above One has granted his approval for marriages as young as sixteen. It leaves more childbearing years."

I looked at the yarn to avoid revealing the horror in my eyes. I chose white and pink yarn.

"You do know how to knit, Bryn?" Grace asked.

"Yes, my mama taught me from when I was little. I'd taken a break for a few years until I got pregnant with Lu—Abra. It was like riding a bike. Came right back to me."

"You've ridden a bike?" Lilly sat forward, her eyes alive with excitement.

I nodded. "Yeah, it's lots of fun."

Grace looked at me with disapproval. " The world above is not discussed here. Greed and vanity are mortal sins."

Lilly shrunk back into the couch, and I recognized the momentary death of hope. It seemed clear why Lilly bore the most visible abuse. Her dreams were the most visible of the group. I had once been Lilly, and I refused to be her again. I wouldn't stay in a place of lingering darkness. I started knitting a blanket. I could at least make the best of this and create a blanket for Luna. Grace offered me a seat on the couch next to three other women, and she took the matching blue chair. She pulled out a basket from underneath the chair full of yarn and knitting needles.

"Talitha is going to have her baby soon. I'm going to make her a blanket," Mallory said. "I'm not sure color since we don't know what it'll be yet. What color do you think I should choose, Bryn?"

Grace sent Mallory a nod, and it made me wonder if Grace had told them to actively include me.

"I love yellow. Like Grace's rug. It reminds me of the sun." I didn't look at them as I said it.

"I've meant to replace it for some time. I should probably do that on the next supply run." Grace took that moment to roll up the yellow rug.

"You've seen the sun!" Lilly's face lifted.

I met her eyes. "Yes, and stars. Those are the best."

"Bryn, I realize you are new here, but I must ask you to refrain from speaking of life outside of our community. Those are pagan things, and we can't allow ourselves corruption."

I looked at her a second, realizing she didn't deny anything about the world. She didn't snap at me and tell me it was radiated. They also had admitted at my wedding that they let people go out into the world to steal children. Something was very off.

"But they are things of nature which means they are creations of the Above One. Doesn't that make them good?" I feigned inno-cence.

"Bryn does have a point," Felicity said.

Grace pursed her lips. "They have turned pagan because they are corrupted by the evils of a world in sin. We are underground because it provides escape from the spiritual toxins we'd find in natural air. We will no longer discuss evil things in my house. Am I clear?"

All the women nodded, but I used the conversation to analyze the women. Lilly needed to come with me, and I didn't think it would take much to convince her. Felicity was a possible ally as well. Grace seemed to have control of Mallory, and I needed to keep vigilant around both of them. I got a good portion of the blanket done before the clock on the wall read noon. I heard Luna crying from the back.

"Ganesh will be here soon. I think I will gather Abra's things." I walked down the hall and found Deborah bouncing Luna on her knee.

Deborah caught sight of me. "She's so sweet. Mama says this is good training for my own little one."

I stepped inside and sat across from them. "Your mother told me that you were getting married soon. How do you feel about that?"

She looked at the ground "It is a blessing to submit to a husband and bear children for him." She kept a stoic tone as she recited a verse that I'd heard my entire life.

"I remember that proverb. It was a favorite of my priest. How do you really feel?"

She looked at me for a few seconds before glancing behind me and quietly said, "I'm scared. Have you really lived above ground?"

I nodded. "Yes, and it's a wonderful place. Full of the sky. That's the best part. That and my real husband. He is kind and loves me, no matter what."

"He doesn't hit you when you do wrong?"

"He'd rather die first."

"Bryn, Ganesh is here." Grace stood in the door, and I froze.

Why had I been so open with Deborah? I needed to be more careful. My head felt foggy, and I was slipping up. I couldn't afford that.

Deborah handed me Luna, and I smiled, hoping I could give Deborah hope. I met Ganesh at the front door, and we headed back to our den. I started making lunch. I pulled peanut butter and jelly from the cupboard and bread from the box on the counter. Actual cooking was a rarity in the cave because supplies had to keep for long periods. We were lucky to have bread from when Ganesh left to get my medicine. Soups from a can with added spices were usually the best that could be done.

Ganesh reached around me to grab plates but stayed close for an extra few seconds. His touches were becoming more frequent, and they always made me squirm. I needed to escape before he demanded more.

He nuzzled into my hair. "You smell nice."

I moved away to set the table. "Thank you. Brigid brought me some new soaps and a bottle of shampoo."

"Make me a list of things you like toiletry wise. I'll get what I can on the next supply run."

"That's kind of you. Thank you."

"Yeah, I want you to be happy here and have pretty things." He brought the sandwiches over and grabbed my hand. "Dear Above One, we thank you for this bounty. Thank you for friends like Grace, who are welcoming. I pray you will help Bryn find happiness here with me. Protect our child as she sleeps that her breath will remain. Amen. "

"Amen," I repeated and let go of his hand.

Ganesh poured water in our glasses. "How was it? Were the women kind to you?"

"Yes, quite kind. Deborah, Grace's daughter, watched Abra. She's being married soon when she turns sixteen."

"Yeah, that's normal now. It gives more time for children to be born."

I nodded. "Yes, that's what Grace said."

"Bryn, I'm trying to be patient with you, but it's expected for you to fall pregnant before Abra is one."

"She's not even two months. I needed a little more time. Please."

"I'll make it special, and I'll be gentle."

I set my sandwich down, no longer feeling hungry. "I can't. Not yet. Please."

"Can we at least kiss. I promise to leave it at that for now."

"Maybe you should ask for a different wife."

He let out a frustrated sigh. "I don't want a different wife. You fascinate me, and you're beautiful."

"You could find those things in someone else. There are women far more pretty than me here, I'm sure."

"That's not true. You haven't met most of them. Do you have any idea how gorgeous you are?"

I shook my head. "I look awful. I saw myself in the mirror."

"You look sick. Your beauty is still very obvious."

"Thank you for saying that. I know you and the elders believe my marriage to Lachlan is over, but I promised him until death do us part. How can I be righteous, breaking a marriage covenant?"

"Because it wasn't a true covenant. It wasn't ordained by the true God." He shoved his plate, and his chair scraped the floor as he jumped up. "I want to be with my wife. I want to kiss you and hold you. You keep denying me that right. I could beat you and make you, but I haven't. That should say something to you."

"If you did, you would lose me forever. I can't give you what you want."

"The first night they brought you in Brigid had me carry you. As I brought you through the tunnel and into Brigid's den, I knew I wanted you. I couldn't rid you from my mind."

"Ganesh—"

"Don't say it. I'll leave you to clean dinner." He sat down on the couch and started reading. How much longer could I hold him off?

I rubbed my head. I couldn't think straight with this headache. What was wrong with me? I didn't want a different husband here. Ganesh was the best I could hope for. I felt almost drunk or hungover like I couldn't stop things pouring from my mouth. I went to bed, hoping when I woke up, it would be gone.

Soulless

Bryn

Someone knocked on my front door, and I opened it to find Brigid.

I opened the door wider. "Please come in."

She sat on the couch next to me. "I've come to check on you. How have you been feeling?"

"Better. I had the energy to knit with a few of the other women."

Brigid clapped her hands. "That's wonderful. I'm glad to see you are settling in. I will examine you, and then I need you to give me a urine specimen."

"A urine specimen?"

"Yes, I need to check you for infection and pregnancy. I do this for all the women. We need to mark any pregnancies in the book as soon as possible. It also helps us to know who is performing their duty."

"Right." I awkwardly studied the green on my ugly couch.

She gave me a cup, and I started to leave to take care of it in my bedroom.

She grabbed my arm. "No, I must see you pee in it."

"No one else is here for me to trade with."

"It's standard. You shouldn't be shy. I saw a lot more of you when you were sick."

If she was trying to make me feel better, she was doing a terrible job. I complied and handed her the sample. She took it over to the counter and put two sticks in it then set them both on the counter. "Let's hope this is positive. It'll go a long way, proving the Above One has forgiven your transgressions. It will also reflect positively upon your husband."

I wanted to punch her in the eye really hard and tucked my hands under my thighs to prevent action. We waited for a few minutes before Brigid picked up the smaller stick. "No, sign of infection. Let's see about the other one." She picked it up and carefully examined it. She shook her head, and her face fell in disapproval. "It seems you haven't been blessed this month. I will have the priest speak with Ganesh. He needs to try harder this next month."

All I needed was for the priest to push Ganesh into being intimate with me. Ganesh believed the priest talked to God, and anything that the priest said should be followed to prevent damnation. What chance did I have against a man who wanted to sleep with me because he found me attractive and felt he had a God-ordained right to.

Brigid packed up her bag. "I'm pleased you have made company in the community. For showing such a promising effort, I'd like to invite you to the canning drive. I think your participation will be a welcome sight for everyone. It's tomorrow after lunch and morning prayers."

I opened the door to let her out. "I'll be there. Thank you for the invite."

She reached over and placed her hand on my stomach. "I pray blessing upon your womb." She turned and left.

I closed the door and shuddered from her touch. I started making lunch because Ganesh would be back from the daily men's meeting any minute. I chopped up tomatoes and put several between the bread and poured water into his glass. I followed it up with opening one of the chip bags Ganesh had brought back. Luna screeched from her blanket on the living room floor. I picked her up and bounced her on my knee.

"I can see your daddy when I look at you. I miss him. I want you to know he loves you so much. We're going to make it back to him. I promise."

The front door opened, and Ganesh walked in with a tight jaw. He put his straw hat on the hook and sat at the table. "This looks great. Thank you." He picked up his sandwich and began devouring it. "This bread is so good." He barely finished his bite before speaking.

"I'm glad you like it." I sat across from him.

He reached over the table and put his finger into Luna's tiny hand. My heart clenched as he took her. She was going to see him as her daddy. It seemed she already did.

He smiled at her. "How's my beautiful, Abra? Are you treating your mama fair? She's getting so big." His smile faded as he looked up at me. "What's wrong?"

I scratched my tear away, hoping he would think I had an itch. "Nothing."

"Are you feeling okay? Has Brigid checked you out recently?"

"Yes, this morning. Everything looked good."

"Was she upset about you not being pregnant?"

I looked at Luna smiling at Ganesh. "She mentioned it is all. What do they do to people who don't get pregnant?"

"The woman is punished."

"Punished how?"

"Time in the pit. If the behavior isn't corrected after the third time, you are expected to go out into the world and bring the children of others into the fold."

"How can you go out into the world if it is radiated?"

He looked at me with a slight grin. "We both know you know it's not."

"Why did my father tell me that? Why are other girls told that?" I remembered the fifty-four girls who I had to convince to leave because they'd been told the world was toxic.

"The priests encourage this for younger girls, so they don't wander astray. You wandered anyway. You're different, which is why I like you."

"You're saying if I don't bear a child soon, I will be thrown in this pit?"

"Yes, you don't want that to happen. Trust me."

My heart sank with memory. "You're telling me my mama probably got put into this pit three times before they kidnapped us? What does it even mean to get put into this pit?"

He cooed at Luna and kissed her hand. "The pit is solitary confinement. A dark place you can't escape. They use it for other things. Anytime a member needs to be cleansed. Cleansing takes, on average, seven days. The sentences vary based on how heinous the crime. I keep forgetting your father was a guardian and by oath-bound to a life of isolation—a harsh honor for anyone. I need to teach you more of our ways. But yes, your mother was mostly likely punished three weeks in the pit on three separate occasions."

"How do you survive without food and water for a week?"

"You are given a water jug, but you are to fast and pray for the Above one to forgive you."

I watched water drip from the ceiling and onto the floor. It brought childhood reminiscence with it. I used to watch water drip from my ceiling when I should be sleeping. Papa caught me often with the lantern on too late. I hated the suffocating darkness brought in the place. Everything here smothered a person's spirit. I could imagine the horror of the pit.

Ganesh interrupted my thoughts. "What are you thinking?"

Lachlan loved to ask me that question. He'd always wanted to know the thoughts of my heart. I could only wonder at Ganesh's reasons.

Bryn, you silly little bird. Come out of there.

I was a little girl and hiding underneath the coffee table. I popped my head out. "What's a bird, Mama?"

She reached her arms out for me, and I squirmed away. She took me on her lap. "It's an animal that flew in the sky when the world was pure."

"I want to fly. I want to fly in the sky."

She tickled me. "I wish you could. I wish the world wasn't corrupt, and my little dreamer could have every dream."

"Quit filling her head with foolishness!" Papa snapped behind us.

"I'm not. I told her it was impossible." Mama's voice shook.

"You told her what a bird was! The sky! I thought you would have learned by now! What's it going to take? More cleansing?"

"No, I'm sorry."

Papa yanked me by my arm, and it felt like it would rip from its socket. He threw me onto the rough floor of my room. He slammed the door, but it swung open a crack. "Don't ever put foolish thoughts in her head again!"

"I don't want her to grow up like me."

"And how exactly is that?"

"Alone. With dreams all dead."

I heard him strike her again and again.

She sobbed. "This is no life for a little girl. What have we done?"

"We've done the Above One's laws. It's time to gather another child into the fold. Then your precious little bird won't feel so alone. Will this stop your obstinance?"

"Can we condemn another child to this?"

I heard him strike her again and again. Later that night, when Papa let me out for dinner, Mama was gone.

I looked around, frightened. Papa always scared me, and I didn't want to be alone with him. "Where's Mama?"

"She left to be cleansed."

"When will she be back?"

He struck me across the face, and I became a ball on the floor. He kicked me. "Don't ever ask questions! Curiosity puts you where your Mama is!" He kicked me again and left me crying alone on the floor.

My thoughts returned to the present with Ganesh. I looked him in the eye. "I'm thinking that I understand why my mama often looked soulless." *The cave suffocated everything.*

"You can have this spot over here!" Lilly patted the chair next to her. "I'm canning the peaches. You can grab something else if you prefer."

"No, Peaches are fine." I sat down and looked at the strawberries that Felicity was canning. I had memories of strawberries that involved traveling the world, and they brought the pull to escape.

Deborah took the seat next to me with some cherries. "I'm happy to see you today. How is Abra?"

"She's doing great. She's with the other children." I pointed to where Mallory was reading to ten other kids of various ages. Luna sat in another lady's lap. "I'm surprised they read to them. We weren't allowed growing up."

Lilly's eyes shot up. "Not even the sacred book?"

"No."

"That's husband preference. It must have been a personal law your papa made," Deborah said. "My friend Annabelle can't read either. Her papa doesn't allow it."

"Some men believe it keeps us women safe. It holds off dreams which are dangerous within a corrupt world," another woman with deep brown eyes and curly black hair joined the conversation. "I'm Cynthia, by the way."

"It's nice to meet you, Cynthia." I opened my first jars, and old memory returned. I'd done this often with Morely, Capri, and Mama growing up.

Deborah sliced up several peaches, refilling our bowl. "Bryn, Abra is the cutest baby. I can't believe how much hair she has."

"Thank you. I was told I had lots of hair when I was a baby too."

Cynthia was pressing apples to make into sauce and paused. "Weren't you a foundling?"

"A foundling?"

"One brought in from the outside world to be cleansed."

"Yeah, I was taken from my real family when I was three."

She returned to pressing apples. "How could you know you had hair as a baby?"

"I returned to my family a few years ago. My real mother told me."

Another woman shook her head. "You have been corrupted, and it will take you time to be truly cleansed from the poisonous air. You must realize anything that comes from a corrupt mouth could be a falsehood. You were probably bald."

I squinted and opened my mouth then shut it. I had no clue how to respond to the craziness.

"Deborah, has your mama finished your wedding gown yet?" Lilly asked.

Deborah closed a jar and grabbed another. "Almost. I'm nervous about my pairing."

"You wish it to be Atticus?"

Deborah's cheeks blushed. "Why would you say such a thing?"

"Oh, no reason." Lilly winked, and Deborah seemed to shrink in her chair.

"Atticus Dunne? The priest's son?" Cynthia filled a jar with the mushed apples.

Lilly nodded enthusiastically. "He's quite handsome. I hope you do get him."

"It's unlikely. The older men get priority. I'd hoped they'd all been used up when my turn came about, but alas, I got Ralph Craig."

I glanced at Cynthia. "Who is Ralph Craig?"

"He's one of the elders and nearing seventy-five. I can't complain. He sleeps a lot."

"You are fortunate you have been blessed with children," Deborah added. "You would think old men couldn't provide that."

"The Above One chooses who to bless, Deborah. Age doesn't matter. Look at Sarah in the Bible!" Cynthia's tone rose, causing several women to look our way.

I wanted more information and for this not to turn into a fight. I played peacemaker. "You have children, Cynthia?"

Cynthia's angry glare at Deborah morphed into joy. "Yes, a little boy named Callum." Her hand moved to her stomach. "I'm having another little one. Brigid thinks about seven more months."

I smiled at her happiness. "That's amazing. Congratulations!"

"I'm sure you're dying to give Abra a sibling."

I looked over at Luna. "Yeah, I'd like that." With Lachlan, I absolutely did.

Lilly practically bounced out of her seat. "You're so lucky. Ganesh is so handsome and in his twenties. He's not old but has more maturity than those that haven't reached thirty. Many of the women have wished for him, but I heard he's turned down many pairings."

I wiped my hands on a towel so I could open another jar. "How could he turn down a pairing?"

"He's a man. They have choices on who they marry. You really are in the dark about our ways."

"Lilly! Her papa was a gatekeeper. That's an expectation!" Cynthia snapped. "It sounds like her papa was even more protective than most."

Deborah got up. "I'm going to go get some more jars." She disappeared out of the room.

Lilly laughed. "Let's see if she remembers the jars this time."

Cynthia shook her head with a scowl. "She's foolish."

I looked between both of them. "Why?"

They both avoided eye contact and stayed silent. They didn't trust me yet. Deborah remained gone for longer than it should have taken to find jars. Curiosity got the better of me.

"I need to use the hole. Can you point me to the closest one?" I pushed my chair back and stood.

Lilly pointed the way Deborah had left. "Right, left, right. Make sure you're back in fifteen minutes. If the men catch you gone, they'll punish you."

"I'll hurry." I walked out of the room and was glad they kept these tunnels lit. I went right and came to the next turn choice. I heard giggling to my right and took it instead. The tunnel opened into a room. I paused at the entrance to watch. Deborah kissed a boy. When they pulled apart, I saw he was young, probably her age. I guessed he was Atticus.

"Debbie, you have a little bit of peaches on your cheek." He brushed her face with his thumb. "Have you been stealing tastes of the fruit? Is that why you taste so sweet?"

Deborah giggled. "Better than when you ate garlic before one of our meetings."

"I always steal a peppermint stick from my mama's pantry before meeting you now. That's the lengths I go for you, my pretty star."

They kissed again, and I retreated back to the other women. My heart ached for Deborah, and I wanted to find a way for her to end up with Atticus. The wheels in my head began turning. I'd felt sad since the moment I found out she'd be forced into marriage so young. It didn't seem so bad if she ended up with the boy she loved and wanted.

"Did you find the hole okay?" Lilly asked.

I sat back in my chair. "I did. Thank you."

I canned three more jars of peaches. I noticed Lilly glancing at Deborah's empty chair with a worried look.

Grace walked in and scanned the room. She made her way to our group. "Where is Deborah?"

"She needed to use the hole," I offered.

"She knows that's not allowed during canning time."

"It seemed urgent."

"I wonder if she's well. I should go to her."

I stood up. "Grace, wait."

She stopped. "Is there a reason I shouldn't go after my daughter?"

Lilly's eyes grew big.

"No, it's not that. I just wanted to ask you something before I forget. I was wondering if children playdates were allowed?"

"Playdates?"

"Mothers bringing their children to each other's dens to play."

"Oh, yes. It is allowed. Do you want to expand Abra's circle?"

I nodded. "I wanted to invite Cynthia's Callum to play with Abra."

"Callum is a bit old to play with Abra."

"He's almost the same size!" a woman yelled.

Cynthia jumped up. "He just hasn't reached his growth spurt yet. He's perfect!"

"Callum can play with Luna if you'd like, but I personally don't see the benefit." Grace stepped past me.

To my relief, Deborah stepped into the room. "Mother, you're early today," she said, sounding almost breathless.

"Yes, are you unwell? I heard you had an urgent need to use the hole."

Deborah glanced away. "Yes, just a little too much water, I think."

"Do you think you need to go see Brigid?"

"No, the hole took care of the issue."

Imperfections

Bryn

Ganesh arrived, and I picked up Luna from the children's circle. I caught up to Cynthia, who held a tiny boy on her hip. He did look much smaller than three, and his head seemed disproportionally large.

"Would you like to bring Callum over to play?" I asked Cynthia.

She glanced around at the other women. "I thought that was just a distraction. You really want Abra to play with my Callum?"

"Yeah, I mean, I know he's older and everything, but I thought we could get to know each other."

She smiled and nodded. "I'd like that."

Ganesh took Luna, and she smiled big. I needed to feel grateful Ganesh treated Luna kindly enough that she wanted to go to him, but that was always tainted by the fact that only another man had a right to be Luna's daddy.

"Did you have a good time?" Ganesh asked me on our walk home.

"Yes, it was fun. Grace is going to tally up the jars we canned, and then we get a share. I hope you like peaches."

"I love peaches. Isn't that right, my little peach." He kissed the top of Luna's head.

"I invited Cynthia to bring her little boy over to play with Abra."

"Isn't he a bit old for that?"

I shrugged. "It was more of an excuse to have time with Cynthia."

"I'm sure she's thrilled. Most of the other women don't want Callum near their kids."

"What? Why's that?"

"Have you seen the boy?"

"Yes, he's little."

"He's more than little. I often wonder how he can stand with that head of his."

I sent him a disapproving look. "That's mean to say bad things about a child."

"He has something wrong with him. The Above One saw to curse him. Cynthia and Ralph must have done something wrong. It's become more and more evident, and soon the elders may vote on it."

"What does that mean?"

"It means if it is established that he has an imperfection, then he'll be set free to the Above One."

My mouth hung open, and it took me a minute to regain composure. "Set free? He'll be killed?" I almost whispered it out of fear of the answer.

"He will gain his heavenly body early so his corruption can't continue into adulthood where he'd find no redemption."

"They'll kill him!"

"It's a peaceful passing."

I quit walking and stared at him with my eyes widened. "This is insanity."

"Shhh! Bryn, don't talk like that."

"It isn't right."

"The Above One's will is always right. Even if it's a difficult thing to face."

Angry tears stung my face, and I wanted to punch something. "Does Cynthia know?"

"She has to, but I'm sure she's coping by denying it's a possibility. I've seen her snap at anyone who comments on him."

"She's pregnant. They shouldn't put a pregnant woman through that stress either."

"Well, that's good. See, the child's ascension wouldn't be so bad with a replacement on the way."

I grabbed Luna from him and quickened my pace to our den. I got a bottle out and started feeding her on the couch when Ganesh caught up to us.

He stood over me with anger flashing in his eyes. "Don't ever disrespect me like that again! You're lucky no one saw you stomp away from me like that. You want to challenge me? Do it in this den alone. Do you hear me?"

I took a deep breath to keep myself from screaming at Ganesh. I couldn't allow anything to happen to me until I got Luna away from these psychos.

"Do you hear me?" Ganesh yelled.

"I hear you."

He shook his head and stormed off toward the bedroom. For the rest of the day, he stayed in the bedroom reading. I kept to the living room with Luna. The days crawled in the damp dungeon. That night to my relief, Ganesh slept on the couch, and I got the bed to myself. He left for the men's meeting before I got up. The one good thing about being stuck here was Luna could have my complete attention.

Midmorning, I opened my door to find Lilly, Deborah, and Cynthia with Callum on her hip. I let them in, and we went to my living room, where Luna played on her blanket.

Cynthia set a bag of toys down in front of Callum, and he quickly moved a wooden truck across the floor.

"I hope you don't mind that I invited Lilly and Deborah." Cynthia sat down across from where I sat in the chair.

"I thought I could keep the little ones busy while you ladies talk. If that's okay anyway," Deborah said.

"That's very nice of you. Can I get any of you water or tea?" I stood to head to the kitchen.

They all said they were fine, so I sat back down. Deborah sat on the floor with the children. She bounced Luna on her knee while running a second car next to Callum's.

Lilly glanced around the room as if searching for something. "Has Ganesh left for the day?" I nodded, and she continued. "We came because we wanted to talk to you." She looked at the other two. "We wanted to talk to you about forbidden things."

I smiled. "My favorite subject."

Deborah and Lilly laughed. Cynthia looked slightly stricken before slow amusement displayed on her face.

Lilly continued. "We know you escaped the caves before. All of us have reasons we want to leave, but we're terrified. We were hoping you could tell us what it's like above ground."

"I'd love to." I spent the next two hours telling them all I could about the world. They stayed captivated on me the entire time.

Callum brought his chubby hands to his face before flinging them outward and saying "A boo! A boo."

Luna smiled, and Callum repeated the action. The second time Luna smiled, Callum giggled and looked up at Cynthia. "Mama! The baby wuvs me!"

I told myself I wouldn't burst into tears. He was the sweetest baby boy. I couldn't let them kill him. I didn't know how I'd stop them, but they weren't killing him. All three women watched me watching the children.

I met all of their eyes one by one. "Why do you want to leave the cave?" I needed to hear their reasons and see the look in their eyes. I needed more proof they weren't spies for Brigid and Grace.

Lilly sat forward. "I'll start. I just found out two days ago I'm pregnant with my first."

"Congratulations!"

"Thank you. It was expected. It was my last chance before they would declare me barren. My husband made sure that wouldn't happen. I ummm..."

I grabbed her hand. "Don't tell us anything that makes you uncomfortable."

She nodded. "I grew up here. I've known nothing else. When you left Bryn, it created a giant controversy. Someone in the community spread word that the guardian's daughters had rebelled and left into the corrupt world. We were told you were killed. Somehow, word got out about your sisters and you being alive. The whole radiation thing unraveled with the rumors. This was all confirmed when they brought you back in. Talitha says she saw your picture on the magic boxes and knows it's you. One of the elders was confronted with this by a brave woman who spent ten days in the pit for it. They couldn't deny things anymore. They told us the radiation had always been metaphorical for the spiritual poison of the world. I've always wanted more. So many of us have. You've become our hero. You did what none of us have been able to do."

Cynthia watched Callum as she spoke. "You've probably noticed my boy is different. Brigid keeps commenting on it. Ralph has stopped acknowledging him. That's not a good sign. I can't let them hurt him. Not when there is an abundance of places I can keep him safe. We were going to wait to get to know you better, but I can feel Callum's time running out. My heart is telling me to run with him, but I don't know where to go."

I turned to Deborah. "And you? Why do you want to leave?"

Her eyes welled. "There's a boy, Atticus. I found out yesterday they are marrying me to Marvin Gallen. He's in his late seventies. Me and my boy both want out before my wedding night in two months."

"Do you think it can be done? Do you think we can get out?" Lilly looked at me with such hope in her eyes.

My eyes landed on the children before moving to the three women, two of which carried more children to be brought into the cave. I now knew why all of this had happened. "Yes, it can be done."

We were starting a revolution.

Church for the week arrived, and Ganesh led us toward a log in the front. I felt uncomfortable as that was usually reserved for the highest members. Ganesh put his arm around me, and I saw the priest nod at him, which made me squirm. The Priest lifted his arms, and everyone did the tedious chanting that I hated more than anything.

When it concluded, the priest began giving announcements. "Today is a wondrous day. We are forgoing the main service to make an announcement that will be held as the utmost important declaration in decades. As most of you know, The Above One has spared Bryn Moretti a life of corruption twice. This shows how gracious and kind he is. His extended mercy is because of the child born to Bryn. Abra Moretti has been declared a holy child. Since that realization, it has become clear she is a gift much greater than that. She is our first oracle in more than forty years. Bring the child forward."

I squeezed Ganesh's arm. He shook me loose and sent me a stern look. He took Luna from my arms and brought her to the priest. I wanted to scream, throw things, and grab my child away from the man who seeped evil with every word he spoke.

The priest raised Abra into the air. "Behold this angelic face. The blue eyes that shine brightly against her immense dark hair. Her beauty reveals how we have been blessed with one who speaks directly to God."

Luna wiggled, and I wanted so badly to run for her. I trembled in my seat as he held my baby under her armpits, dangling her for all the see like she was a freakin lion in a cartoon movie. The room burst into cheers. None of them questioned this insanity. They were all unbelievably brainwashed. My eyes caught Lilly and Cynthia. The strained looks on their faces told me they at least knew this whole thing was a sham.

"Behold the perfect child gifted to us by the Above One!" He jerked her forward, and I started to rise.

Ganesh held my thigh so firmly to the seat that I knew it'd bruise. Luna couldn't hold her head upright for long, and it lulled slightly back. A wail ripped from her, and as she squirmed the priest dropped her. I screamed as Brigid caught Luna seconds from the floor. She gave my baby back to the priest.

I couldn't handle it. "Give my baby!" I fought against Ganesh. "Give her to me now!"

All heads snapped to me, and the priest looked ready to burn me at the stake. He lowered Abra, and she continued to scream. He handed her to Brigid and made his way to me. The punch hitting my cheek knocked me out cold.

Empty Beds

♥

Lachlan- Two months earlier

The police finally let me back into my house. I didn't go back for an additional three days because the thought of walking into where my family was ripped from me felt unbearable. I moved to our bedroom and took in the scene of our unraveled room. I picked up Luna's baby blanket that still laid in the bassinet. It was a soft baby pink with stars and moons knitted throughout. The skill and care Bryn had used to craft it was intricate.

My chest heaved involuntarily, and I sunk to the ground, still holding the blanket. They came into my house and took my wife and daughter. My entire world collapsed in minutes. My world was as frail as a newborn's first cry. I curled into myself, cradling the blanket I wished wrapped around my daughter. Grief, torment, guilt, and agony were what made up the form I was buried inside. This body that wanted nothing more than my girls back in my arms. Only a heavy emptiness was what my arms held. I melded into my sorrow for hours until a voice pulled me from the vacancy consuming me.

"Brother, I got you. I got you." Ryo helped me sit.

I looked into his eyes. "I'm so broken without them. There's no way to ever fix this."

He put his hand on my shoulder. "There is, and that's getting them back. I swear to you, Lachlan, the biggest oath I could ever swear. We're getting them back."

I gripped Luna's blanket. "What if they're already dead?" An anguished cry tore from my mouth because part of me thought they were.

Ryo waited until I calmed to speak. "You know how Bryn is always talking about her gut feelings? I have a pretty strong one, and it tells me both of them are still alive. It tells me they need their husband and daddy not to fall to pieces. They need him whole to bring them home. That's what you need to see. Them home and never them buried. You need to use the anger I know you have and vanquish the bastards who took your wife and baby. I'm right with you. I'm pretty angry myself that they took my darling. I'm angry they took my niece. We need to use that to take these people down. For that reason, neither of us can ever give in to this heavy grief."

I nodded, and Ryo helped me to my feet.

Present

Bryn and Luna had been missing for three months, and I couldn't afford to feel anymore. Every night without them, my heart became more battered. I focused myself and placed all my energy into finding them. The hype had died down, and Adely and Koa had returned to their lives with their families.

Thane asked if Capri could stay while he traveled for business, and of course, Anna and Donovan welcomed her with open arms. They were two of the most generous people I'd ever met. I hadn't left yet because I couldn't go home to either of our houses and look at all the reminders of Bryn and Luna. Two empty nurseries were enough to turn me into nothing.

I stayed in the guest house with Bryn's older brother Cole. He and I had turned a spare bedroom into our recon room. A map of the cave system hung on the wall, and different colored pins were pushed in according to our guide. Blue pins meant tourist spots, green meant nonpublic but explored, and red meant unexplored. The map was external only since no one knew what some of the internal areas contained. We'd be going in blind. Every day I stared at it for hours, writing down any patterns I thought I saw.

Most mornings Cole and I went to a rock-climbing facility where an older man named Davey taught us all he knew about spelunking. Ryo and Thane joined us when they could. I studied every possible piece of equipment we would need. I felt confident we could take on the dangers of the cave and live through it.

Cole sat in the chair next to me and handed me a bowl of popcorn. Staring at the map together had become our nightly routine. "I think we're getting closer to narrowing down the best part to try first. We take enough camping gear that we could stay out there until we find something."

I looked at my notebooks of patterns and back at the map. "Yeah, I think it makes sense to go to that big pocket of red over there. You think that's what about a hundred square miles?"

"At least. But what if they are over there in the second pocket. It's clear on the other side," Cole said.

"We check out both and hope it's not in one of the smaller pockets. I'm thinking we've gathered all the information we're going to, and we need to make our move."

"We already have most of the supplies ready. Plenty of guns and knives."

I ran my fingers through my hair. "If we find them, I'm taking that whole damn cult down."

Cole gave me a fist bump. "Totally in on that. And it's when not if. I'm not coming back without my sister or niece."

"I have a meeting with the lead detective in three days. If he has no new information, we leave the next morning."

"Sounds like a plan. I've been waiting almost twenty years to kick these bastards' asses."

Cole left, and I continued to stare at the map. Too much of the cave system was unexplored, and that made finding Luna and Bryn seem impossible. I didn't care if it was harder than finding Pluto in the night sky. I would find them if it took the rest of my life.

I sat across from Detective Lambert as he pulled up Bryn and Luna's case on his computer.

He finished typing and glanced up. He rested his fingertips together. "I'm sorry to tell you the trail has gone cold. We've sent people looking in the cave and have found no leads. It's just too large, and the terrain is unexplored and dangerous."

"Are you telling me that my wife and daughter are considered a cold case after only three months?"

"Not exactly a cold case yet, but headed that direction if something big isn't found soon. They seem to have vanished without a trace."

I bit my cheek, giving myself a second to seethe. "Yeah, exactly as the first time my wife was kidnapped when she was three. They took her back into the cave."

"Yeah, probably, but I already explained why that's an issue."

I stood up, shoving my chair forward. "Thank you for absolutely nothing." I stormed out of his office. I reached my truck and dialed Cole first. "Detective Lambert basically said the case is dead in the water. He wouldn't say they are giving up on Bryn and Luna but acknowledged they would if no leads were found soon."

"Time?" He asked simply.

"Yeah, I'm calling Thane and Ryo. Let's meet at for one last training."

"Alright. See you in an hour."

We hung up, and I relayed the information to my friends. We all met up with Davey, and he went over all the equipment we would need.

He placed everything on a cart. "I'm giving you some backup oxygen tanks. I know it makes sense they are somewhere close to an entrance, but you should never go into an unexplored cave without oxygen."

Cole and I took it all out to my truck and loaded it. Ryo and Thane followed.

I gave Davey a hug. "Thank you for all of your help."

He patted my back. "You bring your beautiful girls to see me when you get them back."

"I will for sure."

The plan was to leave in the morning, and I went home to get plenty of sleep. I didn't sleep much anymore, but tonight I had to try. I needed all the energy I could muster to get my family back. I found Anna in the kitchen of the main house.

I told her what the detective told me and watched her shoulders slump. Her green eyes that matched Bryn's held a long-term sorrow and carried the deep bags as extra emphasis. She'd always looked so put together since I'd known her. Lately, I'd seen her with disheveled hair and wearing her bathrobe over pajamas. She hadn't gone to work since the trade show the night that we'd lost the girls.

"I'm going after them, Anna. Tomorrow morning. Cole, Ryo, and Thane are coming with."

She knew we'd been training, so her eyes held no surprise. "I'm worried about all of you, but I think you're our only hope for getting my babies back."

"I'll have Cole's back. I won't let anything happen to another of your children."

She lifted her head from the ground. "You watch your own back then too. You became my son a long time ago." She hugged me.

"I'm bringing them home, Anna. I promise."

"If anyone can, it'll be you. Check-in with me when you can."

I went to bed and touched the part of my bed that shouldn't be empty. "I'm going to find you, baby. I'm going to bring you and Luna home." I told her the promise I told her every night since I'd lost her. A restless night led to morning. I got up early and loaded a duffle bag with my personal items. Ryo and Thane pulled into the driveway. Anna and Donovan came out to the drive to see us off.

Anna waved all of us over, and we all piled into her arms. "All of you are my boys. My sons. All of you come home."

We climbed into my truck and drove toward Kentucky.

The Pit

Bryn

I woke up back in the den with Ganesh in a chair next to my bed. His jaw looked tight, and he glowered.

I groaned as my cheek seared pain. "Luna!"

He moved in front of me. "Brigid has Abra at the rest of the ceremony."

I forced myself upright. "You left her!"

"You gave me no choice! You have no right to be angry. This is all on you."

I pushed him away. "He was hurting her!"

"He would never hurt the holy child."

"He almost dropped her! He didn't support her head!"

"She is fine!"

I jumped out of bed and ran for the door. Ganesh grabbed me around my waist and tossed me on the bed. I fought against him but couldn't budge.

He kept a firm hold on my shoulders. "You are going to get us both thrown in the pit. If you want to keep Abra safe, the best thing you can do is comply."

"My baby!" I cried. "Without her, I have nothing here to comply for."

"They're bringing her back soon. You need to calm down."

I quit struggling against him, and he released me. I turned my back away from him.

He pushed my hair behind my ear and touched my shoulder. "Bryn, I promise she'll be back soon." A knock hit the door, and Ganesh rose. "Stay here!"

I tiptoed out of bed and peeked into the living room. To my relief, Luna smiled at Ganesh as he took her. Out of all the men here, Ganesh was the only one I trusted with Luna. I didn't want him in our lives, but he seemed to really care about her.

"Have you dealt with your wife?" Brigid snarled. "She disgraced you today. On such a glorious day."

"Yes, she has been punished," Ganesh said with his voice full of tension.

"The elders are deciding if they will pursue community punishment against her."

"She is my wife. I have dealt her punishment. Community action is not necessary."

Brigid crossed her arms. "You insisted you would have better control of her. You need to break her spirit. I suggest you withhold food and give lashings twice a day. Hard enough to draw blood."

"You can leave my house, woman! How I handle my wife is none of your concern."

Brigid turned to go before pausing and turning back around. "You are showing her too much love. This will be your downfall." Brigid left with a slam of the door.

I ran back to the bed as Ganesh moved toward the bedroom.

As soon as he appeared in the room, I ran for him. "Give me my daughter."

He handed me Luna and sat down in a chair. "Bryn, you have to do better about not vocalizing things. If he'd really dropped our baby, I'd have been the first to challenge him. But Abra is fine, and things could have been a lot worse for you. I'm scared. If you don't watch it, they will hurt you. They may hurt you in a way I don't get you back."

"Why do you stay here if this place scares you? If this place would punish you, for the way that you live your life?"

He moved over to the bed and took my hand. "Because my soul, yours, and Abra's souls are way too important. This life is a flame. It's short. I can't stand the thought of you or our baby in damnation."

"They're going to kill a child because he was born different. Not bad, only different, but he's also the same. He's just a little boy." I shoved a tear away.

"They are sparing him, Bryn! If he carries his curse into adulthood, he will be damned. Letting him be damned is far more cruel than a peaceful passing."

I gaped at him. He actually believed all of this to the core of him. He really thought they were saving Callum's soul by killing him. I couldn't stop the tears. His blind faith was stirring conflict in me. Ganesh wanted with all his heart to be a good man, but the cult had twisted good into ugly and horrific.

Ganesh wiped one of my tears. "I know all of this seems terrible to you. I understand you won't agree, but please, if you can't stay quiet for yourself, please do so for Luna. If they take her from us, we have no control over what happens to her. You want to vent and holler do it here with me. But never again in public."

I looked at the grey comforter on the bed. My tears kept landing on it, turning it darker. I met his eyes. "The problem is that some things are too terrible to stay silent for."

His face fell. "I will try to hold the elders off on a decision on the boy. I just worry for his soul."

"Thank you."

Ganesh left to sleep on the couch. I put a sleeping Luna in her bassinet, landed on my bed, and fell apart. I had to pray Ganesh could hold the elders off long enough for me to figure out how to get Callum out of the cave.

Ganesh splashed me with the dishwater and smiled.

"Eww! That's disgusting. It's dishwater." I wiped my face with a towel.

He splashed me again. I scooped up some of the water and flung it at his face. He scooped up some of the suds and smeared them on my hair. It dripped down my cheek. I returned the favor by launching bubbles on his shirt. He scooped another load, and I ducked. I ran to the living room, and he chased me with a handful of soap.

I laughed and bolted for the bedroom. He ran in after me and backed me to the corner. He smeared the bubbles on my chest and kept his hand there a little too long. He cupped my face, and we stared at each other. He leaned in and kissed me.

I turned my head. "Stop! I can't."

He gripped my face hard and forced a kiss. "I'm growing impatient. We've been married three months and still haven't consummated our marriage. It's not natural."

"I'm already married to someone else."

He threw me over his shoulder. "You're married to me!" He flung me on the bed and was on top of me.

"Stop!"

He held my hands down and kissed me. I squirmed but could barely move.

Tears rolled down my cheeks. "Please!"

"You're my wife. I have a right to be with you. Your marriage to him is no longer valid. I've been so patient with you. How long must I wait to claim what's mine?"

"If you do this, I will never accept you."

He lifted himself up and sat on the end of the bed with his hand to his head. He stormed out of the room. I heard the front door slam. Luna screamed, and I pulled myself together to get to my daughter. I fed her and calmed her before quickly putting diapers and milk in a bag. I placed Luna in a homemade sling and hurried out the door.

I didn't know how long I had until Ganesh returned, and I hoped the community followed the rules about not leaving their homes for the rest of Sunday. I made it to the chapel and ran behind the podium. I grabbed the book and flipped through it quickly. I found the map but didn't take the time to look at it as I ripped it from the book. I stuffed it in a tiny inner pocket of the bag and zipped it closed. I went out an archway opposite from the one that led to my quarters.

I found a secluded area and studied the map. I used G. Moretti, the chapel, and Grace's den to figure out the rest of it. I burned it in my memory and gave myself hints to remember the important locations. The exits were far. It would take a lot to get to them. The community was larger than I'd thought. There were four more pockets. There had to be hundreds of members between the four of them.

I tucked the map back in my bag. I needed to meet with the other women somehow, so we could make a plan. I looked toward the path that led to the exit and the path that led back to my den. I headed back to my den. I couldn't leave without the women and Callum. If I did, it might anger Ganesh enough that he'd let them kill the boy. The walk would be long, and who knew how fast I could get help back here. I couldn't abandon these women who were relying on me.

I opened my front door to find Brigid, the priest, and Ganesh all in the living room. Ganesh had his face buried in his hands. The priest and Brigid looked ready to murder me.

"Give me the baby," Brigid said in a deadly calm voice.

The priest moved toward me. "If you love your daughter, give her to Brigid."

Ganesh looked up at me then and his eyes pleaded. He was crying.

I let the priest give Luna to Brigid, who, to my relief, carried her to Ganesh.

The priest stepped closer to me. "We came to see that you were punished, and your husband looked stunned when we found your den empty. Bryn Moretti, for your defiance of the Above One's ways, you are hereby sentenced to a week in the pit. If you resist, we will remove Luna from your care and give her to a more worthy family."

I held out the diaper bag, and Ganesh took it. I had to hope he wouldn't search it too thoroughly, but the map was better with him than them. I let them lead me from the room. They forced me through the winding paths for what seemed at least a mile. We came to a large opening. The priest put a ladder into the pit.

"Climb down." He shoved me forward.

I did what he said. Brigid brought down two jugs of water and set them next to me. They climbed back up the ladder, removing it once they were at the top. They left, taking the light with them. I slumped on the ground and shook. I started to lose track of time, but I knew it had probably been days. One of my water jugs felt like it might be half empty. I'd conserved it as much as possible.

I sang and slept to pass the time, but there was no way my sanity was staying intact. I had a lot of time to think, which allowed me to come up with a plan. We needed a secret way to get messages to each other. I also thought about Rachel Slater and her delusions. It seemed she'd been thrown in the pit a lot. I felt pretty sure that the isolation and abuse had caused her to snap. Guilt tugged at me when I thought about my coldness at our last meeting. I moved my finger across the dirt and sang "A Million Dreams" for the fiftieth time. I no longer even tried to stop the tears. They grew, as did my despair.

"Mommy." I heard a voice and looked through the darkness. Something glowed and grew brighter. "Mommy." It was a small child's voice. The little blonde-haired girl appeared in front of me.

I stared at her until I realized her brightness hadn't made me wince. My eyes hadn't needed adjustment from the darkness. "Who are you?"

"I'm your little girl."

"Luna? Have I been in here that long?"

She laughed. "No, your other little girl."

I sat up. "Aurora?" I'd miscarried a daughter about two years ago.

She nodded.

I reached my hand out to her, and it went right through her. "I'm dead?"

"No, your mind wants to see me."

"You're a hallucination?"

She nodded.

"Can I hallucinate your father?"

She grinned. "I'm not sure it works that way. I've come to tell you something very important."

"If you are a hallucination, how important could anything you say be?"

She frowned. "You need to listen to me. It's important."

"Okay. What is important?"

"You aren't better."

I glanced around me. "I know. I'm in a pit."

"No, you're sick. You're still sick."

"They're just headaches."

"Look in the mirror." She spread her arms to the side.

A mirror with a brass frame appeared, and I walked over to it. "Why am I yellow?"

"You're sick. You're still very sick. You will die unless you run."

I sat back down next to my water jugs. "I want to run, but I have to take them all."

"If you take them all, you will die."

"Will they be free? Will your sister be free? Callum?"

"Yes, but you will die."

"Why?"

"Because you're still sick. You're running out of time. You will only get sicker." She pursed her lips as though frustrated with my denseness.

"It's them or me?"

"Yes, you could leave with Luna and be safe. But Callum will die. Many will die."

"This is my purpose?"

She nodded. "This is your purpose. You can forsake it and live or embrace it and die."

"What will happen when I die?"

"You will be with me."

I smiled and nodded. "I love you, Aurora. Watch over your daddy for me."

"Always." She faded, returning me to darkness.

I snapped my head up, realizing I'd fallen asleep. The dream was more vivid than any dream I'd ever had. Aurora may not have visited me, but I could feel in my gut that her words were true. I was still sick.

Acceptance

Bryn

I hummed, "Twinkle Twinkle Little Star" and rocked back and forth. Something had been crawling on my skin for probably hours. At first, it scared me, but I accepted its presence. My mind wandered to memories of Lachlan, and I wished I'd hallucinate him.

"I felt that! The baby kicked my hand," Lachlan said in bed one morning. "I want to have ten more of these."

I looked at him wide-eyed. "You want ten more kids?"

"Yeah, why not." He kissed the back of my neck.

"Lots of reasons."

"Name five."

I stared at the blinds letting in the sun. "It's a lot of work. We can't give them all enough attention. We'd have to have fifty nannies to go on vacation. We'd never sleep. Our house would be chaos."

"The best chaos there is."

"You can't be serious."

He moved his hand to find a better spot to feel the baby. "This is so amazing, though. It's going too fast. The baby is going to grow so fast. I don't want to miss any of it."

"You do have school, but I'm sure you'll get a lot of time in between."

"I'm just going to take him or her in one of those baby slings to classes. No one will mind. It'll probably earn me better grades. Bringing a baby is like a bribe of cuteness."

I laughed. "I don't think anyone will see it that way."

"I'm going to be one of those dads who stays up at night with the baby. I won't get to see them enough, otherwise."

"You would get no complaints from me."

He started tickling me. "We're going to be parents, Bryn! Parents! We've got our happily ever after."

I squirmed. "Stop. Stop." I turned over and kissed him. "Stop the torture, and there are more kisses."

"Yes, Ma'am!"

I kissed him, and we fell into each other. This really felt like happily ever after. We were untouchable. We'd had all the bad and deserved only good.

After our kisses and touches ended, I pushed myself against his chest. "Maybe two more."

He put his hand back on my belly, and the baby obliged. "Deal." His arms brought me serenity.

I talked to Lachlan, wishing he could hear me. "I wonder what you're doing right now. Are you at work? I hope you're still doing the things you need to do to graduate. You'll need to provide for Luna still. We have lots of family, so I think you'll be okay. I know it will hurt, but Luna will help make it okay."

I talked to Ryo. "I know I don't even have to tell you to take care of Morely and Dahlia because that's what you do best. You take care of everyone. Give my family your randomness after I'm gone. They'll need the laughter you are so good at bringing."

I went through the rest of my family. I made it through my sisters. I told Morely to love her life with Ryo and her babies. Not to let my death lessen that. I asked her to keep Jada's house going. I knew that she would. I told Capri to go on adventures with Thane even when her fear told her not to. I wanted her to embrace life. I told Koa not to do anything too crazy that would kill her. I wanted her to make it to eighteen and beyond. I didn't want her to join me in heaven until she was at least eighty.

I told Adely and Dahlia to stay best friends and that they would always be loved. I went through my brothers. I told Cole to keep up with his music because music was life. I told Jace to visit mom more and that I would miss his French cooking. I asked Thane to look after Capri and protect her sensitive soul. I asked him to check on Lachlan when he could.

I got to my parents. "Daddy, thank you for proving that great fathers exist and living that every day I've known you. You never wavered in your love for me. You showed how a real man treats his children. You changed my entire view on fatherhood."

I got to my mom next, and tears streamed down my face. "Mom, I'm sorry my kidnapping happened to you twice. Please get up every morning and see me in the sky. See me in the sun that will touch your face or the fireflies that brighten the night. See me in the ocean waves and feel me in the wind. Let the ocean heal you as you play with Luna in it. I plan to stay a part of all of that. Go back to work and live because I can't anymore. Show Luna everything I loved about the world."

"Rachel Slater, I forgive you, and I understand you. I'm sorry you were tormented to the point you no longer knew what reality was. Any time your thoughts strayed to see this as wrong, you were beaten or thrown into darkness. I understand now why you accepted all of this as your truth. Seeing all of this as truth was all that kept you safe." I shoved a tear away.

I sobbed as I got to Luna. "Dance in the rain, play in the ocean, and live every moment like it might be your last. Don't live it in fear but in wonder of needing to experience all of it. Don't let anyone tell you dreams are wrong. Above everything, do good and be a light in the darkness. Bring others out of their despair. May that be the legacy I left to you. I will always watch over you. Your sister and I will always watch over you. You will never be alone. Remember the stars always fall which means wishes never die. Your daddy taught me that years ago on a group home roof. Never stop wishing for your happy ending. Fight for it. Even though I'm not getting mine, it was worth the fight. "

I full circled back to Lachlan. "Don't close your heart to love. Open it, and you might be surprised by what you find waiting for you. You can survive without me. I know you can because you are the strongest man I have ever met. You survived the isolation that I feel now because at six your mother locked you in closets for hours. You are so much stronger than you think you are. Remember, I'm going to love you until the universe turns to dust. Our love will never end with my death."

I curled up and realized I could accept death. I'd already decided I wasn't going to leave without the women. If that meant my death, so be it. I wished I could prepare Lachlan, but with me gone so long already maybe, he was already prepared for my loss. I let my despair consume as though I could rid it from my system before the final test of my life. I took all of it inside of me and grieved my missed life. I found acceptance inside of the darkest place.

I would lead all of them out of here, and I felt with all my heart that this fate would be a worthy one. I would give my final fight to Luna, Callum, and these women. I closed my eyes in peace.

Light startled me, and I kept my eyes tightly shut. I heard a scraping sound and then arms around me.

"Bryn?"

"Lachlan?" I hoped with all my heart.

"No, I'm sorry it's Ganesh. I need you to climb the ladder, then I'll carry you the rest of the way."

I winced as I opened my eyes and caught sight of the blurry ladder. I stumbled over to it and climbed. I collapsed on the ground. Arms carried me and eventually laid me on something soft. A blanket went over my shoulders, and a soft kiss pressed to my head. I fell back into sleep.

"Her sentence wasn't over yet!" A man's voice bellowed. "We should give you the rest of her sentence!"

"She is my wife! You took my right to decide her punishment," Ganesh roared back.

"She committed a public sin!"

"Three days was enough!"

"First, you call a challenge to the vote on the child and now you remove your wife before her sentence is complete."

"I want a sane wife! Unlike yours, who babbles to herself continually because you gave her to the pit for all small things."

"I am making a challenge to the elders against you, Ganesh Moretti."

"Go ahead, and you can tell them how you put my wife in the pit against my will without a hearing."

The door slammed, and Ganesh let out a yell of frustration. He came back to the room and dropped on his knees next to my bed. "Do you forgive me?"

I looked at him, confused. I couldn't remember what he'd done. "Why?"

"Because I was wrong. If I hadn't done what I did, you wouldn't have run away. I expected you to stay gone, but you came back. Part of me wished you hadn't."

"I don't remember it, so yes, I forgive you."

His brow furrowed. "The pit does things to people. I've seen it. It's like demons live inside of it. I shouldn't have been a coward. I should have taken you out the first day."

I looked at the wall. "It's okay. I found peace there."

His eyes widened. "You did?"

"Yes, and I saw my daughter, who passed. She was beautiful."

"I think I should get Brigid to check you out."

"No, I'm fine. Can you stay with me, please?"

He grabbed a pillow and blanket and laid on the floor. It wasn't until a bit later I realized I'd forgotten something vital.

I sat up. "Ganesh, where is Luna?"

"She's with Brigid until the hearing."

"No!"

"The hearing is this afternoon. They will decide both my challenges on killing Callum and removing you from punishment."

I wanted to run to my baby, but I felt so tired. I closed my eye almost involuntarily and slept.

Ganesh shoved my shoulder. "You need to eat something. We have to leave for the hearing soon." He fed me soup.

I got up to get dressed, and he left me for privacy. I walked over to the mirror and felt grateful I wasn't actually yellow. I stared closer at my eyes. The whites of my eyes did look dull. They were cream, maybe. I picked my brush and ran it through my hair. A wad of hair came out with it, and I stared at it. *I'm still sick. It's okay. I've accepted this.*

Ganesh held my hand as we walked to the chapel. We kept going into a new tunnel until we came into a room with plastered walls. *Who plasters a cave?* Folding chairs faced a tall wooden podium. Men in black robes sat facing the crown of around thirty people. I counted twelve men in robes. Ganesh brought me to the front, and we sat.

An elderly woman wearing white stepped out from the back. Her eyes landed on me. "I wish to speak to the new oracle and her mother."

Brigid came into view and handed Luna to the woman. The woman waved me forward, and I followed her. We pushed through thick black curtains until we came to a room that smelled like the jasmine flowers. A red cabinet ran across one wall, and the plush blue carpet felt soft on my feet. The room looked normal with the red couch and bed. The blue walls made me feel I'd left the cavern behind.

She pointed to the couch. "Sit."

I did as she asked, and she placed a sleeping Luna in my arms.

"We must wait for the child to wake, so I can speak with her. While we wait, I want to talk to you."

"Are you the oracle?"

"Yes, one of three, counting your daughter."

"You're a woman."

She looked down at Luna. "As is your daughter."

"Are all oracles women?"

"No, most have been men."

"How can a woman oppress another woman?"

A small smile appeared on her lips. "You really believe what we do here is oppression?"

"Yes, very much it is."

She got up and pulled a jug of water from the cabinet and brought me some in a glass. "Here drink this. You are looking unwell."

"I have accepted this."

She studied me for a moment. "I guess it is good to accept the inevitable."

"Will you answer my question about how you can oppress women as you are one?

"What you see as oppression we see as obedience. What you see as cruelty we see as mercy. What you see as darkness we see as light. You have strayed, and this is difficult for you to reconcile. Your morals have skewed to call evil good and good evil."

"You cause pain. There is no good in that," I said.

"Pain purifies. Were you not purified in the pit? You say you have accepted your illness. Would that have come about without the pit?"

My toes pushed into the carpet. "No, but only because I would have thought I was still well."

"See purification." Luna opened her eyes, and the woman took her from me. "I must speak with the child alone. She will tell me about your punishment." She took Luna out a different door than the one we'd entered. I wondered if she'd also been thrown in the pit too much.

I wandered the room, looking at abstract paintings of smeared black and grey. Even the art revealed the terribleness of the place. I opened the cabinet and saw dozens of bottles with a clear liquid. They all had a label that said purification on them. I opened one and smelled nothing from it. Maybe it was holy water. Something inside me urged me to put it back because it had a sinister drip to it.

The store creaked as the woman stepped back into the room. "I would not drink those if I were you. Too much, and you will meet the Above One. Only a little at a time is needed for purification."

I closed the cabinet. "Is that what you've done to me? Purified me?"

"Not quite yet. You are still full of impurities. Your daughter has generously agreed to give you mercy. She loves you."

This woman was a loon, but I'd hoped those would be Luna's thoughts if she could speak.

"What does her mercy mean?"

She handed Luna back to me. "She wants you to attend school. She has pointed out the unfairness of you accepting our ways without truly knowing them."

"I'm going to school?"

"Yes, with the children. You will be tested in two weeks. If you pass, you will not have to finish your sentence in the pit. Your husband's challenges will be approved. "

"You will spare Callum?"

"We will give him three months to prove himself perfect."

I nodded. I wouldn't need three.

Plucked Wings

Lachlan

The four of us took turns driving and made it the national park in two days. We headed to the information building to buy permits.

A man sat at the front desk whose name tag read Roger. "You're that husband whose wife and baby are missing," he said.

"Yeah, I didn't know I was that famous."

"You are around here. Police have been around a lot, which has kept us rangers interested in the cave. We've been keeping an eye out."

"Thank you. I appreciate that."

"Tom will be excited to hear you're here. He's a little obsessed with your case. It's upsetting to him that this cult has lived under our noses. Are you here to look for your family?"

"No, I just thought I'd take a nice hike."

Roger frowned. "Oh."

I chuckled. "I'm kidding. Yeah, police have given up, so I need to find themselves."

"I'll call Tom up here. He might have more information for you." Roger picked up the phone and called his coworker.

We bought all the permits we needed and waited for Tom. A man probably in his early forties with a trimmed beard ran into the building, nearly out of breath.

"Lachlan West is here! Where is he?" He looked around frantically, and I saw his badge read Tom. His eyes landed on me, and he hurried over. "I want you to know I've been looking. I check a new passage every day. I'm willing to help in any way I can. I can't believe a cult is living right under our noses, taking women and babies."

I shook his hand. "Do you have the passages you've checked marked?"

"Yes, it's in the conference room. I'll show you."

He led us to a room with an oval table and a bunch of swivel chairs. A large map similar to the one Cole and I had used hung on the wall near a whiteboard.

Tom walked over to the map and pointed. "I've been Xing all the spots that it's not. I've circled probable locations. I haven't had much luck yet."

"This is amazing. Thank you!" This would save a lot of time. I noticed some areas I'd wanted to check were crossed off. "Where do you think is the most promising?"

"These circles over here. It's toward the end of the cave system and pretty far from civilization. If I were going to hide, that would be my pick. It's been my top pick, but it's so far, I haven't been able to get to it yet."

"We'll head there. Thank you, Tom."

Tom beamed. "Yeah, you guys can use this as your war room if you want. We have business meetings once a month, but we just had this month's last Saturday. I'd like to help in whatever way I can. I have a six-month-old. It's been killing me that your little one is missing."

"Thank you. This is extremely generous and helpful." I took a picture of his map with my phone.

Tom brought me his business card. "Call if you need anything. You can have free access to this room."

I called Tom so he would have my number. The other three guys did the same. As always, Thane had two satellite phones, which would help in the more isolated locations. He gave Tom those numbers as well. It was getting dark, so we set up camp close to the information station.

I studied the picture of the map. "I'm thinking tomorrow we split into two teams. We can cover more ground that way. Each group has a satellite phone and calls the other for any clues."

Thane moved the fire around with a stick. "Yeah, that's best. How are we splitting things?"

"I have to go with Cole."

Cole glanced up from his phone. "Why?"

"I promised your mother I'd have your back. I can't do that if you're with Thane or Ryo."

"You think I need a babysitter?"

"I think your mom can't lose another child."

Cole's eyes turned sad as he stared into the fire. "Yeah, I'm worried about her too. She's always gotten up by six because she loves mornings. I kept finding her in bed at noon. Dad has done the opposite. He's thrown himself into work."

I nodded. "I'm also worried about both of them."

Cole pushed his shoe around in the dirt. "This is all so unfair. Our family already lived this."

Ryo, who had stayed uncharacteristically quiet nodded. "Yeah, Bryn has lived this twice."

We all stayed silent after that, watching the glow of the fire dance into the night sky. I retreated to my tent and climbed into my sleeping bag.

I touched the ground. "You're under here somewhere, baby. We're so close to each other. I hope you know I haven't given up on you. Not even for a second."

"Lachlan, promise me you'll finish your degree no matter what," Bryn said. She was on my chest, basking in the sun. We had our swimsuits on, and our legs were tangled together.

I kept my eyes closed, breathing in the flowery scent of her shampoo. "I plan on it. I haven't come this far to quit."

"Promise even if I die or something you will."

I stiffened. "Why are you talking like that?"

"I don't ever want to be the reason you don't become a doctor."

"We're both going to die in our sleep when we're ninety. They'll find us with our arms around each other and smiles on our faces because we passed together."

"Promise me."

I sighed. "I promise I'll finish my degree as long as I'm alive to do so."

"Hey! Don't talk like that."

I laughed and kissed her head. "See how it feels?"

She ran her fingers across my chest. "I don't want you to ever hurt because of me. You'd have to at least still work at the hospital. I don't want your love for me to destroy your future."

I closed my eyes again, feeling lazy. "Your love is the only future I want."

My thoughts returned to the present. Now that I was faced with Bryn's possible death, I didn't know if I could still finish my degree. I didn't know if I could keep my promise to her. She always diminished what losing her would mean to me. I don't think it was because she wasn't aware of how much I loved her. I think it was because she never wanted to think I'd experience that much pain.

"No, baby, I'm not still going to work. I haven't gone to work since they took you. I haven't continued my degree. I can't until I find you. If I didn't have this pain, would our love have any power to it? If I could still go to work and not look for you, would our love mean anything?" If I didn't get Bryn back, I wasn't sure I wanted a future. If I kept Luna, I would make one. If I lost her, too, I would just want to be with them.

I tossed and turned in my sleeping bag, so far, and so close to my girls.

"It's definitely a cave opening." I swung my pack over my shoulder. I adjusted my headlamp.

Cole and I had found our first entrance and were about to head in.

"Did you pack extra batteries for the headlamps?" Cole rifled through his bag.

"Yeah, they're in the waterproof case with the satellite phone."

Cole stepped up to the entrances and peered inside. "It doesn't look like much."

"It's probably a good start then. We want places that don't look like much. These guys are extra good at hiding."

I checked my gun before putting it back in my holster. Cole did the same, and we lit up the darkness as we walked. The musty scent I remembered filled my nostrils. Brown walls extended for miles. We marked the trails as we went to prevent getting lost or re-searching the same tunnels.

Cole placed the latest mark as he looked around the cavern. "I can't believe this is what Bryn was in her entire childhood. No wonder she found the glowworms the best part."

"Yeah, it's pretty bad. I think it's worse now because she knows what she's missing."

We came to a branch and chose left because it looked broader and easier to get furniture down. We disturbed a colony of bats, and they flapped all around us. I laughed, thinking about how Thane would have freaked up. One bat had scared him in the past. This many would have put him into shock.

"Is that a door?" Cole pointed ahead.

I squinted across a chasm. "Yeah, I think it is. It blends well with the cavern. That's exactly what they'd want it to."

Cole stepped to the edge. "That's a pretty deep drop. How do we even get to it?"

"There's a ledge over there that wraps around what looks like another tunnel. Let's keep walking and see if we can find it."

We continued left and found a narrow path. It opened back up, and we found ourselves on the other side of the chasm. I barely touched the door, and it swung open with a creak.

"That's nice. Just more cave." Cole sounded disappointed.

"It leads to somewhere. There isn't a door for no reason."

"Maybe there is. Maybe they put it here as a diversion."

"That doesn't make sense. This is just the entrance. Let's not call this nothing yet."

The scenery of rock grew tedious, and I couldn't imagine living here. I couldn't imagine my firefly living in such a dismal place. It was like they'd plucked out her wings. I was going to make sure they grew back.

"Well, what do you know more doors." My hand felt my gun and then my knife. Blue doors stuck out from the rock around them. These doors weren't meant for concealment. Someone wanted them seen. Brass numbers hung on each door. Two of the doors had dangling upside down numbers.

"Which number are we betting on?"

"For sure, not that one." I pointed at the door with three sixes on it.

"That does seem super appropriate."

"It does. Eerily so."

"You think if we pass through it, a demon will pop out and eat us?"

"Not much would surprise me with the cult." I moved to door 664 and turned the knob.

A tattered beige couch faced a matching recliner. A battery-operated stove sat on a dusty counter. A table had a vase on it with long ago dead flowers that wilted off the sides. We moved to the bedrooms. The first bed had a doll on it, and I picked it up. It had black button eyes and a stitched smile. I wondered if the child it had belonged to had ever seen the outside. We searched the rest of the den and found nothing useful. After the fourth den we explored, it became clear the community had abandoned this area. We came to what I knew was the chapel. Logs pointed toward a wooden podium. My heart leaped at the thought of it still having a book behind it. I ran around the back and found only dust. I let the disappointment slide off the best it could.

We searched every tunnel and room we came to, and the day came to a close with bats being the only sign of life. We made our way back out, and I wanted to scream. I couldn't be so lucky as to find them on my first day searching.

We met back at the ranger's station to mark off where we'd ventured for the day. Ryo and Thane hadn't found anything but more bats. Thane had freaked as I'd expected. Ryo had recorded the whole thing, and we got to watch on replay. I laughed as I watched Thane screaming and falling flat on his stomach. When the video ended, Ryo stared at me.

"What?" I finally asked.

Ryo patted my shoulder. "It's good to hear my brother laugh again. I hope we run into more bats, and Thane can bring more amusement."

"Hey!" Thane hollered.

"Take one for the team."

Thane rolled his eyes, and I grinned, which quickly faded. How could I laugh with my world gone? It angered me, and I went to my tent to call it a night.

Coloring Sheets

Bryn

"**B**ryn, wake up. It's time for school." Ganesh shook my shoulder.

I groaned. "It's too early. I have a headache."

"Another one?"

"They are constant now." I opened my eyes to see his brows creased in concern.

"We should have Brigid bring you a remedy."

"No remedies from Brigid," I said.

I pushed past him, and he left so I could get dressed.

I checked on Luna, who slept peacefully with her hand by her chin. "I love you," I whispered.

Ganesh had breakfast waiting for me, and I ate what I could. Eating had become increasingly difficult, but I needed to keep my strength as long as possible.

Ganesh handed me a red cloth bag. "This is your lunch. The school is in the chapel. Do you need help getting there?"

"No, stay with Luna. I don't want to wake her."

I walked out the door, and the closer I got the chapel, the more people I ran into. I took my seat on a log and watched as children started pouring in. Why hadn't I noticed there were that many children? I started counting and arrived at thirty-six when Deborah's Atticus stepped up to the podium. He gave me a nod, and I waved.

Atticus clapped his hands to get everyone's attention. "Alright, children, find your seat. We have a lot to cover today. First, I want all of you to give Bryn Moretti a warm welcome."

A boy with red hair and freckled skin gave me a toothless smile. "Are you a teacher?"

"No, I'm a student like you."

"You're too old to be a student."

I smiled. "You're never too old to be a student."

"Yes, Jack, Bryn is correct. You are never too old to learn. The first subject is doctrines. Who can tell me the five commandments of the Above One?"

A girl next to Jack raised her hand, and Atticus called on her. She stood up. "One, obeying authority without question is our highest law. Two, dreaming is the worst form of rebellion. Three, the corrupt world should never be ventured into because poisonous air will kill our souls. Four, for a woman to serve her husband and bear children for him, is the only way she can find worth. Five, speaking of pagan things is punishable by the pit."

Atticus put his hand to his chest. "Thank you, Joy. Everyone stand for the pledge. Hands over your hearts."

The children all stood with hands to their chests. "I pledge allegiance to the Above One. I will not question my elders, for they are wise in all things. I will seek purity and not dream of pagan things.

The cave is my home and keeps me safe. I must never desire to leave it as it will condemn my mortal soul to hell's fire."

I glanced around and saw children who had to be no older than five reciting the pledge. All the children sat, and Atticus pulled down a chalkboard. "Today, we are going to talk about the history of our community."

Jack raised his hand, and when Atticus called on him. "Are we going to color pictures of the blood oath ceremony today?" Jack asked.

"Yes, we'll get to that later. First, let's talk about how our community came to be. Our founder Malachi Summet was given a vision by the Above One to come into darkness and live for forty days. During his time in darkness, the Above One revealed to Malachi that he should bring others into the light by bringing them into darkness. Can anyone tell me what year this was?"

Joy raised her hand. "1926."

"Excellent, and how many members do we have now?"

Another little boy raised his hand. "445 last book count."

Atticus looked at his notes. "We are actually up to 456. There have been new babies born or brought into our community."

"They have been spared corruption," A little boy in front said.

"Max, please remember to raise your hand."

We did end up coloring blood oath papers. It was disturbing seeing a five-year-old coloring a knife dripping blood into a bowl. A blood oath is our highest law was printed on the bottom of each sheet. *I thought not questioning authority was? Oh, wait, I'm not supposed to question anything.* I let my thoughts turn sarcastic, wishing I could say them aloud.

Atticus paused classes for lunch, and each kid took out a red bag as I had. I opened mine. I thought about the diaper bag and how I'd hidden the map. Ganesh hadn't found it or at least hadn't mentioned it. I'd removed it from the bag and put it under my mattress but didn't know how often the map was looked at, So far, no one had made any announcements about it being missing.

As I watched all the kids, an idea formed in my head about how we could get messages to the other women. We needed to make boxes with false bottoms, and we needed a code. After lunch, Atticus told the children a story about a woman who wanted to see the sky and ventured into the world.

She walked off a cliff, and her soul fell into hell because she dreamed too much. We even got to color a picture of her falling into fire. The caption on that one was, dreaming leads to hell's fire. I almost wondered if I'd inspired this sheet. If it weren't for the subject matter, it would have been nice that the kids could color. However, they were only allowed to use black, grey, and brown. It made sense because those were the theme colors for cavern childhoods.

Atticus dismissed the class and asked me to stay afterward. I'd seen in movies that usually meant you did something wrong. The kids emptied out, and I approached his desk.

He glanced around the room and focused on a tunnel behind me. "Debbie told me you think you can get us out. I want you to know that you have my help in getting all of these kids out. I'd like to do it on a school day. They allow us occasional field trips if I can come up with a good enough reason. I'll make the request. I'll put that I need volunteers to keep the kid's minds from straying to forbidden things. After that, we get the women we picked and leave. The only problem is I'm not entirely sure where the exits are."

"I can help with that. This sounds like a good idea. I'm going to have Cynthia, Lilly, and Deborah over for another visit. I'll pass this along to them."

I turned to leave, and Atticus stopped me. "Bryn."

"Yes?"

"Thank you for helping. If I lose Debbie, I don't think I could stand it."

"I'm happy to help." I headed back to the den to find Ganesh cooking soup on the battery-operated stove.

He stirred the mixture while also bouncing Luna. "How was school?"

"Amazing. I learned that if I dream of the sky, I will find a cliff that leads to hell. I will then not notice there is a cliff and fall right into eternal flame. I colored it all black."

Ganesh frowned. "It was good then?"

"It was fine." I sat at the table. He handed me the soup and a glass of water.

He grabbed himself a piece of bread and munched on it.

I could see the pan still had plenty in it and wondered why he'd choose plain bread. "Do you hate soup?"

"No, soup is quite good. I don't want to take soup from you."

"I don't mind sharing."

"It's not that. It's soup to make you healthy."

"Why would I need soup to make me healthy?"

Tension built in his face, and he looked away from me. "I didn't want to say anything. I'm afraid you'll take it wrong."

"Tell it to me and tell me how it's meant to be taken."

"I saw your hairbrush, and I see your eyes. Something is still wrong. You get headaches and forget things."

"I don't think soup will fix any of that," I said.

"Maybe not, but I needed to try something."

I looked at my pale reflection in the living room mirror. "That's very sweet of you. Sometimes people just have to get better."

"I have prayed that you will. Do you think you will pass your test?"

"I've only gone to school one day. If they test me on the consequences of dreaming, I promise not to be sarcastic. That's got to count for something."

"It may not be a test on your knowledge." He refilled my water glass.

I downed the water like I'd let my tongue dry in a desert. "What would it be then?"

He refilled my glass. "It may be a physical test. They often do things I don't understand."

I drank the third glass of water. "You mean like asking a three-month-old how her mother should be punished?"

"That only seems strange to you because you have never heard a three-month-old talk."

I scrunched my nose and quickly straightened it. "You're right. That's exactly why it seems strange to me."

"I am grateful the oracle chose to ask Luna's opinion. Luna loves you. I can see that every time she looks at you. She would have never asked for your return to the pit."

I didn't even know what to say to that. It was sweet and crazy, all mixed into one. More and more, I was finding Ganesh lovable. Not in the way he wanted me to, but in the way that I didn't want anything bad to happen to him.

"Okay, class, who can tell me what happened to the boy who fell asleep in church?" Atticus looked tired like he didn't really want to be there.

Joy waved her hand. "Spiders carried him away in his sleep."

I completely guessed right on the coloring sheet of the day. I colored it all black again.

Jack peeked at my paper. "You can't see the boy or the spiders anymore."

"That's because they carried him deeper into the cave."

He seemed to mull that over for a few seconds. "That makes sense. I colored the boy grey and the spider brown. Darkness feels like it swallows you; that's why I never use my black crayon."

"You're right, Jack. It does feel that way. What's your favorite color?"

"My mama has a bright rug, but I don't know what the color is. That's my favorite."

"Maybe bright is your favorite color."

His eyes lit up. "I think it is."

After school ended for the day, Atticus asked me to speak with him again. "I've put in my petition for the field trip. I should know by next week if it's granted. I would invite the women for your meeting at the next service. It should probably be done publicly, so if you are caught together, it doesn't look like a secret meeting."

"That's a good idea. You're right. I think it's time to have a crafting party."

I went home and found Ganesh fixing dinner again. Luna was on her tummy on the floor, trying to reach for a rattle. I sat down on the floor by her and brought her to my lap. She grabbed my face, and I kissed her hand. She had on a cute little pink dress. It was the first time Ganesh hadn't put her in white.

"I love this dress on her. The brightness pops her eyes," I said.

"I knew that you would. In the privacy of our den, it is fine, and I wanted you to be pleased."

"I am pleased. Thank you."

"Come and eat. Tell me about your day."

I put Luna back with her toys and sat at the dinner table. "It was good. We learned about the boy who fell asleep in church."

Ganesh poured our water. "Yes, spiders carried him off. It used to terrify me as a child. I always went to bed early on Saturday nights."

We finished dinner and did the dishes together. I started to feel queasy.

Ganesh watched me. "What is wrong?"

"I don't feel so well." I lost dinner into the dishwater.

Ganesh and I both gawked in horror at the red water.

Vitamins

Bryn

Ganesh carried me back to bed. "I'm getting Brigid."

I grabbed his arm. "No, no Brigid, please."

"I know she is not the kindest woman, but she is our best healer. You need a healer."

"Ganesh, she can't fix what's wrong with me."

He froze. "Why do you say that?"

"I'm too sick. She doesn't have the right medicine to fix my problem. Only the above ground does."

"I will go out and get these medicines then. More antibiotics."

I weakly took his hand. "Antibiotics won't fix this."

"I have to do something. I'm sorry, but Brigid needs to look at you." He placed Luna in her bassinet. "I just changed and fed Abra. She should be okay until I return."

"Thank you." I watched him leave, dreading the moment he would return with Brigid. All the muscles in my body felt like they were cramping. Ganesh had left me with a bucket, and I made use of it two more times. "Lachlan, I don't think I have much longer. I hope you at least get to find out what happened to me, so you don't wonder the rest of your life. I love you." I dozed off and only woke when Brigid entered the room.

She looked in the bucket. "Ganesh, this is nothing to be concerned with."

He looked at her like she'd lost her mind. He was probably right. "She is very ill."

"No, she's being purified."

"She's going to die."

"If she proves herself unworthy, yes, she will."

"You need to do something to help her. Please," he pleaded.

"There is nothing that can be done, but to wait." Brigid bent down and pushed my sweat-drenched hair out of my face. "You must pray for mercy, dear. That is all that will fix this."

Brigid left, and I heard a loud crash like glass being thrown against the wall. I heard it a second time and a third. On the fourth time, I realized it was Ganesh raging. I drifted back to sleep. I woke up with my tongue stuck to the roof of my mouth. I pried it off and called to the darkness, "Ganesh!"

A lantern light came on, and he was at my side. "What is it?"

"I'm so thirsty."

He ran from the room and came back with water. I guzzled it.

He grabbed the glass. "You need to slow down. You'll only throw it up again."

I did what he said and took small sips. "What day is it today?"

"Sunday. Church is soon, but you're staying here. I will take Abra alone."

"No, I need to go."

"You are in no state to go."

"I feel a little better. I miss my friends and need to see them."

Ganesh pressed his lips. "Okay, but if you fall ill during service, I'm bringing you home for rest."

Ganesh left so I could change into my white dress. I looked in the mirror and saw my eyes looked a little yellow. My vision was coming to pass. I needed to invite the women over for tomorrow because my time was slipping fast.

Ganesh carried Luna because my arms were too weak. My mind couldn't focus on anything being said, and I felt grateful Ganesh wasn't like my father, who would quiz on the sermon. If we spoke the wrong answers, we'd earn a smack. When the service ended, I had to think for a minute as to why I'd come to services feeling so terrible. I spotted Cynthia looking at me with a frown, and I remembered.

I walked over to her. "I would like to invite you and Callum for another play date."

She touched my arm. "Bryn, are you well?"

"No, that's why I really need the playdate to happen tomorrow. Can you invite Deborah and Lilly?"

Her eyes studied me for a few seconds. "I will let them know."

Ganesh woke me up. "You have school."

"I'm going to be late today. My friends are coming over because I have missed them. We are doing a crafting party."

"Are you sure that is wise with the test only a week away."

"Yes, Atticus said he will catch me up before the test."

He squeezed my hand. "Alright. Have fun. How are you feeling?"

"Better," I lied.

"Good." He pressed a kiss to my head and left for the men's meeting.

I brushed my hair, and more fell out. I didn't know why I bothered anymore. I put on a fresh dress and went to my pantry to find something to serve my guests. I pulled out our last chip bag and debated whether to use them. Ganesh really liked them with sandwiches, but we'd run out of bread. Something caught my eye in the back, and I reached for it. It was one of the oracle's clear bottles nearly empty. I opened it up and smelled it. There still wasn't a scent to it. Why did we have one of these?

I decided to save the chips and instead would offer water. It wasn't much, but our supplies were running low. I opened my door when I heard a knock. Lilly, Deborah, Cynthia, and Callum stood there, and I let them inside. We sat on the couch, and all three of them looked at me with frowns.

"Atticus says you are quite the student, Bryn." Deborah smiled like she always did when she spoke of Atticus.

"Yes, he's a great teacher. I've made a few cute little friends. Jack sits with me every day."

"Jack Lawson? The little redhead."

I nodded. "Yes, he has the cutest freckles."

"He's a foundling like you," Deborah said.

My mouth hung open. "He was taken from the world?"

"Yes, about a year ago. He is the third in his family because his parents were declared barren. His siblings all attend the school."

I took a second to regather myself. I knew they stole children, but I hadn't really thought about the fact we'd be returning kidnapped children to their parents. I started the conversation and told them Atticus' plan. "Do any of you know other women who can be trusted and would want to come?"

They all three nodded.

"I have an idea. We need to get messages out to each other in code. I was thinking boxes with false bottoms, or maybe we give something out and stay to visit. We'd have to be very careful about who we trusted. I trust all of your judgments on who those women would be."

"What about the canning we did?" Lilly said.

"What do you mean?"

"I'm part of the canning committee to disperse the canned goods. I can deliver the jars and stay and chat with the women we choose."

"That's a great idea. It won't look suspicious with you going from house to house."

Deborah rolled a car next to Callum's. "I can help you."

"Should we make a mental list then." I tried to turn on my brain, so I'd remember the list.

The women gave me the names of fifteen women they believed were trustworthy.

All three women got up to leave, and Cynthia grabbed my hand. "Bryn, you're very ill. Aren't you?"

"Yes."

She closed her eyes, and the other two shook their heads.

"Purification, "Lilly said.

"Yeah, I think so."

Lilly grabbed my hand. "We're going to get you out of here and away from that. Hang on until we can."

I nodded, and as they disappeared out the door, I wiped my tears. There would be no escape for me, but it would be worth it because thirty-eight children, eighteen women, and Atticus were going to be free. I felt too tired to go to school. I fed Luna and got her down for a nap. I took one myself.

"I've made lunch," Ganesh called from the kitchen.

I walked out and sat down. I stared at the soup. "Ganesh, what do you put in my soup?"

He pulled out the can from the trash. "Not much. It's just canned soup. I'm sorry. I plan on going on a supply run soon. We'll have some fresh food in a few days.

"Do you put anything else in it?"

"Yeah, I add a few spices for flavor and your vitamins that Brigid gave me. She said they would make you strong. I mean, we all take our vitamins, but these were a second set because you need strength."

I went to the cupboard and pulled out the bottle. "Is this the vitamins?"

"Yeah, I've measured the exact amount Brigid told me too. She said it was important to keep you healthy. It hasn't worked very well, but I kept it up because I figured you might be worse if I didn't."

"How long?"

"Since you stopped nursing Abra. Brigid said you couldn't nurse the baby on them, but you needed them to stay alive. She said you wouldn't wake up without them. I told her I would provide milk for Abra, but you had to live."

I watched him bounce Luna and didn't have the heart to tell him he'd been poisoning me for weeks. I was pretty sure it would kill him.

I sat down and reached across for his hand. "Ganesh, I don't want any more vitamins."

"You need them. You're getting sick again."

"Exactly, I'm getting sick anyway. Please stop the vitamins."

"Are you sure?"

I sat back in my chair thinking about how I could phrase things. I was going to die anyway. I could feel too much damage had already been done. I didn't want to condemn Ganesh to a lifetime of guilt.

"Yes, vitamins sometimes upset my stomach. I think I'll be able to eat better without them. Can we at least try it?"

"Yeah, I didn't know you were sensitive to them. I'm sorry."

"It's okay. You know now."

He went to the pantry and threw the bottle in the trash. "I'll make you fresh soup." He poured the soup in the garbage and made me a fresh can.

I didn't vomit dinner for the first time in days, and it convinced Ganesh I was right about me being sensitive to the purification potion. My eyes were a yellowish red now, and my skin had taken the tone it had in my vision. It wouldn't be much longer. My test would take place in four days, and I had to hold out until then. We needed time for the field trip to be approved. I didn't know what the test was, but I had to pass it.

I took my place on a log next, waiting for school to start. Jack sat next to me. He'd become my buddy. I watched the other kids pour in, and Atticus took his place at the podium. We recited the five commandments followed by the pledge.

Today's lesson was on a girl who didn't want to get married or have children. The Above One turned her into part of the cave. We colored a rock wall with a girl's face.

"You're going to color the whole thing black again?" Jack asked me.

"Yeah, I think I should."

"I think you should give her a little light. It's scary enough becoming a rock."

I picked up my brown crayon. "You're right."

Atticus dismissed the class and waved me over. "Hey, Deborah wanted to know if you could help her deliver the jars on Saturday. I know your test is the next day, but she thinks you could in the morning."

"Yeah, I can help. As long as she's sure that the other women will trust me."

"They need you. They see you as the leader. Also, I got the field trip approved. It's going to take place next Wednesday."

"We have a week to convince everyone?"

"You have Saturday. I'm not sure *you* can afford to wait much longer." He gave me a knowing look.

"Right. Okay, we'll save who we can."

I needed to get some water. My tongue was so dry, and my desperation grew. I ran in the house, ready to down a jug. I halted when I saw Brigid sitting across from Ganesh.

She looked up at me. "Ganesh says you don't want a vitamin refill." She gave a look to kill.

"They hurt my stomach."

She patted the seat next to her. "Come sit, dear. They are supposed to not be pleasant on the stomach. A small price to pay for health."

I sat down. "My health is poorer since your vitamins."

"You are being purified. Purification is always pain." She handed Ganesh a new bottle. "If you care about your wife's soul, make sure she gets these as I prescribed." Brigid got up and left the house.

I was going to have to tell Ganesh the truth, and I was pretty sure it would crush him.

Impossible Promises

♥

Lachlan

I tightened the rope and descended farther into the hole. We'd searched for almost two weeks with no success. We burned through all the probable areas and were on to the not likely ones. Part of me started to fear we had the wrong cave system. The main reason I didn't think it was probable was that they would have had to move all the cult members through the above ground. This kept me hopeful that we'd eventually find something.

Cole rappelled next to me. "You really think they could be in these? How would they get supplies in?"

"Probably through another entrance. I'm not leaving until I find them or have searched all caverns."

We made it the bottom and started searching the level. I studied a smooth archway. "This looks too perfect to be naturally forming. Don't you think?"

Cole ran his hand over it. "It does look carved and polished. Even if it is, it could just be more abandoned dens."

We'd found two more sets of dens. Ryo and Thane had found one. It seemed the cult alternated its dens to avoid detection. We didn't know how long they stayed in one spot. Bryn had never mentioned moving as a child. We didn't know how long the cult had existed.

We came to a branch and took the right turn because it looked more man-made. If we found nothing, we'd circle back to the left turn. Cole continued to mark as we went. We found more closely spaced archways.

I pointed to my right. "I'll take that one. You take the other?"

"Yeah, sounds good."

I went into my room, and it proved it empty. I turned to meet back up with Cole when he yelled, "Lachlan! Come here."

I ran into the area that Cole was and found him staring at a wall. A banner hung with the words, they shall be purified. "It seems we're on the right track, after all."

"I'd say so. That's a pretty specific saying."

I looked around to see the rest of the room empty. "It also means we were right about rappelling down. I think we're going to have to start thinking that nothing is off-limits. These people are resourceful."

"I guess they could have propelled the furniture and supplies down with rope. It would be worth the effort if it would make people like us think twice about this spot."

Cole had a good point. We moved on and looked at the remnants of the cave people. We found a china cabinet with plates still intact. They had red roses painted over the top. The things that always got me were the toys because they were a reminder of the children being trapped here. It was a reminder of the life my daughter would have if I didn't find her.

I wondered what she was doing by now. I tried not to focus too much on what I'd missed, but instead tried to stay focused on the time we'd have.

I thought back to the last night I had her and how Bryn couldn't get her to sleep.

"I don't know what she wants." Bryn rubbed her eyebrow. She had her eyes closed, leaning against the back of our bed. She'd stayed so tired, and I worried about her.

"I'll take her for a little while."

"You can't feed her."

"I could always give her a bottle, and you could sleep longer."

Her eyes opened. "Don't say it. We're not giving her a bottle."

"Okay. She and I will just have a talk then. Try to get some sleep."

She curled up on her side and looked already asleep. My gut told me it was more than her being a new mother, but no one would listen to me. I picked up a screaming Luna.

"What's wrong with my girl?" I took her out to the living room and googled fussy babies. "It says you might have gas." I bicycled her legs as the Youtube video showed. She screeched, and it horrified me. Maybe I'd made it worse. After an hour of me in a near panic, I texted Ryo because I remembered he'd soothed Dahlia as a newborn. He rushed over to rescue me.

I bounced Luna while cradling her on my shoulder. "I'm such a failure. I promised her I'd fix everything. That I wouldn't let anything hurt her."

"Why would you make such a silly promise?"

"Why wouldn't I promise her that?"

He grinned. "You need to start with promises you can keep. Let me take her for a minute."

I handed her to Ryo. "Why can't I fix everything for her?"

"Your new father gullibility is precious, man."

I scowled at him. "Very funny."

"It's impossible for you to fix everything. She has to learn to live her life without you eventually."

"No, she doesn't."

Ryo laughed as he rested Luna on his forearm and held her outward with her chin resting gently in his hand. His other hand rested on top of her, keeping her stable. She immediately quieted and fell asleep.

I stared in disbelief. "How did you do that?"

"It's a trick my grandma told me about when I called her to ask for tips on calming babies. I wanted to be impressive for Morely after that first night."

"I'm impressed."

"It's serious baby magic. The only problem is your arms get tired fast." He slowly brought her back to a cradle position and rocked her. *"But yeah, as I said, you can't fix everything for Luna. It's not possible. She's like a baby bird. You have to let her test her wings, so she can fly one day. She has to be able to fly when the wind gets tough. I thought I was going to die the day Dahlia fell off her tricycle and skinned her knee. She wailed, and I wanted to right along with her. I ran her inside because I was sure she'd bleed to death. I almost called you because you're basically a doctor."*

"I would have told you to clean it, put antibiotic ointment and a Band-Aid on it."

Luna stirred a little, and he rocked her. "Right. That's the right answer, Dr. West. But I panicked because she was in tears. She looked up at me with the saddest eyes, and I swear my heart fell to the floor. She asked me to kiss it and get her a Band-Aid. That's what I did."

"See you fixed it," I pointed out.

He shook his head and handed me a sleeping Luna. "No, I didn't fix it. She still had the wound. It still had to heal."

"Yeah, but you made it better than it would have been." I smiled at my sleeping daughter, and every part of me filled with love for her.

"My point is sometimes you'll be able to help her wounds a little, but you'll never be able to fix everything that happens to her. It's part of growing up and letting her grow into a strong adult. It's part of the letting go that must happen. Be there for her, but don't drive yourself crazy, trying to keep impossible promises."

Ryo's words were true now more than ever. When I got my girls back, I wouldn't be able to fix their trauma. I could only be there for them while they healed. Luna was little and hopefully wouldn't remember most of hers. I had to stay away from thoughts of Bryn's trauma. I knew how the cult treated women, and if I let my mind stray to what they were doing to her, I'd go mad with rage.

I continued to look through the ghostly cavern to learn anything I could about their way of life. I rifled through a drawer and spotted a little red notebook. I flipped through it and saw someone had written on every page. I stuck it in my bag to read once I got back at the campsite for the night.

We hiked back to the branch and took the left tunnel, which opened up to a vast chasm with clear blue water. The walls were purple and blue swirls, making it look like marble. There appeared the be a tunnel that led through the water.

Cole gaped at it. "That is one of the prettiest things I've ever seen."

"Yeah, Bryn would love this. A part of the cave that is stunning." I took some pictures of it.

I sat on a rock and pulled out our lunch and the map. The problem with the map was the unexplored parts were all external. The internal parts obviously weren't mapped. I handed Cole his sandwich. "I'm thinking we start checking the smaller pockets tomorrow."

"Are you sure? We keep finding signs that they've lived in these big pockets."

"Yeah, the keyword being lived."

"We haven't even made it through a third of our pocket. We should see it through before moving on." Cole tossed me a bottled water.

I thought all of it over. He was probably right. We should cross off an entire area before moving on. "I guess that's a better plan. This is incredibly frustrating, is all."

"That's definitely understandable."

"I mean, I knew it wouldn't be easy. I hoped it would, but almost two weeks have gone by without anything useful. I keep thinking about what their days must be like."

Cole finished a bite on his sandwich and threw a rock into the water below. "I can't let my thoughts go there. They almost take me out."

"Me too." I took in the beauty in front of me, wishing if Bryn had to grow up in a cave, it could have been here.

We ate the rest of our lunch in silence.

Cole walked to the edge. "Are we going to scale down to the water tunnel or keep going up here?"

"I think we keep going up here for now. I doubt they took everything through water."

Cole started ahead of me down a narrow tunnel. My rope loosened on the side of my pack, and I stopped to wind it tight and secure it.

"Ahhhh!" Cole shouted.

I put the rope quickly back in place and ran for him. The tunnel narrowed until I had to remove my pack and push it ahead to squeeze through sideways. "Cole!" His lack of response pushed me faster. Nothing bad could happen to Cole. The thought accelerated my heart rate. My hands and knees scraped against the rough wall until I pushed through to the other side. "Cole!"

I pushed my heels into the ground and grabbed onto a rock to prevent myself from plummeting down the sudden drop. Panic rushed through me. I stabilized my position and took out my large flashlight and shined it into the darkness. "Cole!"

"Down here!"

"Are you okay?"

"Yeah, my hand is flopping at an odd angle, but I'm overall good for the height of the drop."

I secured my rope and rappelled to the bottom. I examined Cole's wrist and cringed at the protruding bone. I did what I could with first aid supplies but needed to get him to an ER for proper surgery. I handed him some Tylenol. "We're going to have to find another way out of here. It's going to be difficult for you to scale this cliff and then the original one. Can you walk? Do you hurt anywhere else?"

"No, I think I'm good." Cole walked in a circle to prove it. "Finding another way out might not be a bad idea. It means we'll get through a deeper portion."

"That's true." I looked at the two tunnel options. "Which looks more promising?"

"Why don't we go right and hope we're right." He examined his wrist. "I'm glad I have my own personal doctor on this trip."

"I'm not one yet."

"Close enough."

We hiked through the right tunnel. My breathing grew heavy, and signs of oxygen deprivation crept in that I recognized from Davey's cave warnings. I checked the levels and realized I was right. *Good ole Davey, thank you for everything.*

Cole and I pulled out the tanks and rigged them like in our training. I helped Cole with his since he only had one useable hand.

"I'm glad Davey had us bring extra tanks because I have a feeling we might use these ones up," Cole said.

"Yeah, Davey knows his cave info. We owe him dinner."

We continued deeper into the cave, hoping we'd find an exit soon.

The Beasts We Hide

Bryn

Lilly and Cynthia loaded all the peaches onto a cart while I sat dizzy on a rock. I'd tried to help, but both of them had sternly sent me to the rock. Deborah had Luna in a sling because I felt too weak to carry her even with sling assistance. Callum moved his truck over the slimy ground. He accidentally bumped my feet.

His lower lip trembled. "I'm sorry."

I smiled at him. "It's okay."

"I weally wuv Aba. Your bebe is so tute."

"Thank you, Callum. I like your truck."

"I wish it was bier."

"You want it to be bigger?"

He circled his truck in the dirt. "Yeah, I wanna ride in it like I do that." His chubby little finger pointed at the cart.

"Callum, come climb in," Cynthia called.

He bounced up and down before reaching the cart. He struggled to make it over the edge, and Lilly gave him a boost. I noticed he'd left his car and brought it over to him.

"Tank you!" He gave me a million-dollar smile.

Someday you're going to ride in a really big truck.

Cynthia grabbed my hand. "Are you sure you feel up to making all these deliveries?"

"I'd like to do at least a few."

"This first den we're going to is Abby Quinn's. She has twin baby girls about a month older than Abra, and boys two, three, four, and five."

"Does she have help?" I asked, stunned.

"No, it's seen as poor motherhood to get help."

"Ganesh always helps me."

They all stopped walking and stared at me.

"Ganesh Moretti helps you with Abra?" Lilly sounded as stunned as she looked.

"Yes, the house too."

They looked at me like I'd told them I'd won the lotto.

"Dang! I knew he was a catch. More than just his handsome looks." Cynthia started pulling the wagon again. "We meant what we said before about him turning down pairings until you."

"I know you said because he was a man, but I would think the elders would still have wanted him married."

Lilly stopped in front of a den. "They did, but Ganesh has more pull than most. No other husband would have gotten away with removing their wife from the pit early."

Before I could ask her more about it, she knocked on the den, and it opened to a pale, exhausted-looking woman. I thought my convincing argument would be to tell her nannies were allowed above ground.

Lilly held up a jar. "We've brought canned goods for your family."

"I didn't participate in the canning drive," Abby nearly whispered.

"We are giving them to everyone because we have an abundance."

"That is generous. Come in." She let us in like Lilly said she would. It was customary to accept company when a gift was given. Once we were inside, I noticed substantial bruising up her arm. I wondered how many more her clothes hid. Her boys all sat on the floor, doing nothing. The middle boy had a black eye, and another had bruise marks on his neck. It felt eerie to see toddler boys merely looking at the grey area rug. Callum hopped out of the cart and tried to share his truck with one of the boys. The other boys just stared longingly at the truck. No wonder this place bred cruelty.

Abby looked at me. "You're Bryn Moretti?"

I offered her my hand, and she pulled me into a hug. "Bless you. I'm sorry they brought you back to this hell."

Yes, she was coming with us. We stayed with Abby for as long as we could as she cried into my shoulder about the torture her husband dealt daily. We went to the fourth home, and I was wearing out. There would be no way I'd reach all fifteen women. I pulled the strength to visit one more.

A woman probably in her sixties opened the door. She embraced all of us and stopped with me. She studied my eyes. "They've put you in purification?"

I nodded. "Yes, I think I'm at the end."

"Yes, you have the look of the end." She ran to her cupboard. "Take these when you get home. Take two twice a day. They will hold it off a bit. Not forever, but a bit."

"Thank you."

"Also, when you get home, look for a bottle of clear liquid. It has no taste or smell. Dump it out and replace it with water."

I smiled at her. "That's perfect. Why didn't I think of that?"

"It fogs your brain. I can't believe you're standing, honey."

I wouldn't have to tell Ganesh, after all.

Lilly sat across from the lady and took her hand. "Edna, how would you like to see the sky?"

Edna's eyes lit up. "I would love that."

We got Edna too. Deborah helped me back to my den with Luna. We dumped the poison, rinsed it out, and filled the bottle with water. Ganesh could remain blissfully unaware of his role in my death.

Deborah fed Luna. "I have Abra, Bryn. Why don't you go back and sleep?"

"Are you sure?"

"I'm so sure."

I hugged her. "Thank you, sweet girl."

Deborah squeezed back, and I stumbled to my room. I flopped on the bed and was out.

I opened my eyes to see Ganesh on his knees with his eyes closed. He was mumbling inaudible words. He finally opened his eyes and met mine. "Thank the Above One, you're awake!"

"I needed a nap."

"You slept all day and late into the night. I couldn't wake you to eat. I was praying."

"I'm just drained. Ganesh, can you make me a promise?"

"What's that?"

"If I can no longer be yours, you will find someone who loves you in the way I've never been able to."

He pushed my hair from my eyes. "Bryn, don't speak this way. I don't like it."

"Promise."

"I promise I will keep my heart open."

My eyelids drooped, but I forced a smile. "That works. Tomorrow is my test."

"I know. It was another reason I was praying."

I ran my hand over his stubble and held his cheek. "Thank you for protecting Luna and me."

"I failed several times."

"You were not what I expected from the men here."

"The men here did not have the mother I had."

"What do you mean?"

"My father was a cruel man, but he died when I was five. My mom asked to never remarry. She, as you, knew the harshness of the men here."

"They granted her request?"

He sat down on the floor and leaned his back against the bed. He spoke toward the wall. "Yes, it was not a normal thing, but for her, they did. She raised me alone and taught me the ways of the Above One. She also taught me that there was a better way to treat the wife I would someday get. She said someday they would ask me to marry a vulnerable, scared girl and to never use that against the girl. She taught me many more things about how I should treat this girl. For many years, I avoided my pairing."

"Why?"

"Because I knew a beast like my father lived inside of me. I knew without control, he could be released. He was what you saw the day they threw you in the pit. He was what emerged from me when I almost forced you into things. I wanted to think I could be like my mother wanted, but I knew my father lurked there too."

"I think we all have our own beasts. We all have a monster we could release if we don't cling to the good. Why did you want me? You said it was because I was pretty, but you haven't kicked me out in my worst state."

He turned to face me. "I meant what I said about you being beautiful. But I didn't tell you something before because I knew you thought our ways are crazy. After I carried you to Brigid's den, it was like I heard my mother telling me that you were the girl who needed me. That I needed to protect you because you had much bigger things to do here." He laughed almost to himself. "I probably sound insane to you."

I held his hand. "No, your mother knew I wouldn't survive this place without you." I grew too tired then and fell back to sleep.

Ganesh woke me up. "Bryn, I must leave early. Deborah and Atticus are here to make sure you get to your test safely. Atticus wants to quiz you."

I got dressed and met Deborah and Atticus in the living room after Ganesh left. I went to the cupboard and took two of the silver pills Edna had given me. I'd taken two before I'd passed out yesterday, and my fatigue had improved. I sat down across from them. "How did it go?"

Debbie's eyes told me they had good news. "We got all fifteen, I think."

"You think they'll keep a secret?"

"Yes, it helps they don't know all the details. We told them to be travel-ready Wednesday. We're going to take the cart to Abby's so all her kids can ride in that."

"That's a great idea. I think it's big enough Callum could ride too."

Atticus jumped in. "I can get us more carts. I'll claim that I need it to transport lunches and books. We can put the younger ones in the cart to prevent fatigue for the women or a little one getting lost."

"Atticus, don't ever let anyone tell you you're not amazing."

Deborah gave him a quick kiss. "I tell him that every day."

Atticus quizzed me on possible questions. I now knew the cult history, folklore, and laws by heart.

Deborah put Luna in a sling and hooked arms with me. "You look a bit stronger today."

"I think Edna's pills are giving me enough strength to fulfill my purpose."

"Perhaps, enough strength to reach above ground medicine."

I wished that to be true and remembered my words to Luna. The stars always fall, which means wishes never die. If I could see the night sky one last time, I would wish for Lachlan's happily ever after. That would be the final act of my life.

Notebook

♥

Lachlan

We were yet again at a branch in the tunnels. These always felt like deciding fate. Cole had started to look tired miles ago. The pain wasn't helping his endurance, but he didn't complain. I pushed Tylenol when enough hours elapsed. It was far from enough for his injury, but it was all I had.

I looked at my watch. "Ryo and Thane are probably a bit freaked by now." Our satellite phone wouldn't work this far underground. The time we should have met up with them passed hours ago.

"Yeah, hopefully, we find something promising soon, " Cole said.

"I think we should call it a night. I know they'll probably worry, but we need the energy to keep this up." I checked my instruments. "Oxygen levels are good here. This is a good spot." I unrolled our sleeping bags and would use my jacket as a pillow. I started to resettle my bag when I spotted the notebook. I pulled it out and started reading the first page.

These are the words of Zachariah Bronze, regretful apprentice and brother to Jared Bronze. Malachi Summet has condemned us all to hell.

He is the devil disguised as an angel. He convinced ten families to join him in the darkness. He has stolen many more since. Children are pushed because they are how his power grows. We never find light and are bound to medicines to keep us alive. Notably, the most important family names are Summet, Moretti, Slater, Bronze, and Feldman. In that order, does their authority rank. They have placed us all in bondage and hold authority that exceeds all others. They each hold a different role. These are the founding members. The most powerful of which are Summet and Moretti. They make all the laws. Malachi's granddaughter is the first oracle of our people.

His great-granddaughter Virginia Malone, who is a pure light, was given in marriage to Robert Moretti, making the union a powerful one. They had a son Ganesh who Virginia shielded from cruelty by living the rest of her life alone. He holds an innocence that the other men do not have. She shielded him from many dark practices. She sheltered him from the power he holds as a descendant of an oracle, a Summet, and a Moretti. I believe she did this to prevent the power from corrupting him. She was murdered by James Slater when she requested to leave with her boy. Slater killed her for the request.

The Slaters are the line of guardians. Slaters determine who arrives and leaves the community. The boy was sixteen at the time his mother was killed. The boy never knew Slater killed his mother, but I have seen all. James Slater is one of the evilest among us. At the time, he had three daughters, one of which was mine. As punishment for killing a descendant of Summet, he was sentenced to never being able to acquire a son to fulfill his line.

It was fortunate he had no sons at the time, or they would have been killed. It is said his wife had a preference for daughters. I believed it to be she didn't want to bring more harshness into the fold as she was a kind woman. She lost her mind in torture and could not reconcile. Rather than brutality being given by her line, she had unknowingly condemned her daughters to torment.

Jared Bronze is in charge of procurement, as is our family line. He brings all into the fold for approval by James and Jared Bronze himself approves all the kidnappings of children. He sometimes sells children to members if they don't want to trouble themselves with seeking out sons and daughters. This used to be my responsibility but I forsook it long ago. Jared is a bringer of sorrow and slavery. He sold my own daughter to James Slater. An act which I could not prevent as Slater holds great power. They would have killed the child if I'd fought.

Feldman is an enforcer and is the priest of priests. His hand is dark and far-reaching. His line is the educators. They ensure the children follow doctrines. It is an expected duty of his descendants. I write these things to leave behind to be found when our den moves. May someone someday free my people.

I will never see liberty. I am in the final stages of my purification. Beware, Brigid Feldman, as she is the bringer of painful deaths and kills in the same magnitude as she heals. She is not a doctor though she is all we have as such. She is wife to the priest of priests. They pretend you can survive this, but no one does. They say it was because we were unworthy of purification. They poison us with something that can't be remedied by natural medicines. It yellows the skin, makes our hair fall to the ground, and lastly, we throw up our own blood as though they have forced a blood oath upon us. A blood oath to die for their evil ways. Take heed to any who stumble upon the horrors of Summet. Run! For he shall find you in the darkness and drag you into the pit of hell.

My final prayer is that a God-ordained person will one day find my final testament, free my people, and deliver my words to my daughter Morely Slater. Jared Bronze insisted that as his apprentice I defile girls. The first he placed me with was a young girl named Olivia Garcia. She was beautiful and innocent. I couldn't bring myself to harm her. We talked each time Jared sent me to her. Over many months, we fell in love. Our marriage would never have been allowed. In fact, it was highly forbidden. Bronze declared cage girls the lowest class. I was expected, as his brother, to fulfill his duties when he couldn't, and therefore, my class was of the highest.

Our daughter was born, and I wasn't allowed to claim her. Olivia was sent to Nevada to the cruelest of places. I was put in charge of the children for five years to stay close to our daughter. I taught her to read when she was four. I was quite proud of how quickly she learned at a young age. I wanted her to have the gift of knowledge which was denied to so many of our women.

After five years, Jared gave Morely to the cruelest of our families. He made me hand her to them. When no one was watching, Rachel asked me the child's name, and I told her Morely.

Somehow, she made sure my daughter kept the name. I don't understand how because the Feldmans always chose names. Morely means meadow, and her mother named her after the place that held her happiest childhood memories. It was the one piece of her mother she was allowed to keep.

I don't know what happened to Olivia. I have long feared Jared killed her to punish me. I watched Morely grow from a distance. I want her to know she was wanted and born of great love. My own purification prevents her death. It was the punishment going to be given to her for losing her sisters. I took it in her place by enacting one of our laws that allows punishment to be endured by another. Each member is allowed one case of this. Never have I found a more worthy reason.

Daughter, if you someday read this know, I am honored to give my life for such a beautiful soul. Do not weep for my action but rather rejoice that I have taken a step toward my redemption. For that, I thank you, my Morely.

In my death, I wish that three people may cross paths with my daughter. May the first bring her kindness and laughter all the days of her life. May the second be one of bravery who shall rise up and lead her to freedom. May the third be one of mercy who delivers my message into her hands. For these people, I pray eternal blessing from the hand of God. I go to my death in peace that I have released this in the hopes that my words will be found.

The notebook held no more. I took a minute to process everything I had just read before looking up at Cole. "I think I just struck gold." I handed him the notebook.

He read it and looked up at me with a giant grin. "The three people he wanted Morely to cross paths with are Ryo, Bryn, and you."

I absolutely had struck the best kind of gold. I placed the notebook in my waterproof case where it would stay safe until I could give a daughter the message from the father she'd longed to know. Morely would know she was born of a beautiful love story and always wanted.

Cole and I woke in the morning and hiked five miles before sunlight pierced our eyes. We followed it to an exit and called Ryo and Thane, who drove us to the ER. We sat in the waiting room, waiting for Cole to get out of surgery.

Thane shook my shoulder. "You gave us a giant scare, brother. Terrible things were going through my head."

Ryo opened his eyes. "Yeah, I lost a lot of sleep over it."

I pulled the notebook out of my backpack and handed it to Ryo. "This made last night worth every bit of your worry."

Ryo read it, and when he looked up, his eyes watered. "Other than Bryn and Luna, this is the best thing you could have found. It's going to give Morely the answers that have haunted her. I've held her so many nights when she cried over not having a family looking for her. This explains it all. Thank you, man."

A nurse found us and took us back to Cole, who looked exhausted but in good shape. This would complicate our search, but I felt grateful that it was only his wrist and not his life.

I started to step out of the room. "Cole, I need to check in with your mom. I'll be right back."

"Can you not tell her about this? Let her find out when she sees I've come back alive."

"Yeah, that's probably best." I stepped into the hall and dialed Anna.

She answered, sounding sleepy. I glanced at the clock and saw it was one in the afternoon. "Lachlan, how are things? Any luck?"

"No, but we still have a lot of cave to check. I'll let you know as soon as I find anything. How are you holding up?"

"I'm tired."

"Anna, I'm not giving up. Please don't either."

"I won't. You're what's holding me to hope."

We hung up, and I knew her saying she was tired was code for her falling apart. I knew the feeling all too well. It contained an exhaustion that outmatched any other.

Test

Bryn

I returned to the auditorium with plastered walls. The turn out for my test was significant. I started to head to the front when someone grabbed my hand and pulled me into a corner room. I began to fight until I realized it was Ganesh.

"You startled me." I gasped, trying to calm.

"I'm sorry. I just needed to see you before your test. You're going to do great. I'm not going to let them put you in the pit again. You have my word."

"What choice will you have if I fail?"

He pulled me into a hug. "I will figure something out."

I put my arms around his waist. "Ganesh, If it comes down to it, and you have one choice, save Callum."

"I'm meant to protect you."

"You were meant to protect me so I could accomplish what I need to. Save Callum."

He pulled back, and conflict crossed his eyes. We walked into the auditorium hand in hand. As we walked to the front, he gave my hand one last squeeze. I turned to look at him, and he nodded. I stood in front of the podium with my back to the crowd, as Atticus had told me would be expected. The elders sat in their chairs, and the crowd chatted behind me.

The oracle walked out from the back in her white dress. Silence fell on the room. Her long grey hair flowed freely behind her. "Bryn Moretti, please step forward. I will take you to your test. I will have my final ruling at the conclusion."

I followed her back to the room with the red cabinet. I'd expected to answer questions in front of the community.

The oracle handed me clothes. "Change into this gown."

I already had on a plain white dress. The one she asked me to change into was a white fleece nightgown. I quickly obeyed, and a woman entered the room and washed my feet, hands, and face with an ointment that burned and smelled of cinnamon.

The oracle pointed to the bed. "Lay"

I did as she asked. She had me get under the white sheets and quilt. A small table sat next to the bed with some type of incense on it. The woman who had washed my feet lit the incense but put a glass dome over the top, snuffing out most of the smell.

The oracle approached my bed. "You are about to enter into a dream state. As you leave this plane of consciousness behind, focus on four objects you need to find. When you return here, I will ask you the four things and their meaning. If you guess correctly, your husband's challenges will be accepted. If you fail, you will serve the rest of your time in the pit, and the vote for Callum will be carried forward."

"What was the point of school?"

"The four objects were in your lessons. If you paid attention, the dream will bring them forward. Must you ask any more questions?"

Now was as good a time as any to ask the one bugging me for weeks. "Yes, why did you abolish the hoods for church?"

She pulled the blankets to my chin. "That was your fault, dear."

"My fault?"

"Yes, the hoods were meant to prevent distraction from vanity during church. They equalized everyone. When you left, we realized a closer community would help prevent rebellion. We became open in all things."

"Even about the world not being radiated."

"See, we are evolving into a happy place."

"Right."

She snapped her fingers. "Close your eyes."

I did as she said, and a deep citrusy plant smell flowed into my nose. I floated up through the cavern and out to the above ground. A forest of pine trees surrounded me on all sides. Droplets of water dripped from a few of the branches. Dried pine needles crunched, and sticks snapped under my feet as I walked toward an unknown destination. I glanced up, and the branches of the trees wove too tightly together for me to see the sky.

A fox peeked out from a log, and our eyes met. "Are you one of the things I must find?" I asked him. He darted away from me. Purple flowers tossed dirt into piles as they bloomed with each step I took. It was as though my movements grew them from seedlings. An abundance of blue butterflies fluttered around me, swirling like a soft tornado and making my hair fly into the air.

Roots from a tall oak rose from the ground and entangled my arms. I tugged, trying to break free. The more fear rose, the tighter the branches wrapped.

"You must calm the fear that has the power to suffocate you," a voice that sounded more like an echo carried past my ears.

I relaxed my limbs, giving in to the struggle, and the roots retreated back into the earth. A woman dropped slowly from a tree branch until she stood in front of me. She wore a pink sundress and a straw hat. Her face held a familiarity I couldn't place. "I am your guide. I have come to help you find the four things and understand their meanings."

I stepped closer to her and smelled lilacs. "Thank you. I could use all the help I can get. The oracle didn't offer many clues."

"Her mind has long left her. She talks to things that are not real."

"Isn't that what I am doing now?"

She smiled and started walking away from me.

I hurried after her, hoping she could offer more tangible assistance. "Do you know what we are looking for?"

She kept walking and didn't look at me. "Only you know that."

"I don't know anything. I have to pass this. If I don't, a little boy will die. I can't allow that to happen."

"You must calm the fear that has the power to suffocate you."

"You're saying I need to quit focusing on the results because the fear of the results will cause failure."

"You learn quickly."

"I guess I will just follow you then because I don't know what direction to go."

She stopped. "Are you sure that's wise?"

"No, not at all. I'm not always wise."

"Humility is a start."

I stared straight ahead at the cottage. "I know this place. I went here with my husband about two years ago."

"Shall we step inside?"

"I'd love to."

The round wooden door creaked open, and a damp flowery scent filled my nose. I stared into the eyes of the long-dead bear rug. It creeped me out as it had the first time, but my toes appreciated the softness. "Help me! Help me!" a haunting voice called from the back room. Fog made it challenging to see the path, and I stumbled into the next room.

"Help me! Help me!" the voice called again.

The fog parted to reveal Morely's face trapped in rock. I beat the stone over and over, but she remained trapped. The woman appeared next to me. "Help me free my sister! Please!" I pleaded with her.

"Must I repeat myself for the third time?"

I stopped hitting the wall and took in my surroundings. A massive hammer leaned against the bed. I had difficulty lifting it, but once I had it to my shoulder, it felt weightless. I drove it into the stone, and it cracked. Morely shook free and vanished.

The woman touched my shoulder. "What have you learned?"

"To calm my fears."

"No, what does the woman mean. What is the deception that the oracle wants you to see? Once you know that, you will find the truth."

"The woman didn't want to get married or have children."

"That was her motive. What was her sin?"

"She was selfish? She didn't care about the community."

"Yes, you have found the deception. What is the truth?"

"She was selfless because she wanted a life of solitude over having those that she loves suffer because of the cult."

"Good. Let's continue."

We stepped outside and onto a beach. Spiders pushed through the sand and crawled over me. The feeling from the pit pounded my mind. I started to scream until the woman gave me a stern look. I closed my eyes and let them finish their journey over my body. I shuddered but stayed calm enough for the spiders to pass. I spotted Ryo at the end of the beach and ran for him. The spiders skittered past me until they reached him and pulled him away from me.

"Bryn! This is kind of an uncool thing that's happening. I could use a little assistance."

"Ryo!"

"Darling, help me out here!"

Stay calm. Stay calm. I practiced my breathing techniques. I looked around the beach as the spiders pulled Ryo into the sand."

"It'd be nice if you could save me before I'm eaten by sand," Ryo complained.

"I'm working on it!" Something shiny caught my eye, and I hurried over to it. I freed the golf club from the seaweed. I started squashing the spiders one by one with the metal head.

"That was my toe!" Ryo screamed at me.

"Next time, free yourself from spiders!" I squashed the last of them, and Ryo faded.

"What is the sin committed?" The woman took Ryo's place in front of me.

"He was slothful because he slept in church."

"Yes, very good. What is the truth?"

"The community shows no mercy for those in need. He needed sleep, and they dealt him too harsh of a punishment. Resting his body and missing one message was not worth him being eaten by spiders."

"Good."

Ahead of me appeared a grand waterfall, and I stopped my advance.

"You must move forward," my guide said.

"I can't. Not without Lachlan. The rock behind it is scary without him. With him, it is peaceful and a reminder of how he shields me from dark memories."

"You must conquer it without him."

"I can't. He's my safe place."

"You must step out of safety to survive this."

My entire body shook. "Why can't I just hallucinate my husband?"

"I have already answered that."

"I was talking to myself!" I hollered back.

I pushed through the water and plummeted into a pit. "I knew this was a horrible idea!" I screamed at my guide. The darkness dispersed, and heat scorched my skin. Flames leaped to life and danced around me as I fell to the gate of hell.

"Not seeing a way out of hell!" I looked up, and the northern lights flickered as the fire consumed me. I let the glimpses of the lights calm me. A strong wind extinguished hell's fire, and my guide balanced on a nearby log.

I didn't wait for her response. "This was a two-fold sin. The woman had the sin of greed and pride. She wanted more, even though her life was sufficient to keep her alive. The truth is she had the courage to follow a path she was told would destroy her. She found freedom from those who called her dreams, greed and pride."

"Good. The fourth thing awaits."

"Please be Lachlan," I whispered.

"It is not."

I sighed. "You could have let me hope a little longer."

She grinned. "Let's keep going."

To my dismay, we returned to the cave, and a priest stood in front of an ornate wooden table. On top, sat a brass bowl. The priest held out his hand, and I approached. He grasped my wrist so tightly that I thought it would fall off. I struggled, and the priest glared. He kept one hand on me, and the other pointed to a deep hole. Above the hole dangled a platform holding Callum, who was trying to reach his floating truck.

"Stay still! You will fall!" I yelled, but he teetered toward the edge. I turned back to the priest. "Let me go!"

"Make a blood oath for eternal servitude to the Above One, and we shall free you to spare the boy."

I relaxed my hand and let him cut my palm. Once my blood dripped into the bowl, I returned to the forest, where a blue-eyed man stood with his hands in his back pocket. I ran for Lachlan, and he spun me around. Our lips crashed together.

When we parted, he kept me against him. "I missed you. I missed you so much!"

"I missed you too. The thought of your arms was all that kept me sane," I said.

"The thought of you in my arms was all that kept *me* sane."

We kissed again until Lachlan pulled back and pointed at the sky above. Stars fell all around us, striking the ground in explosions of color. I closed my eyes and wished for Lachlan's happily ever after. When I opened them again, he was gone. I fell to my knees and wept the loss.

"Are you sorry I brought him here?"

"No, seeing him was worth the sorrow his parting brought."

She gently touched my face. "You are ready to pass your test."

She started to fade, and I called out to her. "Wait! Do you have a name?"

With a nod, she said, "Virginia."

Wednesday

♥

Bryn

I floated for an unclear amount of time. Panic swelled as I realized Virginia hadn't gone over the fourth deception and truth. I was going to fail! *Calm the fear that has the power to suffocate you.* Why would she leave me to the last reason? It finally hit me. She needed me to conquer the last one on my own. All of this was about stepping through my fears. *Think!*

My mind strained to come up with the purpose of the blood oath. I repeated the priest's words in my mind. *Make a blood oath for eternal servitude, and we will free you. That's it!* I had my reason. Blind devotion leads to freedom is the deception. The truth is that blind faith only leads to slavery. I pictured Virginia looking proud of me. As soon as the answer came to me, I located my body and merged.

I opened my eyes and nausea rocked me. "I need a bucket!" I cried into the air. The foot washer rushed one over to me, and I gave up my breakfast.

The oracle stood over me. "Gather yourself and rise."

I sat up slowly, but the room spun and my weakness returned. The drugs had probably aided the poison. I stumbled to my knees. The oracle yelled something to the back room, and two women rushed in to help me to my feet.

The oracle pursed her lips. "You must walk out to the community on your own to pass the test."

I forced myself to move forward and made it to the other side of the curtain, where she allowed me to sit in a chair that faced the elders. She took the middle chair that looked more like an elaborate throne. "Bryn Moretti, you have received your test. Tell us the four things and their meanings."

I cleared my throat and spoke as loud as my exhaustion allowed. "The first thing was the woman trapped in rock. The meaning is she was selfish and didn't care about the community." The elders and oracle's eyes widened, and I continued. "The second was the boy carried off by spiders. He was slothful, and that was worsened because he committed his sin on a holy day." They all looked like they were coming unglued as I got to the third. "The third was the girl who fell from the sky into hell. She had two sins. Greed because she wanted more even though what she had kept her alive. She had pride because she thought she had the right to dream." Horror displayed on all their faces, and I didn't understand why. I finished the last one. "The blood oath, which is the highest law. It means that blind devotion will lead to freedom."

Silence followed until the oracle rose to her feet, looking as pale as her dress. "How? How were you not suffocated by fear? That's what the elixir I gave you accomplishes. Who helped you?"

The test had been rigged. I hesitated, unsure if I should mention my guide.

Her face grew angry. "Tell us who helped you or fail your test."

"I had a guide named Virginia."

Gasps filled the room.

"The dead speaks to her. She is a prophetess," a man shouted.

"Silence!" one of the elders yelled. He rose and stood in front of me. "You are a seer. It is well known only seers have guides through this test and can clearly articulate what they saw. We can't punish her even though we would like to."

The rest of the elders nodded.

The oracle stepped forward to address the crowd. "We hereby grant Ganesh Moretti's challenges. Bryn Moretti will be released to her husband. Callum, the boy of imperfection, will have three months to turn himself around. That is all. Return to your lives and mention this no more." She left and was followed out by the elders.

I stayed seated in my chair, too stunned and weak to move.

Ganesh sat on his knees in front of me. "You passed! You passed! I was told that it was impossible. My mother helped you."

I looked up from the floor. "Your mother?"

"Yes, her name was Virginia."

An eerie feeling crept across my skin, and I wondered if I'd lost my mind being underground too long. I tried to stand and stumbled on stage. Ganesh carried me home and put me to bed, where I slept. I woke up later and took two of the silver pills. I sipped water and went back to bed. Ganesh cared for Luna. I'd tried to protest.

"Your daughter needs her mother healed. Go sleep," he'd said.

I slept until the morning when I felt slightly better. I took more of the pills and knew I'd have to thank Edna. Ganesh put on his hat, and someone knocked on the door.

"Why do you always wear a hat underground?" I stopped his advance with my words.

"Because the men's meeting is somewhere, I need it." He went to the door and let in Deborah. "Thank you for helping with Abra." He left.

Deborah picked up Luna from her bassinet and made her a bottle. "No one can believe yesterday."

"I can't believe yesterday."

"Did you really talk to Ganesh's dead mother?"

I shrugged. "I keep trying to remember if he told me her name in the past. I can't recall him doing so, but my mind is all out of sorts."

"Are the pills helping?"

"Yes, better than anything else."

"Good."

I shifted uncomfortably on the couch. "I need you to have something, but my legs are cramping pretty bad. I know you have Abra, but can you go look under my mattress. There are two pieces of paper."

"Yeah, no problem." She set Luna down and went back to my bedroom. She returned. "You tore this from the book. My word Bryn, you really are the bravest person I know."

"The other is a replica. I've drawn it over the last few weeks. I want us to have two copies, just in case. You and Atticus memorize it the best you can. Show it to Lilly and Cynthia if possible."

"Definitely. Why don't you go back and sleep? I have Abra until Ganesh returns."

"Are you sure?"

"Yes, we need you as well as possible for Wednesday."

I went back to my bedroom and sipped on water until I got the entire glass down. I would do no one any good if dehydration killed me. I slept until Ganesh insisted that I eat soup for dinner. He fed me and stayed silent until the bowl nearly emptied.

He gave me the last bite. "Did my mother tell you that you would be healed?"

"No, I don't think I will be. I think my purpose is almost concluded. She helped me with the test so I could fulfill it."

"What is your purpose?"

I closed my eyes slowly and opened them again. "To save Callum."

"She wanted you to save Callum?"

"Yes."

His face lit up. "The boy must not be truly imperfect. He will grow into his head, and his soul shall be spared." He let out a breath as if all his worries had dispelled. He looked back at me, and they returned. "I don't want you to leave with my mother."

"I know, but you will be fine. Remember your promise. Remember to keep your heart open."

His arms went around me, and he held me. "Bryn, I told you the first night that my actions were first and love would follow."

I returned his hug. "I remember."

"It turned out to be right. I love you. Even if we will never truly be man and wife. I truly love you."

"I love you too, Ganesh." And I unexpectedly did. I loved him the way I loved Thane and Ryo and even Cole. I loved him the way I loved family. I felt pretty sure by his words that he felt exactly the same way.

Wednesday morning, I had to remind myself of every reason to exit my bed. Every physical system in my body pleaded for the mercy of rest. I had one final task before I would rest with Aurora.

Today would be a good day despite the sorrow my passing would bring those I loved. I took three silver pills, figuring I needed extra strength. It didn't matter at this point if it was too much.

Ganesh read a book on the sofa, and I caught his eye. "Why are you dressed? You look much too sick to leave your bed."

"I need to go to school today. I have people I need to see. I want to take Abra with me. I was hoping you could carry her for me on your way to the men's meeting."

"How will you get her home?"

"Deborah will be there today. She can help me take her back." I grabbed the diaper bag and sling.

"Alright, but don't stay long. You need rest."

He fed Luna and changed her. We walked toward the school, and when we arrived, Deborah spotted us and took Luna from Ganesh. I hugged him extra tight, and he kissed the top of my head. I started to walk away from him, but he stopped me.

"Bryn?"

I turned to look at him. "Yes?"

His mouth opened and closed. The look in his eyes told me somehow, he knew this was goodbye. His eyes welled, and he quickly exited the room.

Cynthia walked in with Callum riding happily in the cart. Abby's four boys were with him. Abby had both her girls in a sling. She was a super mom to me. The children trickled in, all bursting with excitement for the field trip.

Jack tugged on my shirt. "We're going to see glowworms today."

"I know. It's a good day."

"The best!"

"Yes, the absolute best." I looked around the room. "Deborah, where are the other women?"

"All those who want to come are meeting us in the canning room. It's more private. No one ever goes in there except to can."

Atticus clapped his hands. "Children, line up."

All thirty-six kids calmly lined up in a perfect row. Their obedience would bend in our favor today. After today, they would get to be kids. We walked to the canning room, and I stared stunned at the overflowing room. There had to be at least a hundred women and children.

"I thought we were bringing fifteen?" I whispered to Deborah.

"Word spread."

"What if the men know?"

"We carry on anyway. As of now, no one has stopped us."

Urgency strengthened me, and I helped load the smallest children into the carts. Twenty-four little ones would ride securely.

I scanned all the faces. "Has anyone seen Lilly?"

Cynthia looked with me. "I haven't seen her. I'm getting worried."

Atticus walked over. "I'll go find her. Why don't the rest of you start up the tunnels? Get as much distance between the rest of the men and us."

Deborah grabbed his hand. "No, what if you're caught with her alone."

"I'll go with him. The rest of you get going. I have a copy of the map," I said.

Atticus shouted to the children and pointed at Cynthia and Deborah. "Miss Cynthia and Debbie are going to start the field trip. Listen to them as you would me. I will catch up soon."

The room began to empty. The women and children went right toward liberty. Atticus and I went left. I looked behind me at the stream of people escaping. This was a mass exodus. We made it to Lilly's den and got no answer. Atticus opened the door, and we found Lilly on the floor, savagely beaten. Atticus didn't think twice.

He scooped her up. "Let's get going."

She groaned, and I knew she was at least alive.

Revolution

Bryn

Atticus held Lilly as we hurried to catch up with the others.

Lilly clutched her stomach. "My baby!"

I grabbed her hand. "We're leaving. A hospital will check you both out." We caught sight of the last of the group headed down the expected tunnels. Something hit me out of nowhere. "Atticus the cameras! I forgot the cameras."

He gave me a tight smile. "I took care of them this morning. They always check them on the way back from the men's meeting, but hopefully, we'll be too far ahead when they notice them disabled. I'm going to go see if there is room on one of the carts for Lilly."

That was probably best. Lilly wasn't very big, but it would better if Atticus didn't wear out. As a man, he was the only one able to have a gun. We needed his arms free. The farther we walked, the more adrenaline started to wear off, and I was having trouble keeping pace. We still had miles to go, and I didn't think I could make it that far. I thought about riding in a cart, but they were so far ahead. I didn't know if I could reach one or if there would be room. Atticus would be lucky to find a place for Lilly.

"Bryn!" I looked up to see Deborah jogging back to me. She had Luna in a sling, and I was glad because I wanted to see my baby one last time. "Atticus found room on a cart for Lilly."

"Good."

She studied me with intense worry. "It's only a little farther." She grabbed my hand. "You've made it this far. Don't give up. You're going to see your family soon."

A woman slightly ahead of us spoke with another woman. "I wonder what food they have above ground."

"It'll be like right after our husbands leave on supply runs. The food will probably be fresh. I can't wait to feel the wind. I haven't since I was a little girl."

"I never have. Is it cold?"

"Sometimes, but it will be so worth it even if it is."

"Feeling anything at all will be nice."

I wanted to sleep so badly, but I knew if I surrendered to the feeling, I'd never get back up. I pushed myself to see the sky one last time. It was the best I could hope for to use my first motivation to leave this place. Seeing Lachlan felt too much to hope for. We said goodbye in my dream. It had almost felt like a shared dream as though he'd really held me. I took one step after the other as muscle spasms set in.

"Deborah, do you have my pills?"

She searched through a bag on her shoulder and pulled them out. I swallowed two, wondering if they would kick in fast enough. I started to slow, and Deborah pulled me along.

She looked at the map. "Only a quarter of a mile. We're so close. So close."

We walked about twenty minutes more, and my strength felt nearly depleted. I wasn't going to make it. I could feel myself draining. The walk had proven too much.

Cynthia ran back to us. "We've found the exit, but it's small. We can only crawl through one person at a time. We've already started."

"We need to get Bryn there now," Deborah said.

I shook my head. "I can't crawl through it. My muscles don't have the strength. How will we get the babies through?"

"We made a line and are passing them through from one person to the next. I need to get back to Callum." Cynthia hugged me. "Stay strong, Bryn. I know it's not ideal, but we can always put a blanket under you and pull you through. That's what we're doing for Lilly." She took off toward the front of the line.

Slowly we moved forward, and my heartfelt lighter with each movement forward because it meant another person had escaped. My legs shook uncontrollably, and I collapsed on the ground.

"Bryn!" Deborah screamed. "Bryn, get up! You have to get up. They'll find us soon. The men's meeting is almost done."

"Deborah, I'm not going to make it. Get my daughter out of here. Her real name is Luna Sky. Get her to her daddy. When you get to a town, ask for the police. Tell them you have Luna West, a missing child. Her father's name is Lachlan West. The police will know how to find him." Each word was an effort, and exhaustion consumed me.

She tried to help me up but realized I couldn't move and just held me. "I'm not leaving you. We need you to lead us out."

I touched the top of Luna's head. "You're already led out. Get my daughter out of here. I'm too weak. You have to be strong for all of them." I closed my eyes.

Luna started crying, and Deborah bounced the sling. "Bryn, she needs you."

"She needs out of this cave more. She has lots of family to care for her. Get her to the stars, Deborah. Let her make star wishes. Remember, the stars always fall. There will always be places for wishes and dreams. This is your revolution, Deborah! Get out and today the cult will be overthrown. The world will no longer ignore your cries. The cult ends today. Go for Luna's sake. Go for Atticus. Go so all of this will end. I'm begging you."

That's what today was, our revolution. We might not have raised sword or gun to fight, but each of these women woke up today and fought against the ideals ingrained in them through years of slavery. And today with every part of me, I knew the cult would experience the end of the teachings of Summet.

Deborah wiped her tears. "Don't give up. I'm going to send someone back for you." She let go of her hold and stood up.

I watched her take my baby away before I surrender to rest. Time passed, and I opened my eyes long enough to make sure they all continued. Once the last one disappeared from view, I kept my eyes shut. Everything felt distorted, so I didn't know how long had passed when sharp voices made me stir.

"There's the traitor. I'll strangle her!" I recognized the priest's voice. "The rest of you get the women and children. I'll deal with this one myself."

I felt too weak to turn my head. Someone roughly dragged me. My back scraped against the ground, but my muscles hurt badly enough that the scraping felt like nothing. I didn't resist. I'd done what I'd set out to do, and it wouldn't be much longer.

"Stop!" Ganesh yelled. "Don't touch her! She's suffering enough!"

"She stole our women!" the priest roared.

"Our women left by choice because of our cruelty. My mother taught me of the mercies of God. The god you serve is not one I want anymore. Let her go, or I'll shoot."

I opened my eyes and watched as Ganesh pulled a gun on the priest.

"You'd shoot your priest? That will earn you eternal damnation."

"That might be the case, and I've earned it for staying silent too long. Let go of my wife, or I'll send you to hell first!"

The priest let go of me, and I crumpled back to the ground. Ganesh dropped to his knees and cradled me in his arms. "I'm sorry, Bryn. I'm so sorry. Please forgive me."

I forced my hand to his face. "There's nothing to forgive." Something shiny caught my eye as the priest moved for it. "No!" I gasped.

Ganesh whirled around and pulled his gun in the same motion.

Two deafening booms slammed through my ears.

Ganesh fell, clutching his abdomen."

"Ganesh! Ganesh!"

His hand moved into mine. "Shhh!!! Today we both leave with my mother."

A tear rolled down my cheek, and light took my focus off Ganesh. Aurora held her arms out to me, and I reached my hand to her.

Last Time

Lachlan

A lmost three weeks of searching the cave and not sign of the active cult anywhere. What if we had it all wrong and they didn't take her back to the cave? Cole pulled out his guitar and started singing "Fireflies" by Owl City. It was one he'd taught Bryn, and she loved it.

I looked over at Thane and Ryo and saw the same worn defeat in their eyes. How long should I keep them out here? There was no return to life for me without finding Bryn and Luna, but the guys had their own lives. I'd give it another week, and then talk to all three of them about going back without me.

My satellite phone rang. I glanced at it to see Tom's number and quickly answered. "Hey, Tom."

"Lachlan, one of my rangers called. A bunch of women showed up at his station. It's a twenty-minute drive from your campsite. I'll text you the location."

"Is Bryn with them?"

"He doesn't think so, but Lachlan, they took him back to a small cave entrance. There are dozens of women and children. He says the hole is so small that they can only come out one at a time."

I jumped up. "We'll be there in ten."

"Careful. If you crash, you'll make it in never."

We hung up, and the guys looked at me as I told them the news. We were all in the truck with knives and loaded guns within minutes. Thane wouldn't let me drive, which was probably best. He pushed the speedometer. Hope nipped at my heart, but I pushed it back because the expectation of disappointment grew stronger.

"Are we close yet?" I asked for the tenth time.

"Five minutes," Thane said.

I thought about my little moon and how big she had to be by now. *It doesn't matter. All the time you missed doesn't matter as long as she's safe for you to have years with her.*

"Wow!" Thane yelled.

I jerked forward as the car slammed to a halt. Dozens of people stood in the middle of the road. Thane pulled over, and we hopped out. In the distance, sirens blared. I swung my backpack over my shoulder in case we needed first aid. The almost doctor in me couldn't leave it.

I ran up to the first woman. "Did you come from a cave?"

She clasped her shaky hands together and nodded. "We all did."

I pulled out my phone. "Have you seen this woman?"

She looked at my phone like it was a bomb. "That's Bryn Moretti."

"Moretti?"

"Yeah, Ganesh Moretti's wife."

I thought for a minute and remembered it was the name from the notebook. Then the reality of her words set in. I blinked, trying to calm myself down. They had married my wife to another man! I had to slow down my breathing. I could deal with what all that meant after I found Bryn.

"Where is she?"

"I'm not sure. She was leading us out, but I haven't seen her since she told us to stick together."

"Did she have a baby with her?" I was terrified of the answer. My heart couldn't take Luna being dead.

"Yeah, Abra. She's adorable. Deborah was carrying her because Bryn was too weak."

"Too weak. Why?"

"She's been really sick for a long time."

The guys and I spread out, calling Bryn's name. I couldn't focus on her being sick and too weak to hold Luna. At least someone had seen her alive today.

"Bryn!" I shouted into the crowd of ladies. I shouted her name over and over.

A girl pushed through the crowds with a cloth bundle in front of her. "You're looking for Bryn?"

"Yes, my wife."

"Are you Lachlan West?"

"Yes!"

"She told me to give you your daughter." She lowered the cloth to reveal a baby I didn't recognize.

She had a head full of dark hair as Luna did, but this child was so much older than the one stolen from me. She handed me the baby, and when familiar blue eyes peered back at me, there was no doubt in my mind this baby was Luna.

My body shook as I wept with my daughter in my arms. All the time lost to us both, but I had her. My daughter was in my arms, breathing. "Bryn. Where is Bryn?" I finally choked out.

"She's in the cave. She couldn't walk any farther. I didn't want to leave her, but she begged me to get her baby to safety. I wasn't strong enough to help them both out. I'm sorry."

"Can you show me where this cave is?"

"Yeah, it's not far."

I turned to find the guys and saw they were right behind me.

"Luna!" They all cried at once.

I nodded. Tom stood next to Cole, and I handed him Luna. "Can you help Cole get her out of here?"

"Yeah, not a problem."

I kissed Luna one last time and turned to Cole. "Take care of your niece. I'm going after Bryn."

He smiled at the bundle in Tom's arms. "I'm going with you. I need to get my sister out of there."

"Your arm will slow us down if the tunnel narrows too much. I need someone I trust protecting my daughter, so I can keep my mind on Bryn. Get Luna in the truck and drive her back to the ranger station. I don't want her out here if there is a firefight. Load as many women as you can."

"All the rangers will help with our trucks. Police should be here soon."

Cole gave me a fist bump. "Okay! Go! Kick some cult ass!"

The girl ran down the path. We pushed through the crowd with Ryo, and Thane behind me. We turned on our headlamps. We came to a small opening in the earth. No wonder we couldn't find them. This entrance was barely noticeable.

She pointed at the hole. "You have to crawl for a while. Once you get to where you can stand, follow the path until you come to a drop. Go right, and it will wind quite a ways. Follow it until you come to a three-branched path. Take the left one. I left Bryn on the second curve. The men were almost done with the meeting. I don't know what you'll find."

"You get far away from this entrance." I heard sirens back toward where I'd left Cole and Luna. "Tell the police, the ones in blue shirts, that armed men will be coming out this entrance. Tell them we need a medical helicopter."

The girl ran back toward the other women. I crawled through the cave and pushed my bag in front of me. Usually, the close space would have terrified me, but finding Bryn dead scared me more.

We made it to the drop and turned right. On the third curve, I could hear voices. We drew our guns and hid behind a stalagmite. At least a couple of dozen men marched past. We waited a minute after the last one left. We ran again, following all of the girl's instructions. Three heaps on the floor caught my attention. I ran to them and stopped when I saw the scene. One was clearly dead with a gunshot wound to the head.

The second was a man bleeding from his abdomen, holding his hand was the woman I loved more than life. I crashed to my knees and scooped her into my arms. Her hand let go of his. She didn't look right, but I knew the low lighting might distort things. "Bryn!"

She groaned, keeping her eyes shut. "Lachlan?"

"Yeah, it's me. I have you now. You're safe."

A tear slipped from her eye. "Luna?"

"She's safe. Cole has her."

"I'm not going to make it." Her breathing was ragged, and she weakly lifted her hand. "Save him."

I stared at the man whose hand she'd held. "Who is he?"

"The man who kept Luna and me alive. Save him. I love you. Take care of our daughter."

"No, you're going to be fine. I'm going to get you help."

"It's too late. I can feel it. They...." She had to pause to catch her breath. "They poisoned me for a long time. It's too late now."

"No, we're going to get you to a hospital. It's going to be okay."

"I love you," she gasped.

I brought her closer to me. "I love you too. So much, Bryn. I never stopped looking."

She finally opened her eyes, and the whites were dark yellow, which meant severe liver damage. With a great deal of effort, she touched my face and gave a faint smile. "I knew you wouldn't. I told them you wouldn't." She closed her eyes again.

"Bryn? Bryn!" She no longer responded. I scooped her in my arms. "I don't think she's breathing. I finally get to her, and it's too late." My legs wobbled.

Ryo held out his hands. "Give her to me."

"I can't."

"Give her to me. You save this man. I'm running ahead with her." Ryo took Bryn from me and ran off before I could protest.

Thane stayed with me. I shut off my emotions and went into ER mode as I did at work. I bent down and pulled out my first aid kit and a blanket. I used what I could to stop his bleeding. Thane and I carried him after Ryo and Bryn. We made it to the part of the cave you had to crawl through, and I stared at the hole. We couldn't drag Bryn across the rock.

Ryo handed Bryn back to me. "You wait here. I'm going to make sure we can get medics in here."

"Be careful. It's probably a war zone out there." I watched him disappear through the tunnel and cradled Bryn close to me. She barely weighed anything at all. She'd always been tiny, but I could tell she'd lost significant weight. I felt for a pulse, and my body relaxed as I felt one.

I kissed her forehead. "I'm so sorry, babe. I'm so so sorry."

Too many minutes passed, and I debated trying to maneuver Bryn through the crawl space. Voices interrupted my debate. A medic crawled through pulling a rope. An orange stretcher followed and then a second medic. They took Bryn from me and laid her on the stretcher, wrapping her with a blanket and securing black straps around her. A second set of medics appeared for the man, and they took Bryn and the man through the tunnel. I hurried after them.

Match

♥

Lachlan

We made it outside to find no firefight. It seemed the men didn't locate the exit, and I figured they must have thought the women and children went a different way. The small exit size probably helped them overlook it. Bryn and the man with her were given priority in the helicopters. Several women and children were taken by ambulance in various conditions. The rangers and police were driving the rest.

Tom picked me up and let me know Luna was taken by ambulance to the closest hospital. She'd looked fine when I'd seen her, and I hoped it was a precaution. I held my phone in my hand, shaking. I had to call my in-laws. I didn't know what to tell them about Bryn. Did I simply tell them we found her or tell how she was? They'd probably ask. I dialed Anna.

"Lachlan, how's it going?"

I choked up, trying to get the words to come out. "Anna, we found them. Both of them are alive."

Silence followed for enough seconds that I grew concerned, and I realized it was because she was crying too much to speak.

She regained composure. "How are they?"

"They're both being taken to the hospital. Luna looked perfect, and they just wanted to make sure."

"Bryn?"

I took a deep breath. "She's not in as good of shape, but she's alive."

"Okay. Okay. We can handle alive. Thank you! Lachlan, thank you so much. Donovan and I are on the next plane out."

We hung up, and the ride the hospital took too long. Ryo and Thane were in the back seat, and none of us said anything. Cole had ridden in the ambulance with Luna because they'd taken her before I'd left the cave.

I texted him. *How's Luna?*

Cole: *She's doing well. Happy and giving me lots of smiles. She doesn't appear to have any injuries. They think she was well cared for.*

I let out a relieved breath. Thank God they took care of my baby girl. If only they had done the same for my wife. Who knew the extent of what they had done to Bryn? Tom dropped us off at the hospital entrance.

I sat in the ICU waiting area, staring at the large fern that grew in the corner. Ryo and Thane sat with me. Cole gave me regular updates on Luna. I couldn't wait to see her, but I needed to know about Bryn first.

"Lachlan West?" a doctor stood in the doorway, calling for me. I jumped up, and he asked me to follow him to a consult room. He pointed to a chair. "Have a seat." He closed the door, and terror gripped me that he was about to report Bryn's death.

"How is my wife?"

"I'm afraid, not well. She has multisystem organ damage. We've started her on treatment, and in time we'll see if the lesser damaged organs can heal. The problem is her liver. She is in complete liver failure, and we don't believe anything can be done to preserve the organ."

"Is she going to die?"

"It's a real possibility. Her liver seems to have taken the brunt of the poison, which is good news for the other organs. Her only option at this point is a liver transplant. We have to try to get her a bit stronger, but she will need a new organ as soon as possible. The biggest problem is the donor list is very long. A live donor will be best."

I didn't even hesitate. "Sign me up for testing. I already know I'm a blood type match," I said.

"You should probably take time to think about this."

"It doesn't sound like my wife has time. I'm ready to do all the screenings now. I'll talk to her family and see if anyone else wants to be screened as well. When can I see her?"

"Soon. The nurses are getting her settled. I'll have them get you in a little while."

I went back to talk to Thane and Ryo.

Thane raised his eyebrows. "How can you give her your liver?"

"The liver has the greatest regeneration ability for any internal organ in the human body. The liver can be shared, and both halves return to normal size in both the donor and recipient."

"Sign me up for screening."

"Me too. If my darling needs my liver, it's hers," Ryo said.

I thanked them both and called Bryn's parents and sisters and got the same responses. With all the people willing to get screened, we were bound to find a match. A nurse took me back to Bryn's room. Fear and excitement pulsed through me as I entered her room. She slept on her side with an IV in each arm. Her skin was a sickly yellow color, and her hair looked significantly thinned.

I watched her heartbeat on the monitor as I wheeled the recliner next to her bed. She looked much too fragile to touch. The sight of her brought so much emotion. Each one overwhelmed me to the core. I felt joy and sorrow to the same degree.

"Are you going to hold my hand?" she whispered with her eyes still closed.

I grabbed her hand. "I didn't know you were awake."

"I'm too tired to open my eyes, but it's like your presence was worth waking up for, so my body did. How's Luna?"

"She's doing great. Cole is spoiling her."

"Good."

"Baby, why don't you sleep?"

"I'm afraid this will all be a dream."

I pushed my lips together. I had to keep it together. "It's not a dream. I promise. I'll be right here."

She said nothing else as she drifted back to sleep.

Someone knocked on the door of Bryn's room, and I looked up to see Anna. I waved her into the room.

She looked Bryn over. "Has she woken up at all?"

"Yeah, she's been awake a little." I handed her a tissue and gave her my chair. I pulled another close.

She wiped her eyes. "I know I've said it already, but thank you."

I nodded. "I would have stayed out there no matter how long it took."

"Any word on matches?

"No, I had my screenings done. I expect to hear back any time."

"Mine are scheduled for later today. I've been trying to reach Jace, but he's hiking the Andes. Don doesn't qualify. They eliminated him right away due to the heart trouble he had a few years back."

"One of us is bound to match."

"Why don't you go visit Luna? Cole told me you haven't gotten to yet. I'll stay with Bryn."

"Are you sure?"

"Yes, I'd love some time with my daughter. I haven't seen Luna yet, but I'll go when you get back."

I kissed Bryn's hand. "Your mom is here. I'm going to go see Luna. Don't worry, I'll be back soon."

Bryn didn't even stir as I left the room. I hoped that she would wake a little to see Anna. Mother and daughter needed their reunion.

I had to purposely slow myself down as I exited onto the pediatric floor. I jogged the hall, checking every number until I found hers. Cole cradled Luna, feeding her a bottle. She wore a tiny hospital gown with colorful animals all over it.

Cole spotted me and stood up. "Here's your baby. You guys really should have named her joy. I'm going to go see Mom and Dad."

I sat in the rocking chair, and my eyes stayed fixed on Luna. "Your mom is with Bryn."

"Do you think they'll let me see Bryn?"

"Probably. She doesn't wake up much."

"That's okay. I only want to see her. I need to see for myself we have her back." He left the room.

Luna reached for my face, and I kissed her hand. She smiled, and milk rolled down her cheeks. I dabbed them with a bib.

"I'm pretty sure you have everything beat when it comes to beautiful things. Daddy loves you so much. I hope you knew that every second we were apart. I can't believe you will be four months next week." She cooed, and my heart melted onto the floor. "Is that right? You have so many stories to tell me. I want to hear them all. Every single thing you want to tell me for the rest of your life. It will always have top priority." Luna smiled again as if she understood every word I said.

My phone rang from an unknown number. I answered. "Lachlan West."

"It's Dr. Sallow. We have your test results back. You're a match for your wife. We need you to come in for some more tests."

"Yeah, I can come in right now." I hung up and called Anna. "I got my results back. I'm a match."

"Are you serious? What are the odds of that?"

"Actually, pretty good. Spouses are frequently living donor matches. They are often the first to get tested. It helped that I have type O negative blood."

"Looks like you're saving my baby again. We owe you so much, Lachlan."

"I'm honored that I get to do this for my wife. I wouldn't want anyone else to. I have to go in for some more tests."

"I'll come stay with Luna if you want," she said.

"What about Bryn?"

"Ryo is with her now."

We hung up, and I waited for Anna to show up.

She marched into the room on a mission as she had the first day Luna was born. "Where's my baby?"

I brought Luna to her, and Luna rewarded Anna with a grin. She had to be the happiest baby ever, and she looked so much healthier than I'd expected. Anna returned Luna's gesture, and it was the first smile I'd seen on Anna's face in weeks. A mother's heart had another piece put back into place. I left them to chat and made my way to the lab. After that, I had psychological testing and a few other screenings. My phone rang again, and I saw a number I hadn't seen for a long time.

"Detective Miller, how's it going?"

Ryo and I had worked with Detective Miller months ago to take down a trafficking ring and save Morely from her abusive ex-husband.

"I wanted to give an update on the cult case and ask you a favor."

"Sure. What's up?"

"I was wondering if Jada's House had any openings?"

"I'm sure it does. I'll check with my sister-in-law, but last time I checked, we were down to five girls. We expanded last year, and we have capacity for sixty."

"The women and children rescued from the cave are asking to stay together. There is no other available facility with that type of room."

"How many are we talking?"

"A hundred and twelve. We're still DNA testing all the children to see if they match kidnapping cases. It's a big possibility that some won't be there long."

"Let me talk to my staff, and I'll get back to you. I think we can make some arrangements with some of the rooms. I'll call you right back." I hung up and dialed Morely.

She didn't give me time to say anything. "Lachlan, how are Bryn and Luna?"

I gave her a quick update and told her what Detective Miller had said.

"Yes, we'll take them all. We can set up extra beds in the gym. I'll call in all the volunteers and make this happen."

"Thank you, Morely."

"You worry about my niece and sister. I have this."

I called Detective Miller back and told him it was a go. "You said you had an update. Was it just about the women?"

"No, we got warrants to go in after the cult. A hundred and thirty men are in custody. Jared Bronze is one of them. I caught my big fish."

We'd finally done it. We'd taken down the cult once and for all. I finished all my tests, praying I really would save my wife from dying of liver failure.

The Window

Bryn

My body didn't feel like it belonged to me. Some other force occupied it, keeping me trapped in something painful and bleak. Consciousness found me occasionally, but it always felt like a mistake. A heaviness weighed me to the bed. I reached my hand out, trying to find Lachlan's. Since he'd found me, I'd expected to wake up back in the cave—like my illness had created a cruel joke.

"Sweetheart, I'm here." I heard my mother's voice.

"Mom!"

She gently pushed my hair back. "I'm right here."

I opened my eyes. She looked different as though a sadness had settled into her eyes that refused to leave. Not the type of sadness because I was in the hospital, but the kind that took weeks to stay that lodged.

"Mom, are you okay?" It was a silly thing to ask, but I was so worried about her and wanted some kind of answer.

"I don't think okay is the right term, but being here with you makes this moment wonderful. At this moment, I'm okay."

"I'm sorry." I closed my eyes again.

"What could you possibly be sorry for?"

I forced the lead weights over my eyes to open. "That you had to go through me being stolen twice. I didn't want that to happen to you." I burst into tears.

My mother moved onto my bed and carefully cradled me against her. "Bryn, I'm sorry that happened to you."

I fell asleep right after that, and I woke up to Ryo sitting in the chair next to me, reading some type of anime comic book.

"That looks like important reading," I said.

"Crucial. It's great seeing your eyes."

"They make an occasional appearance now."

"I'm lucky they did for me. Can I get you anything?"

"A Ryo hug."

He looked hesitant. "I can't swing you around, darling. Your nurse will have my head."

"A gentler Ryo hug then."

He treated me like china, which was exactly how my body felt. If I made one wrong move, I'd be pieces on the ground.

I rested my chin on his shoulder. "You give the best hugs."

"You're kind of a favorite of mine." He kept his arms around me for a long while. "I missed my best friend."

"I missed you more than my foggy brain will allow me to express."

"I think your arms are doing a pretty good job," he said.

I fell asleep in his hug. I woke up with him back in his chair with his head tipped back, sound asleep. I didn't feel that his neck could tolerate that long, so I woke him. "Ryo!" I tried to shout, but it came out as more of a squeak. I tried three more times.

He jolted awake and rapidly looked around. "What happened?"

"I saved you."

"From what?"

"A crick in the neck."

"Saved my neck and gave me a heart attack. Doesn't seem a fair trade."

"You'll thank me in the morning." A bench backed up to the window that closed curtains covered. "Ryo, can you carry me to the window. I want to see the sky. We've missed each other a great deal."

"Am I supposed to move you?"

"Yes, because I've approved it."

"I feel so much better knowing you have a medical degree and can make these choices."

I rolled my eyes at his sarcasm, which made me smile. The cave people always stared at me when I spoke sarcastically. Ryo and I spoke each other's language.

"I'm the dying one. You have to do what I ask."

His eyebrow shot up like it did when he wasn't tolerating my crap. "I will move you to the window if you quit insisting that you're dying."

"It's true."

"I guess you get to miss the sky a bit longer." He sat back in his chair and returned to his comic.

"I'm going to let your neck get all the criks next time."

He shrugged. "I have a good chiropractor." He casually flipped through his comic book.

"Lachlan would move me with no conditions."

"Lachlan isn't here now, is he? Also, Lachlan would walk over lava and let his feet melt off if you asked him, and you'd still be sitting here acting like you have no life to fight for."

"I'm too sick."

"Yes, that we can agree on. That's why I want you to fight, so you aren't too sick anymore and I still have you. Tell me you plan on living to ninety, and I'll carry you to the window."

I looked at the curtains. "Fine! I plan on living to ninety. I hate lying to you, but you left me no choice."

Ryo scowled. "Since you gave me half, I will give you half. I'll open your curtains."

"You frustrating, man child."

"It's what you love most about me." He flung open the curtains dramatically. "My lady, I give you the sky."

Sunlight streamed in, and I smiled contently as I drifted back to sleep.

The next time I woke up, Lachlan was at my bedside. His face went from deep worry to happy when he saw me awake. "Hey! Good morning, beautiful."

"Can you hold me?" I scooted over, and it took a great deal of strength.

"Are you sure?"

"I just put all I had into scooting over. I'm sure."

He climbed in with me. I snuggled closer and breathed in the scent I'd missed more than many things. His arms always felt different than anyone else I ever hugged. It's like he was my match, and they were made to fit only me. I buried myself in his chest and felt myself drifting almost immediately.

He woke me back up with words. "Has the doctor spoken with you?"

"No, I think I'm sleeping every time he comes in. I think I even sleep through the exams and tests. Either that or they've done nothing with me since I've arrived."

He moved his fingers over my arms, which was one of my favorite touches. "They have you on medicine that is taking care of the poison. They think you can recover from a lot of the damage. However, your liver is too far gone. It can't be fixed."

"That's what my hallucination meant."

"What do you mean?"

I told him about how I'd seen Aurora in the pit and what she had said.

He processed my words for a minute. "They put you in a dark pit for three days?" His voice broke.

"Yeah, it seems it was true. I think I need a new liver to live."

He kissed my head twice. "You do. You need a liver transplant."

I looked at him, horrified. "Someone has to die for me to live?"

"If that were the case, the person would already be dying anyway. It's their final beautiful gift to the world. But no one has to die for you to get a liver. A liver can be shared because it grows back."

"It grows back?"

"Yeah, it's an amazing organ. I had a bunch of screenings and tests. I'm a match for you."

"I've known you were my match years ago."

He laughed. "I mean, I can give my liver to you."

"Won't that hurt you? What if you die?"

He brought me closer as if trying to tenderly hold onto me in a storm. "Yes, there will be pain for me, and yes, I could die. But the risks of me dying are low. They are definitely low compared to the risk of you dying without a new liver."

"You can't do this for me. I don't want you in pain because of me. I don't want Luna to lose both parents."

"Bryn, I have to do this for you. I'm your match. We don't have a ton of time to find another one. I want you to listen to me when I tell you that If we don't do this, I'll be in so much more pain. The pain level will be so much higher in a way I'm not sure how I'll recover. We're each other's matches in all things. I can't be condemned to live as half a man."

"That scares me. What if I'm fated to die, and we are tempting fate to take both of us?"

"You are convinced your vision is set in stone, aren't you? Is that why you keep insisting you're going to die?"

"Yes, I thought I had two choices. Run and live or save everyone and die."

He brought his lips to mine, giving me soft kisses. "Yeah, there was no universe my wife would have run. Your heart is too big. They're bringing all the women and children to Jada's House."

"They are! Are we ready? I need to make lots of phone calls. Do we have room for this? I can talk to Morely about making some accommodations. I could call the contractor and see if they have time to add some rooms on quickly. We have the land for it. We'd have to push through permits for that. I think we have enough money."

"Bryn!"

I caught my breath. "What?"

"Morely has it covered."

"All on her own?"

"All on her own with dozens of volunteers. All that you should stay focused on is getting better. Extreme isolation, especially in darkness, can cause hallucinations. They can seem incredibly real.

In fact, that's how the brain processes hallucinations. It processes them as reality. I think your subconscious knew you were sick and was trying to let you know."

"What if it was really Aurora, and she wanted her mommy with her? You can't blame a child for wanting their mommy."

"No, I could never blame anyone for wanting you, Bryn West. You are the easiest person in the world to love. Please let me do this for you. Please let me be your husband and follow my vows of protecting you."

"Are you sure you really want to go through with this?"

"I've never been more sure of anything in my life. The last time I was this sure was when I knew I wanted to marry you. The time before that was when I was sure I was in love with you. Both times I was more sure than I was about the sun bringing warmth. Pretty damn sure and both times those things proved to be the absolute best conclusions I'd ever arrived at. So, yes, my firefly, I'm so sure of this decision. I passed the psychological screening so you can't say it's insanity either."

"How long?"

"As soon as the doctors feel you are as strong as possible. Get lots of rest, so that can be soon."

My body took me back into slumber, and I woke to Ryo once again next to my bed. We stared as we squared off.

"Ryo Bae Paik, I want to go to the window."

He smirked. "That sounds like a serious problem."

"The most serious of them all."

"Your husband was here. Why didn't you ask him?"

"Because I want to take you down."

His eyes narrowed. "I could do this for days. Say the words and I will take you to the glass that views the world."

"I plan on living to ninety."

He said nothing immediately. "Hmm... I was waiting for the but to that. Is it coming, or can I proceed?"

"Lachlan is giving me his liver."

"I heard. I have a slight feeling he may love you."

"Me too."

Ryo carried me to the window. He did everything with care to not disturb my wires. The event took a really long time, but he got me there. He sat next to me to make sure I stayed secure. I leaned against the glass and watched the night sky. I sat there until I saw a star fall. I asked it to let the surgery work so my family could stay complete. For the first time in weeks, I wished for Lachlan's happily ever after to include me again.

Confrontation

♥

Lachlan

B ryn babbled a lot in her sleep, but the one that bothered me the most was when she called for Ganesh. We hadn't spoken about him yet, and I had a feeling he was the man I'd saved. Her IV kept her hydrated, but I still tried to encourage water. Food was a bigger struggle. She tried to nibble on things, but they made her queasy easily. The effort often sent her back to sleep.

Sleep brought more mumbling about Ganesh, and each time I wanted to find the guy and have a boxing match. I kept trying to keep my mind from going to where it wanted to go. The things he probably did to her made my stomach churn. If he was the man I'd saved, why had she wanted me to save a man who'd done the dark things that filled my mind? I wondered if it was Stockholm syndrome.

I held her cup while she took sips of water. "Bryn, I wanted to ask you about something. It's probably a sensitive topic, so if it bothers you, let me know, and the conversation is over."

"I want you to always feel free with me."

"I do, but there are certain stresses I won't put on you."

"Lachlan, I feel safer with you than anyone else in the world. Ask me whatever you want."

"Who was the man you asked me to save?"

Her eyes widened. "Ganesh! How could I forget about Ganesh? Did he live?"

I tried to calm the storm rising inside of me. "I'm not sure. I'll check this afternoon. A girl told me he was your husband."

Her cheeks went red, and she looked at the blanket. I knew her look of shame, and I wanted it erased.

I lifted the glass to her lips again. "We can stop talking about this."

She finished her drink. "We can talk about it. We need to. I want you to know they made me marry him. They threatened Luna if I didn't, and I never once accepted it."

"Babe, not for a second did I think you chose this. Not for a second did I doubt your faithfulness."

"We never made it official."

My face showed too much surprise too quickly.

She continued. "He was a gentleman and protected me the entire time. You know how you said Luna looks so well taken care of?"

"Yeah, she looks amazing."

"That was thanks to Ganesh. He took care of her while I was sick."

Anger was building in me. Not at Bryn—never at Bryn. But at the fact that another man had cared for my wife and daughter. The man had stolen that time from me.

She caught the look that showed too strongly. "You're angry with me." Her eyes welled, tearing me in two.

I pushed her tray out of the way and climbed in next to her. I held her face. "Never in any universe would I be angry with you over any of this. That will never be the case. Not even for a second. Don't even consider that a possibility."

She closed her eyes, and I hated myself for bringing it up. I needed to visit this man and have a discussion. I waited until Anna made her daily visit. Bryn kept sleeping as the changing of the guard occurred.

Anna took the chair next to Bryn's bed. "How is she?"

"Extremely tired still."

"Any word on surgery?"

"Her kidney levels are looking promising, but her liver ones are worse. They think next week."

"That's so soon and so far."

"I feel the same way." I stepped out of the room and went to the information desk. Ganesh hadn't restricted visitors, so the lady gave me his room number. I stopped outside his room and collected my thoughts. *I will not punch this man!* I repeated the thought several times and stepped into the room.

He sat up reading what looked like a Bible. I studied him and couldn't believe how built he looked. Did they have weight building classes in the cave? Even sitting, he looked like a giant, and it made me angry. Bryn wouldn't have stood a chance against anything he'd tried. I knocked on the door jam.

He glanced up. "How can I help you?"

"May I come in?"

He nodded.

"We need to have a little talk about the fact you married my wife."

His face stayed neutral, and not even brief surprise flashed across it. "How is Bryn?"

"What makes you think you have the right to know? You think your marriage was legit?"

He raised his eyebrows in an almost amused expression. "If I say yes, am I going to have to fight you?"

"Maybe."

"According to your ways, she is your wife. According to my ways —"

I clenched my fists. "Don't finish that sentence."

He smirked. Probably because he believed he could take me down. He'd find himself surprised. Weeks of MMA training would prove him wrong.

"Can I help you with anything?" He kept the almost grin on his face.

"I needed to meet you. I'm trying to figure out if I need to press charges on you and have you locked up with the rest of your cave brethren."

"If you do, it will have been earned. I didn't protect Bryn as well as I should have. I love her, but I should have protected her much better."

"If you loved her, how did she end up in a pit for three days?"

The smirk dropped and he studied his blanket. "I have no excuses to give. I paid for my cowardice every second she was in that pit. I have no excuses. I made so many mistakes, but I do love her."

The heat rose through my face. "If you love her, how did she get slowly poisoned for weeks?"

His eyes widened in shock. "Poisoned?"

"Yes, she's in the ICU right now fighting for her life because your people slowly poisoned her."

"That's impossible. I prepared all her food. I'd never have let that happen."

My voice rose. "But you did!"

His breathing became heavy as if the reality of something was setting in. "Brigid's vitamins." He looked at his blanket in horror, and the tears falling from his eyes caught me off guard. He held his forehead and finally looked at me. "I did poison her. I'm so sorry. I'm so so sorry. I have no redemption from this."

"You really didn't know?"

"No!"

I closed my eyes and gave myself a minute. "Then, if you didn't know, there is nothing to seek redemption for."

I turned and walked out of the room, feeling worse than when I'd walked in. My frustration and anger needed put somewhere. I couldn't go back in to see Bryn until I'd cooled off. The meeting hadn't gone as I'd expected, and I didn't really know what I'd hoped to accomplish. I only knew I hated the man who thought my wife was his—the man who'd stolen my time. I went to the ICU waiting room and stared at the fern as minutes ticked past on the clock overhead.

"You really like that plant, man." Ryo stepped in front of me, which broke my gaze.

"It's calming my rage."

"If you need someone to hide the bodies, I'm your man, but I have to tell you I have a stiff back from sleeping in chairs. I'd rather not tonight."

"I went and confronted Bryn's cave husband."

"Oh... Should I get the shovels? Do you have him stuffed in a closet somewhere?"

"He wasn't what I expected. I think Bryn has Stockholm syndrome over him. She calls for him in her sleep." I told him about the entire interaction.

"Bryn told us he kept her and Luna alive. If he protected her in a scary time, it makes sense she has some attachment."

Fire lit my eyes. "It should have been me!"

Ryo sat next to me, so we were eye to eye. "You're right. It should have been you. But your wife ended up with someone who it sounds like kept her safe among wolves. It should have been your time, but since it couldn't be, another man guarded your wife and made sure Luna still smiles."

"You think I should thank him instead of killing him?"

"I don't think you necessarily have to thank him, but maybe don't kill him."

I fixated on the fern again. "I think I already did."

"You killed him?"

"I'm pretty sure." I told Ryo about the conversation about the poison. "The look in his eyes. I didn't want to see it, but it was clear as day. I crushed him. He hadn't known, and I let my anger get the better of me."

"It's understandable. If someone forcibly married Morely, I'd have trouble keeping it just a conversation. I know this because I went through it with Patrick. None of this is going to get easy overnight. It's not just Bryn who has trauma to work through. You need to face your own too. Talk to someone if you need to."

My phone went off with a call from Anna. I picked up quickly. "Is Bryn okay?"

"Bryn is sleeping. Some doctors want to talk to you about her. I'm not sure exactly what they want to say."

"Tell them I'll be right there."

I hurried back to Bryn's room to find four doctors waiting for me. Anna was in the big chair and asked if she could stay.

"Yes, please do," I told her.

She had a right to hear whatever this was as much as I did.

Dr. Sallow stepped forward, shook our hands, and introduced the other three. "Your wife is running out of time. We're going to schedule the surgery for two days from now."

I looked at Bryn, who didn't even wake while we talked. "Is she strong enough?"

"She may not be, but it's now or never, so to speak. We will sign consents and go over everything tomorrow to prepare both of you."

The doctors left and, Anna and I split up people to call. All Bryn's sisters but Adely were flying in. Anna had reached Jace, and he was catching the next flight to us. I felt scared, but none of it was for myself. I had no fear of dying. I only had fear that I would lose Bryn.

Morely made it first. The volunteers all insisted she go, and things were pretty much arranged. Not only that, but she hadn't seen Ryo in weeks. Ryo and I sat in the waiting room while they took Bryn for some tests. I spotted Morely come off the elevator.

Ryo leaped out of his chair and ran for her. "I missed every part of you, Dove!" He kissed her, and they stood in the middle of the hallway hugging. Hospital staff maneuvered around them as though hugs of that magnitude were a daily occurrence.

He kissed her belly and took her hand. "I missed little lamb and Ollie too."

Morely was ten weeks pregnant when Bryn went missing. Now the baby was due in eleven. Her belly was a visible reminder of how long Bryn had stayed captured.

I looked at Ryo, and he nodded. I unzipped my bag and pulled out the notebook. "Morely, when we were searching the cave, I found something rather important about your past. It's a letter from your father."

She looked back and forth between Ryo and me. "My father?"

"Yes, it has a lot of answers in it." I handed her the notebook.

She looked frightened. "I think I'll wait to read it when my emotions are a little more stable. Thank you for this, Lachlan."

"You're welcome. I'm glad I found it."

Ryo pulled her against his side and kissed her. "You need me there when you read, say the word. You want privacy. I can handle that too."

She grabbed his hand. "I definitely want you there. I don't think I can read it without you there."

"Then, I'm definitely there."

Two days until surgery and it felt like the biggest day of my life. It would be the first step toward my family reclaiming our lives.

Deepest Sleep

♥

Lachlan

An entire team of doctors and medical personnel arrived in Bryn's room to go over consents and talk about how the surgery would go. I got her awake when they arrived. Ten minutes in she was back to sleep. I had to wake her another three times to get through the entire thing. We got the consents signed, and all the bloodwork for both Bryn and me completed.

Her brain fog had increased, and she often woke up confused. I kept going back and forth over it being the right time for the surgery. She seemed so weak, but I didn't think that was going to get any better. She slept against me with hours to go before the surgery, and I couldn't sleep. I could only savor holding her and pray it wouldn't be the last time.

Anna carrying in Luna, woke me up. "I thought it'd be good for both of you to see her before they take you back," she said.

The doctors released Luna a week ago with a clean bill of health. Bryn's family had taken turns caring for her and bringing her to see us. I knew no matter what happened today, Luna would be well-loved for the rest of her life. In the last few days, Bryn had stayed more awake with Luna in the room. As soon as Luna would leave, Bryn would fall into an even deeper sleep as if forcing herself awake for her daughter took all her strength.

I slid out of bed and took my baby, who was wide awake and babbling. "Yes, absolutely. Thank you, Anna." I looked at the clock and realized we had an hour left until they'd arrive for one of the scariest days of my life.

Anna turned on the light to rouse Bryn, but it was unsuccessful. She'd slept through blood draws and other tests in the past, so the light not waking her wasn't a surprise.

I handed Luna back to Anna and sat next to Bryn. "Sweetheart, your mom has Luna here. They've come to see you before the surgery" I ran my hands down her arms and tried a bit more. I put her bed in a sitting position, and she slid against me. "It's getting so difficult to wake her anymore."

Anna's eyes were full of worry. "I know. I think the doctors are right, it's now or never."

Anna brought Luna over and placed her in Bryn's arms. Luna let out a loud babble, and Bryn moved and, with seemingly intense effort, opened her eyes.

"Hey! Look who has come to see you before surgery," I greeted her, helping her to hold Luna.

"Baby daughter, I love you." She kissed Luna, smiled weakly, and they carried on a conversation.

Her breathing became heavy, and I picked up Luna and said my own bye for now. I refused to let my mind wander to the possibility of her being an orphan by tonight. Over the next hour, Bryn's family all came in to see her. I sat in the chair, watching her talk to each of them.

Morely, Capri, and Koa all piled into bed with her. They all figured out a way to fit, and all three grabbed her hands.

Koa, who sat directly on Bryn's right, kissed her cheek. "We decided we're going to do what you always did for us. We don't promise it will be good."

All three sisters sang 'A Million Dreams', and Bryn smiled through her tears.

When they finished, Capri kissed her other cheek. "We still have so many more dreams to live together. That's how we know you're going to come through this surgery fine."

"Yeah, you're totally going to slay liver failure and not the other way around," Koa added.

Bryn laughed, and it was a wonderful thing to see. Koa and Capri started out of the room, and Bryn grabbed Morely's hand. "Morely, thank you for all your work at Jada's house. I know you will carry on with all of it for as long as I can't." Bryn touched Morely's stomach. "I can't wait to meet you, little Ryo." She looked up at Morely. "Do you know what the baby will be?"

Morely nodded. "It's a boy. It really is a little Ryo."

Bryn's face lit up. "I'm so so so happy for both of you." The sisters embraced.

Bryn's brothers visited with her a bit and made her laugh, followed by her parents. Anna tried hard to stay brave and not cry.

Bryn squeezed her hand. "You can cry if you want, Mom. It just means you love me a whole lot." They held each other and cried for a few minutes.

Anna held Bryn's face and looked at her intensely. "I'm going to see you tomorrow. I'm going to see my beautiful daughter healed. I love you so much."

They cried for a few minutes more. Nurses started to trickle in and prep Bryn. They told me I'd have to be prepped in my own room soon, but Bryn and I would get to see each other before the event. Ryo walked into the room.

He plopped next to her. "Morning Darling, I've come to remind you of your promise. I gave payment, so you have to keep up your end of it."

She leaned her head on his shoulder. "I'm keeping it. I plan on living to ninety."

"That's my girl." He put his arm around her. "When this whole thing is through, you and I have a date for roof golfing."

"I think maybe we could have a rematch for lego houses."

"You're on. You're buying me lunch this time. I don't care how awesome your star view is. I'm winning this time."

"Morely told me the baby is a boy. I was so happy to hear that my heart leaped."

"Would it have sunk if it was a girl?"

She laughed and shook her head. "No, it's just really nice that there's going to be another of you. Someone who can make people laugh in their darkest moments. You bring more healing than you realize, and you never let me wallow."

"Wallowing is for quitters. I just remind you of who you are. I'll see you tomorrow, darling." Ryo looked up at me. "By the way, we're naming the baby Oliver after your middle name, Lachlan."

My face lifted in surprise. "After me? Why would you do that?"

He looked at Bryn and grinned. "Because today, you're going to save our best friend."

Bryn wiped her eyes with a tissue. "That is so amazing of you both."

Ryo kissed her head, and they hugged. He got up and waved me out into the hall, pulling me into a hug. "You had better come out of that surgery room today. Do you hear me?"

"I hear you. I have every intention of waking back up alive. Save all your prayers for Bryn."

A nurse walked up to me. "Lachlan, let's get you prepped."

Ryo gave me another hug. "See you soon, brother."

"See you soon."

The nurse took me to a room, and that's when reality set in. I changed into a gown, and she got my IV started. "This is a wonderful thing you're doing for your wife."

"This is nothing. She's given her entire life to loving me through everything. I want so many more years of that."

"You are one of the sweetest men I have ever met. We need more of you in this world. They should come to get you in the next half an hour. Can I get you anything before then?"

"My wife."

"They're getting her ready. We'll definitely let you guys see each other beforehand."

"Thank you, that's all I need." I sat back, trying to calm my pounding heart.

Anna texted me to ask my room number and a short time later Donavon and her both found me. Anna gave me a hug. "I'm so grateful you were destined to meet and love my daughter. I know you said this can be common for spouses, but I think it's more than that. After everything she's gone through, she needed a man with a heart as good and kind as yours."

"I needed her. I don't know how anyone can't be good with Bryn by their side. I don't know how anyone can't be kind when they see her pure heart. She brings good things out in me. She makes me want to live up to the happiness she spreads to everyone."

Donovan stepped forward and hugged me while patting me back. "If I had to go searching for decades for the man that I wanted to love my daughter, I couldn't find a better man than you. You've come so far from the boy we met at the hospital. You make me so incredibly proud."

I choked up then. "Thank you for being the parents I never really had. You showed me how to be a father to my daughter."

A man stood in the doorway. "Lachlan West."

"Yes?"

"I'm here to take you back."

My in-laws gave me one last hug, and the man in blue scrubs wheeled me to a preop room. I tapped the sidebar on my bed, anxiously wanting to see my wife. I could be completely fine as long as I saw her before they put us both under. A nurse came in and asked me a bunch of questions, followed by the doctors and anesthesiologists.

Everyone kept acting like I was the most selfless person in the world. What they didn't know was I was selfish. Seeing Bryn suffering and the thought of never seeing her again killed me. Her death would break me. Her so sick was crushing me. I'd told her the truth that without her, I'd become half a man. The last few months had proven that correct.

Two nurses pulled the curtains back, and one popped the brake on my bed. "It's time."

I sat up. "No, wait. I need to see my wife."

"We're taking you to her now. We're going to let you drift to sleep together."

I relaxed as they wheeled me through three sets of doors. We traveled into an operating room, and I saw her staring at the wall, looking terrified. They wheeled our beds close together and put down the sidebars. Her entire face relaxed when she looked into my eyes.

I grabbed her hand. "You are as stunning as when I saw you in that cute little pink dress at the dance. It was so worth putting up with dress duty for."

"That's one of my most favorite nights. We almost kissed that night."

"I should have made my mover earlier."

She smiled. "The rain kiss was worth the wait."

"That we can agree on."

We both turned on our sides and kissed. She felt so fragile against me. She felt much too fragile for major surgery, but we had no other choice. All of our hands held tightly together.

Dr. Sallow stood at the end of our beds and smiled at us. "Alright, love birds, it's time. Lay on your backs, and we're going to put some medicine through your IVs. You'll fall asleep quickly."

We both laid back but kept our hands intertwined.

"I love you, firefly," I said.

"I love you more than the sky. Remember until the universe turns to dust."

I rubbed her hand with my thumb. "Until the end of time."

Our eyes stayed locked on each other as we drifted into the deepest sleep.

Impossible Things

♥

Lachlan

*T*he salty air always brought peace. *"Where's your jacket?"* I asked
Bryn.

*She sat on a rock a few feet from shore. Her chin rested on her knees,
and the skirt of her yellow sundress flapped in the wind. The October chill
left her visibly shaking.*

*I tried again to get her attention. "You're going to get sick, staying out
here like this."*

"It will be worth the illness."

I let out a short laugh. "Why is that?"

"The air makes me feel alive."

"It's only giving you goosebumps."

"Goosebumps also make me feel alive."

"You said last night I made you feel alive."

*She turned her head to me. "You also give me goosebumps. You are as
important as the wind. You both have done the same thing to me."*

*I waded out in the water to join her on her rock. A little crab scurried
past my toes, not stopping to pinch them. I watched the seagulls soar
overhead, looking for their afternoon snack. The ocean waves swelled*

and crashed on nearby rocks. Clouds covered the sun, promising colder weather.

When she didn't finish her statement, I broke the silence. "How am I the same as the wind?"

"The wind brought me miracles. You and it are exactly the same. You were my miracle since the first day you bandaged my hands."

"That's funny because I always saw you as mine. Before you, the highlight of my week was pizza day in the cafeteria. Once in a while, they let us play soccer. Then this girl arrived and shook up my entire world. She showed me pizza and soccer were nothing compared to how rain merges with your hair or the one soul that calls your name across miles of earth. You made me a poet, a lover, and you brought me to life. I will spend the rest of my life clinging to everything you make me see differently."

Sharp pain in my stomach yanked me harshly from my memories. I tried to swim back to the rock with Bryn, but a dense fog drew me from the perfect October day.

"It's okay, Lachlan. We're giving you some more pain meds. You should feel some relief soon," an unfamiliar voice said.

Where had Bryn gone? Why wasn't it her voice talking to me?

A loud beeping brought me closer to reality. I needed to wake up and find something out. Before I could figure out what, I fell back to sleep.

I opened my eyes in a strange room. Wires seemed to cover every part of me, and my throat felt like I'd shouted for a week straight. The light of the sink and blue glow from my monitors lit up the room. A nurse sat on a tall stool, typing into a computer.

"My wife." My raw throat made my words a whisper. I tried again. "My wife. I need to know about my wife. *Please*."

The nurse turned around. "Let me get the doctor."

Her words scared me. Why couldn't she just tell me if Bryn had survived? I looked down at my bandaged abdomen. I'd never felt happier to see myself wounded. They'd gone through with it. At least they'd given her a chance. I waited too long for the nurse to retrieve a doctor and grew aggravated. I only needed someone to tell me she lived through surgery. How hard was it for them to let me know? I pushed the call light three times out of urgency.

A nurse ran in. "How can I help you?"

"I need to know how my wife is. I need to know now." All these words were killing my throat, and a dull ache had set in at my incision.

"I'm not your nurse. I'll get someone." She left the room.

If someone didn't return soon, this call light would keep getting pressed. I tried to locate my cell phone and found nothing personal in the room. They'd put me in a stranger's room. I felt distant from it like I still slept.

After way too many minutes and five call light pushes, a doctor stepped into my room. "Hello, Lachlan, how are you feeling?"

"Impatient enough to create a giant ruckus if someone doesn't tell me about my wife soon. I'll force the strength to climb out of this bed and find her myself."

"Fortunately for your surgical area, you don't have to do that."

I stared at him, waiting for more information. "Are you going to tell me?"

"I don't actually know how your wife is." He walked over to the computer.

"Why is my surgical area safe from my rash decisions?"

"Because I'm going to look it up."

Frustration made me want to rip out my IV and throw it at the wall. I didn't because I needed the pain meds to concentrate on Bryn. "Tell me how she is before I fall apart in this bed."

The nurse put her hand to her mouth and looked like she might cry.

"What is your wife's name?"

"Bryn West. How slow is your computer? Is it a dinosaur, or do you love torturing patients?"

The doctor chuckled, and I thought terrible thoughts about it being worth no pain meds to throw my IV at him.

The nurse studied my monitor. "Lachlan breathe a little slower for me. Your heart rate is pretty high."

"Because I'm terrified right now. Hearts race when they are experiencing extreme terror."

"Dr. Richardson, please tell him how his wife is. I can't take it anymore, either."

"Sorry. System outages are the pits."

"What's really the pits is not knowing if I still have the love of my life," I snapped.

The nurse teared up then. "If he doesn't get it soon, I will track down your wife's doctor myself."

The doctor tapped the platform that the computer sat on. "I can't seem to gain access to her file. I'll see if I can figure out what's going on."

A cry unexpectedly flew from my mouth. "Does that mean she's dead?"

"I think our system is just down. It happens now and then. I'll find out right away." He hurried from the room before I could scream at him. It wasn't fair of me. I was sure he probably would have seemed very nice under different circumstances, but fear and pain brought out anger. How hard was it for this hospital to answer yes or no on Bryn's survival.

I stared out the window as tears wouldn't stop. In the last hour since the doctor left, I'd convinced myself she'd died. I pictured sending Luna to kindergarten, putting her toys together on Christmas, and Saturday morning cartoons, just the two of us. I imagined how much of hole all those things would have now. I pushed away thoughts of an intricately carved casket being lowered into the ground.

Anna and Donovan would probably buy Bryn her own statue. Ryo and Thane would help me find function again, but I'd really be a zombie appearing to be human as I shuffled about my day. I'd be a shell trying to function for my daughter. I could pretend until she was eighteen and had a life of her own. What were eighteen years? I'd live for the day I'd get to join Bryn in the afterlife. My death would make me smile because the best day in decades had arrived.

"Lachlan." I turned my head slowly at the sound of Ryo's voice. He wasn't crying. Maybe that was a good sign, or perhaps he was in shock.

"Bryn?" was all I could get out.

He sat in a chair next to me, taking too long. "She survived the surgery."

My chest rose and fell dramatically in relief. I looked into his eyes and suddenly saw the but. "What's wrong?"

"They almost lost her, and she's in a pretty fragile state. They aren't sure she'll pull through."

"They need to take me to her. Now!"

He nodded. "I told them that. If anyone can pull her back to us, it's you."

"I can't lose her, Ryo. I can't. Not after everything."

The nurse from earlier stepped into the room. "I've made arrangements for you to be brought to your wife. You won't be able to get too close to her, but you might be able to reach her hand."

"That's enough. I just need to see her and let her know I'm there. Thank you! That's everything."

"It's the least we can do after what you've done for her."

The nurse left to finish the arrangements, which took too long because hospitals ran as though a sloth and snail had collaborated on acceptable time frames.

They wheeled me into my wife's room, and I couldn't tell her location because of the tubes and wires covering her. My initial anger had fizzled into exhaustion, but sleep could claim me as soon as my hand held my wife's. They maneuvered the beds together and locked them in place. I couldn't get close, but I scooted to the edge and found her hand. A peace settled over me at its warmth, and I slept.

I woke up to find our fingers intertwined. I stared at her ghostly face, seeing her beauty even now. "Bryn?"

She didn't open her eyes, but she squeezed my hand.

"I love you," I whispered.

"I love you," she whispered back.

Slowly, equipment began to be removed from both of us, and we kept creeping closer to each other as the days passed. They made me get out of bed and move around with a walker and physical therapist's assistance. Bryn still wasn't strong enough due to some bleeding complications. She'd proven over the last four days the strength of her fight. I started to feel that she'd recover.

I inched down the hospital hallway. They'd let me wear navy pajama pants and bottoms for the adventure. I made it to the door that led to the stairwell and turned around to return to the room. I passed the elevator and caught detective Miller stepping out of it.

"Detective!" I called.

He hurried over. "Just the man I was looking for."

"Did I miss your calls?"

"No, I wanted to tell you this in person. I don't imagine you should stand too long. Let's sit down."

I made it over to the open waiting area a few feet away. Detective Miller stayed patient with my lack of speed. He sat next to me, and we both turned slightly sideways to see each other.

"We've caught the woman who poisoned your wife," he said.

"You did? That's great news!"

"Yes, it's all thanks to a man named Ganesh Moretti."

I stiffened. "I've heard of him."

His eyes widened. "You have?"

"Yeah, Bryn told me about him."

"He turned himself in and said he needed to pay for his crimes. I asked him what they were, and he said complacency. I didn't know how to charge that. Aiding and abetting maybe. Anyway, he said he wanted to help us take down the cult. He used different words, but that's basically what he meant. He gave us so many secrets that we found an additional three pockets of the cult. We have enough evidence to take Brigid Feldman to trial. As well as most of the other men we have in custody."

My cheeks hurt from the magnitude of my grin. "This is the best news. Thank you for letting me know."

"How's Bryn?"

"Fighting."

"She's good at that. I never met someone who had to fight so hard for everything, but still found wonder everywhere."

I smiled. "That's my girl."

I said goodbye to Miller and returned to Bryn feeling a little lighter. I found her at a slight incline with her eyes open, staring out the window. It was the most alert I'd seen her since we got her back.

I got myself into bed and snuggled close to Bryn. "How are you feeling?"

"I feel hopeful because someone let in the sun today. The sun used to be an impossible thing for me. Thinking about how the sun exists always brings me hope for impossible things. I think I'm going to live to ninety."

We spent the rest of the morning staring out the window and feeling the warmth of the sun tell us we'd yet again found our way back from the dark.

One Step Forward

Bryn

My Physical Therapist, Emmett, waltzed into the room like I was his favorite patient. "Good morning, Ms. Bryn. I think we're going to make it to the hall today."

"You sound so hopeful. After yesterday, that says a lot about your optimism, " I said.

"I am an optimistic person, but it is more than that. You have survived chronic poisoning and a liver transplant. You are strong."

"I've also survived having a gunshot wound to the chest and two kidnappings, but I think physical therapy might be what does me in. The final straw, so to speak."

He lowered the bed to keep me from having to hop out. "This is why you're my favorite patient. Such spirit!" He helped maneuver me to sitting on the edge of the bed with my feet on the ground.

"You say that to all your patients, Emmett. I can tell."

"I don't know what you're talking about. You haven't met some of them. This is a hazardous occupation. I have objects thrown at me quite regularly. Your lack of object throwing moved you to the top of the list."

"I do promise to never throw objects at you despite the infuriating positivity you bring to our sessions."

"I appreciate that. Again, this is why you are my favorite. Let's try to stand. Don't worry, I won't let you fall."

"The person I trust most in the world told me that once when I learned to ride a bike. It didn't turn out well. I'm not sure I can trust a guy I met three days ago to keep that promise." I grinned at him.

"That's just a rite of passage when gaining bike riding skills. That person knew you had to experience it. I'm occupationally obligated to keep you from gaining new injuries."

My feet started their daily tingling, and it became uncomfortable. "Is it normal for my feet to tingle so much?"

He looked up from where he was focusing on my foot placement. "Is this new?"

"No, I've had it for weeks. Back when I could walk, they'd go numb and make me trip."

"You've never mentioned this before. It's not in your chart anyway."

"No, I haven't mentioned it."

"It's not unexpected. It's common with Thallium poisoning, but you need to speak up with all your symptoms. It's important."

"I've had brain fog for weeks. I could barely remember my name at times. Sometimes the fog still returns."

"That's also understandable. I'll make a note to the doctors. Do you currently have feeling in your feet?"

I wiggled my toes. "They're tingling, but there's still feeling."

"Okay, good. Let's continue."

We worked together, and I made it to standing. "I think we used up my entire session up. Time for me to get back in bed."

Emmett looked at the clock. "Sorry. Another twenty minutes."

"Are you sure? I swore it was naptime."

"You make it to the door, and we can end our session no matter the time left."

"That's not fair because I have to repeat the entire thing to make it to my nap."

"Yes, that's the point. You're already standing. That's the hardest part."

I looked at him skeptically. "I think twenty steps is the hardest part."

"If I admitted to that, it wouldn't motivate you to move."

I took a step forward, and my knees gave out. Emmett caught me and stabilized my position. I took three steps.

"There's no way I'm making it the door in twenty minutes," I said.

"You have fifteen."

"I thought you weren't supposed to be discouraging."

"I'm realistic, and yes, you can get there."

Halfway in and I thought I'd topple, but Emmett kept encouraging me. I made it to the door with five minutes to spare. Emmett surprised me by carrying me to bed. He got me all settled.

"Why did you do it?"

He glanced up from the clipboard he was writing on. "Do what?"

"Why did you not make me walk back?"

"It was a reward for taking your first steps."

Lachlan walked in, looking like he'd never had surgery. They'd released him three days ago, and he split his time between Luna and me. Some of my other organ levels weren't stabilized enough for me to go home. I wouldn't get to go straight home anyway. I'd be at a rehab center for a while since my injuries extended beyond my liver alone. I still had a lot of recovery left. Some things would never be healed, and I'd have to take certain medications for the rest of my life. At night that brought depression, but at night, I also had Lachlan's arms.

Lachlan took the food he brought out of the bag and arranged it in front of me. "How did she do today, Emmett?"

"The queen of survival made it to the door. All on her own, too," Emmett said.

Lachlan's eyes lit up. "You took steps! I'm so proud of you, babe." He kissed me to show me.

"Emmett helped. I couldn't have done it without him."

Emmitt put his hands up. "It was all you. I only made sure you didn't fall."

Lachlan took his spot next to me on the bed. "I'm disappointed that I missed it."

I picked up my cheeseburger. "This was more important. I need-ed this."

"I'm happy you're eating again. I would have gotten you any-thing just to see your appetite returning."

Emmitt told us goodbye, and we ate our lunch together.

"Does Emmitt think your progress is good?" Lachlan asked.

"Yeah, he thinks I have nerve damage."

"Seriously? Why?"

"My feet go numb and tingle a lot. He said that's common with Thallium poisoning. There's bound to be things that last, I guess."

He looked down at my tray as his jaw tightened. "Maybe time will fix it all." I didn't think he really believed it either.

I fell for the fourth time and wanted to stay down this time. Emmett had caught me every time, but I was done with it all. This was my second day in the hall, and yesterday had gone so well. Today, I couldn't feel my feet hardly at all. "I'm done, Emmett. I want to go back to bed."

He shook his head. "You have ten more steps."

"I can't do it. I'm done."

Lachlan moved toward me. "I can take her back."

Emmitt held firm. "Ten more steps."

"She's tired." Lachlan couldn't handle me stressed in any way.

"Yes, and she can nap all afternoon after she takes ten steps."

"I see why people throw things at you, Emmitt," I huffed.

"Ten steps." He let a slight grin show.

I moved my feet forward and fell two more times before my tenth step. Lachlan, who'd stood to the side biting his lip, rushed in and picked me up. He carried me back to bed and tucked me in.

I scooted over. "Are you going to take a nap with me?"

"I think I'm going to go see Luna while you nap. That way, we can have the whole evening together."

"Okay, see you soon." I sent him off with a kiss and rolled over to sleep.

Routinely, I stayed awake most mornings and evenings, but I slept twelve hours at night and three hours in the afternoon. It was still a lot better than the twenty-three hours a day I was sleeping before my surgery.

A knock made me sit back up too quickly, and I let out a yelp as pain struck my abdomen. Thankfully, Lachlan had left. He'd have fussed over it until a doctor looked at me. "Come in," I shouted to the door.

Ganesh stepped into the room and glanced around, probably looking for Lachlan. "Hello, Bryn."

"Ganesh!" I held out my arms for him, and we hugged. "I'm happy to see you. I was worried about you."

He gave me a half-smile. "Why would you concern yourself with me?"

"Why wouldn't I? You got shot."

"I have come to ask your forgiveness. I shouldn't have left you down there. I know now I poisoned you for weeks. Ignorance is no excuse."

"Are you psychic?"

"What's that?"

"Never mind. The point is you thought you were helping me. All your reasoning was to make me better. The only one to blame is Brigid."

"She is going to prison for years. I'm going to testify at the cult trials," he said.

"Lachlan told me. I think I'm going to as well. What are you going to do now?"

He looked out the window. "I'm not sure. I think I'm going to go on a quest to find God."

"What a worthy quest. You'll have to let me know what you find out. You should go to Paris, France, there's this church that lets in the sun perfectly. It makes the entire auditorium beautiful. I felt really close to God both times I went." I wrote down the name on my notebook and handed it to him.

He tucked it in his shirt pocket. "I will make that one of my first stops." He hugged me. "You heal in abundance. I wish you all the joy from life. I will miss watching Luna grow."

"Thanks to you, she gets to grow with unlimited options for her life. Find your own happiness. Keep your heart open."

"That is a promise I intend to keep." He squeezed my hand and slipped out of the room.

I returned to my side, determined to sleep off the physical therapy fatigue.

"She's sleeping," Morely said.

"I'm not asleep." I turned back over to see Capri and Morely standing by the door. "Sit down. We can chat."

Capri stood next to my bed. "I can't stay. I have to catch my flight, but I plan to come see you at the beach house soon."

"I'm going to miss you."

"Yeah, Thane and I have been talking. We think we might move close to you guys. His dad has a Boston branch, and he could work out of there. I'd like to help with Jada's house."

I yanked her into a hug. "I would love that so much! Lachlan and Ryo would be thrilled to have Thane close again. They're always talking about how incomplete they are without him."

"We want to be closer too. We'll probably make the decision within the next couple of months as soon as he's able to talk to his dad." We told each other bye, and Capri left.

Morely moved a chair closer to my bed and sat. "I wanted to give you an update on Jada's house before I head back."

I rubbed her belly and felt Oliver kicked my hand. "He's strong. Dahlia is going to love him."

"She already does. She plays her little music box next to my belly when I tell her goodnight. She always tells him she'll see him soon."

"She's the cutest. I've missed her."

"She's missed you every day. Every night she prays to see Auntie Bryn again."

I grabbed a tissue and wiped my eyes. "She's the sweetest little thing. Anyway, back to your update."

"We have most of the women settled, and several have asked about you. It's going well."

"I can't wait to see them all."

"You worry about getting better. I promise they'll be plenty to be involved in once the doctor says you're cleared."

"I still have a long road, but at least I have a road to go down."

We talked for about twenty minutes before she had to leave. I almost got turned around to sleep when Lachlan walked back in. My nap was shot at this point, but it was all the best reasons for it to be shot.

I sat up straight. "That was a quick Luna visit."

"I never left. One of your doctors caught me in the hall. While I'm talking to him, I see Ganesh walking down the hall like he just left your room. I'm not sure how I missed him going in."

"Oh no! You're not in jail, so they either haven't caught you, or you didn't fight him."

"I didn't fight him. I walked him out to his car to make sure he kept going, and we had a long talk. It ended with me thanking him."

I don't think I could have been more surprised. "You thanked him?"

"Yes, we came to an understanding. I don't think we'll ever be best friends, but I think I probably would have lost you without him. He's also the reason the cult can't torture anyone else. He deserved a thank you."

"I knew there was a reason I loved you more than the sky." I gave him a lengthy kiss.

"Oh, yeah? I think I like where this is going."

"Yeah, your heart does the right thing even when your pride tells you differently. It's really attractive, your heart is."

"Does it earn me more kisses?"

"Absolutely." He climbed up next to me, and we kissed. It was so much better than a nap.

Going Home

♥

Bryn

I sat in my brand new hot pink wheelchair waiting for Lachlan to pick me up. We were flying home today after eight weeks in rehab. Morely was due to have her baby anytime, and I'd pushed myself so I could be there to see him. I could walk farther than I could when I'd started physical therapy, but neuropathy had increased. Doctors thought that with continued physical therapy, I might eventually have full use of my feet again. No one could promise anything.

Until then, I got to enjoy the wheelchair, which wasn't completely bad because it was colorful. I worried about going home because our apartment had a lot of stairs. I wouldn't be able to get myself and my chair into Jada's house on my own. I'd have to attempt without the chair or wait for help. I said nothing because I didn't want everyone to worry about me.

"Wow, that's so bright. So pink." Lachlan stared at my wheelchair. He looked as though he had mixed feelings on it. I couldn't blame him. I did too.

"It's making me excited about using it, so don't knock."

"It's perfect then. Are you ready?"

"I'm beyond ready."

Lachlan had already flown back several times to get things ready for me. Luna was with my parents at their Massachusetts home. I hadn't seen her in person in two weeks. Mom Facetimed me every night, so Luna and I could talk. My heart ached to have my baby back in my arms. She'd turn eight months in two weeks. I felt I'd missed most of her first year, and it tore me apart.

Lachlan wheeled me to the exit, and the staff at the rehab center were lined up to cheer and clap my release back into the world.

Emmett gave me a hug. "You keep taking steps. One right after the other. I'm going to miss my favorite patient."

"I'm going to miss you too."

Lachlan had recovered quickly from surgery, and doctors had cleared him to return to regular activity after six weeks. Almost four months later, he could lift me with no issues. His health and strength made me thankful every day. If he'd died or had complications, I don't think I could have handled it.

We took a cab to the airport, and the flight went without any mishaps. I thought my family might be there to greet us when we went to the baggage claim like they often did, but as Lachlan wheeled me off the elevator, no one familiar appeared. I told myself it was fine because I'd see them soon. We got into the rideshare car, and I stared out the window at the drizzly fall day. The orange and yellow leaves reminded me that I'd spent my entire summer inside.

Lachlan took my hand. "Are you warm enough?"

I nodded and kept my eyes on the blackbirds flying overhead. There had to be hundreds of them migrating south. They covered the trees and put on an aerial show, swooping in all directions in coordinated patterns. Telephone wire drooped from the mass bird weight.

"What's wrong?" Lachlan broke my thoughts with his concern.

"Why do you think something is wrong?"

"Because I know every bit of your body language, and it's telling me you're sad."

"I'm not sure. This should be a really happy day. I don't know why I can't agree that it is."

Lachlan scooted over and held me. "All the changes can be over-whelming."

We pulled down the long drive to Jada's house. Trees surround-ed the property on three sides, and the ocean took care of the fourth. I hadn't been here in eleven months. I thought maybe that was my sadness. I felt distant from my dream and hadn't helped anyone in a long time. My first girl Emma had left for college months ago while I was in the cave. I didn't get to say goodbye. I had to hope someday she'd contact me.

We came to the gate and asked the driver to let us out. Lachlan called someone from inside to come to pick us up. Security for all who lived at the facility was top priority. It meant no one made it beyond the gate without authorization. Lachlan helped me into my chair and put my moon quilt over my shoulders. Capri had made it for me. The gate retreated sideways with a squeak, and a blue SUV pulled up.

Unexpectedly, Thane jumped out. Lachlan placed me inside on the seat and loaded my chair. They talked while I watched the ocean to my right. We pulled into the parking lot, and I looked at the large blue house that used to be only a beach house. Over the last two years, we'd expanded and could house sixty women. Ryo and Morely lived in a little guest house close by.

A large banner hung over the doorway, welcoming me home. Lachlan wheeled me through the building, and I expected him to carry me up to our apartment. He kept going through the house. Music playing somewhere close was the only sound. I didn't know how it could be so quiet. We were supposed to have eighty-three women and children. Over thirty children were returned to their biological parents. He hit a button at the back door, and it opened to music and people.

Several children held hands, dancing in a circle to "Sweet Caroline". My eyes followed the line of people to the small stage and saw Cole playing with three other band members. Dozens of people danced, chatted, and nibbled on food from a buffet table. I caught sight of a sign above the stage that read, tonight, we celebrate Bryn West. I looked up to see Lachlan with a giant grin on his face.

The music stopped, and Cole stepped up to the microphone. "About two years ago, My baby sister got a dream stuck in her head. If you know my sister at all, you know that nothing stops her when she sets out to do something. Everything that should stop her, she keeps fighting against. This last year she fought the biggest fight of her life. Her bravery saved hundreds of lives. While she was away reclaiming her life, the rest of us decided to expand her dream."

A screen descended onto the stage, and a video began to play.

Emma had her arm around her best friend, Mia. Both girls were in the first set of girls ever brought to Jada's house. Emma held up a piece of paper. "This is my acceptance letter to college. College was something I thought had been stripped from me until I was rescued. It wasn't just Jada's house that transformed my life. Bryn invested hours into quizzing me before tests and explaining homework questions to me. I wouldn't have this letter in my hand without her."

Mia went next. "I had terrible nightmares when I first came to the house. We have buttons in our room, and these buttons connected to Bryn's phone for us to contact her at any time. It was like she didn't care about sleep or something. Every time a nightmare would steal my night, all I had to do was push a button, and Bryn would sit up with me until I fell asleep. Sometimes she would sing to me until I calmed."

Girl after girl appeared on screen talking about how I helped them and how their life was changed because of the hours I poured into them. The tenth one was Hazel, a girl rescued when Ryo and Lachlan took down the trafficking ring. I'd convinced fifty-four girls, including Hazel, that the outside wouldn't radiate them.

"I want to say if it hadn't been for Bryn being so patient with my cave sisters and me, we probably would have stayed in that room until we starved or they had forced us out. She gave us something important that day. She gave us a choice to leave, and she gave us hope that we could dream for more than survival."

By the twentieth girl, I was falling apart in my chair. The only thing that helped me maintain composure was my desire to hear everything they all had to say. I wanted most of all the updates they gave on their lives. I wanted to know they were all more than okay. I wanted to know they had left our house in a state of healing and had learned how to thrive. The video ended on forty-one girls and women.

Cole paused the video and returned to the mic. "We have secured donors to expand my sister's vision even greater. Twenty homes are in the process of being built. Each of these houses will help keep staff on property. He played the video, and it showed the little neighborhood that would hold the people who'd keep Jada's house running.

He went on. "We have also received funding for three apartment buildings that will house a hundred families each. These will work as transitional houses for as long as the family needs it."

The movie played, showing all the plans to create a community complete with parks and recreational areas. It would be a place where lives could be rebuilt long-term.

"Ladies and gentlemen, I would like you to welcome back the founder and director of Jada's house, my phenomenal little sister, Bryn Dahlia West!" He pointed to me, and everyone turned my way. Gasps filled the air, followed by clapping and cheers.

"Let's party!" Cole shouted.

The music started back up and with it the dancing. I looked around and began recognizing members of the cave community. They'd all made it to freedom.

I grabbed Lachlan's arm, and he dropped on his knees to hear me over the crowd. "Can you take me to the stage?"

"Are you sure? I didn't want you to get worn out."

"I want to sing. Can you help me stand?"

"Yeah." Lachlan took me to the front and carried me on stage. Cole finished the song and looked at us, questioning. "She wants to sing," Lachlan said.

I stood at the microphone with Lachlan's arms tight around my waist. "Hello, everyone! I'm so happy to see every one of you." Cheers erupted. "I'm sorry it took me so long to get back to all of you. I want to sing you a song called 'Waiting on the World to Change'."

Cole started the music, and I sang my heart out. Lachlan kept me upright as I released each note, reaching the end of the song.

"My hope is that when you leave Jada's house and go out into the world, you don't wait for it to change. I hope you change the

world and make it even a little better than how you first found it."
I turned to Lachlan to let him know I was done.

He carried me off stage to more applause. Exhaustion started
setting in deep, and I slouched in the chair. Lachlan moved in front
of me and put his forehead to mine so I could hear him over the
music. "Let's go home and see Luna."

"That sounds really wonderful, but shouldn't we stay and help
clean up."

He grinned. "I see we're back to this. No, Bryn, let's go see our
daughter."

Instead of wheeling me to our apartment, he took me behind the
stage where someone had placed a cheerful house. The Black roof
complimented the yellow siding. He carried me over the threshold
and kissed me. "Welcome home, firefly."

There was enough space to maneuver my wheelchair. He gave
me a tour, and everything I needed was on the first floor. He
brought me over to a side door. He waved his hand, and it opened.
"This tunnel leads to Jada's house. You'll be able to have easy access
to it. However, don't take that as your cue to overdo work. We're
mandating the director gets two days off a week."

"How about one, and we have a deal?"

He gave me a half eye roll.

"There's your mommy," my mom said behind me.

I turned my wheelchair around and held out my arms for Luna.
Mom placed her in my lap.

Luna grabbed my face with a big smile and said, "Mamama!"

I blinked back tears. "Do you think she knows that's who I am?"

Mom nodded. "Of course she knows that's who you are."

Almost a year later, I was finally home.

Blackbird

Bryn

Lachlan looked through his backpack to make sure he had everything. All the events of the past few months had put him behind. Harvard had been incredibly understanding of his situation, and he was back on track to graduate.

He started looking at the bookshelf with a deep frown. "Have you seen my pharmacology textbook?"

"It's in the living room on the coffee table. You left it there after you fell asleep studying. Someone who complains about me working too hard doesn't listen to his own preaching." I smiled.

"The difference is I fall asleep when I work too hard. You stay awake and keep working."

"I take my day off."

"Yes, that's why I caught you emailing contractors on your first day off," he said.

"I was at home in bed. Luna was down for a nap. I needed to keep busy." Our doorbell rang, and I wheeled over to the door. "Hello, I assume you're Bianca?" I let in the woman with neatly braided hair and plum lips.

She looked around and smiled. "Yes, I am. You have a beautiful house."

"Thanks! That's all my mom. She's an award-winning interior decorator. She can't help but make things lovely."

Lachlan shook hands with Bianca. "Thank you for coming. We're excited to have you." He walked over and picked up Luna, who was playing on the floor and brought her over. "This is Luna."

Bianca's face lit up. "We're going to have so much fun, Miss Luna."

Lachlan had hired me a nanny assistant. I'd be able to keep Luna close while still working. The idea of a nanny for Luna had terrified me, but Ryo had known Bianca a long time and vouched for her. I trusted Ryo as much as I trusted Lachlan. He'd never have suggested anyone for Luna unless he felt overly confident. It also helped that we had access to thorough background checks. Lachlan even had Detective Miller run Bianca through all their systems.

Lachlan left for classes, and I showed Bianca around the house, explaining things as I went. I gave her Luna's schedule. I hadn't been out of the house since we'd arrived home a week ago. I decided today I was going to take on the tunnel. Lachlan had installed walking bars on both sides of the tunnel, probably for me to practice walking. My feet felt fine today, and I wanted to test that theory.

"Bianca, I'm going to go to Jada's house for a while. If you need me, feel free to push the button on the wall. It connects to the receptionist, and she can page me."

"Alright, Luna and I will be here practicing her crawling skills."

Luna stayed content hanging out, playing with toys. She had no motivation to crawl. Ryo said she had no need to be mobile being carried around so much. Lachlan and I did have a habit of picking her up at the first sign of distress. I wheeled my chair over to the tunnel and waved the door open. I put on my chair brake and stood.

I felt stable and moved forward, gripping the bar with both hands. Halfway down, my feet started tingling. I looked back toward my chair and then forward at my goal. What exactly had I planned to do once I reached the other side? *I'd hoped my body would work right.* Feeling started leaving my feet. I kept going until my legs gave out, and I toppled to the floor. I could crawl back, but my hands weren't strong, either.

I screamed in frustration. The stupid poison had taken so much from me. It could have taken so much more, but I didn't care. I didn't want to feel gratitude. I wanted to grieve the loss. I backed up to the wall and buried my face on my knees and cried, falling over on my side and letting everything out as I bawled.

"Bryn!" I heard Ryo standing over me, and shame filled me. I looked up at him, and his face grew concerned. "It's okay. It's all going to be okay." I didn't think it would be, but Ryo made me feel it for a few seconds. He held onto me, and I sobbed into his shoulder as he said, "I'm here. I got you." He patiently let me wail.

"I wanted to walk so badly!"

"I know. I know." He stroked my hair. "Let's get you back to your chair, or do you want your room?"

"I want to move myself!" I shook.

"Normally, I would take all the time in the world to help you walk across this tunnel, but we're short on time."

I pulled back to look at him. "Why?"

"Morely's about to have Oliver."

"Why didn't you say that right away?"

"Because you needed your feelings acknowledged. You needed to know that while I can't relate, I can be here for you."

"Take me to my chair so we can get to her. Is she super close?"

"We thought she was in the early stages, but the midwife just got here, and she's at a six already. Second babies usually come faster." He carried me back to my chair. "I tried calling you, but you didn't answer."

"I left my phone."

"You always leave your phone at the wrong times."

"Phones have never been important to me, so they slip my mind easily. Bianca can page me for Luna, and it didn't seem a priority."

He found my phone on the counter, and we continued to Morely. I texted Lachlan to let him know. "Hey, Ryo?"

"Yes, love?"

"Can you not tell Lachlan about this?"

"My lips are sealed."

We went back down the tunnel and into the main house, which bustled with activities. Women were going back and forth to different activities. The cafeteria was full of people eating breakfast, and I longed to be a part of those conversations. I determined then that after Oliver was born, I was going to come and visit everyone. I had a list of people I needed updates on.

We went out a side door and down a little stone path to Ryo and Morely's little white three-bedroom house. Ryo and Lachlan had built a lot of it as a summer project. The things they couldn't do they used our regular contractor for. Morely loved simple and clean. Most of the walls were white, and her curtains a soft blue color. The one place she showed a livelier side was the vase she kept in the middle of her dining room table. I hadn't known for a really long time it was because Ryo brought her a fresh bouquet every week.

"Auntie Bryn!" Dahlia ran for me and climbed up to hug me. She had a little apron over her pink princess dress. "I'm getting my little brother today!"

"I heard, and I'm so excited!"

"I am too! I'm giving him this." She ran over to the couch and brought over a brown teddy bear with misplaced ears. One hung by its cheek, and the other was almost centered on the top. "Nana showed me how to make it. She did most of it, but I did the ears."

"I love it, so will Oliver."

She went back to the kitchen, where my mom had on an apron and was stirring a bowl. "We're making Oliver's birthday cake. You can have some when it's done," Mom said.

Dahlia stood on a step ladder next to my mom. "Nana, can I put the sugar in yet?"

"Yep, here you go." Mom handed her a measuring cup. "You two go be there for Morely. Dahlia and are going to have a blast waiting for baby boy."

We made it back to my sister's bedroom, where she stood slumped against the bed, gripping the mattress. She looked up with tortured eyes and weakly smiled. "I'm so happy you're both here!" Even in labor, she spoke sweetly to us.

"Can I do anything for you?" I asked her.

"Just be here. Please."

"I'm here for as long as you want me here."

"I want you here until this baby boy is finally out. Ryo!"

"Come here." He carefully turned her and let her rest against him. She held his arms and winced. He swayed her slowly back and forth.

We spent the next few hours trying to keep Morely as comfortable as possible. Ryo fed her ice chips and rubbed her back. He was much calmer this time than with me in the attic. I think his bravery stemmed from the midwife and her assistant's presence. Three hours after I arrived, Morely was ready to push. Five pushes, and she brought Oliver into the world. Ryo caught him and turned into a weepy mess. He looked up at Morely, and my heart exploded with love as I witnessed the look they passed between themselves. Ryo handed Morely Oliver, and I sat in the corner, soaking in their moment. I couldn't wait to hold him, but I maintained patience.

Morely blinked slowly before resting her eyes. "Can you go get Dahlia?"

I nodded and found Mom and Dahlia frosting the cake with a blue border. "Somebody is a big sister!"

Dahlia's head snapped up at my words. "I thought I heard him cry but thought it might be the TV."

"Nope, it was him." I held out my hand for her. "Let's go see him."

She sat on my lap as I wheeled us into the room. She leaped off my lap and slowed as she got to her mother's bedside. Ryo helped her onto the bed before taking his place on the other side. I snapped some family pictures for them.

Dahlia's eyes were as wide as the moon in the night sky. "He is the most gorgeous baby I have ever seen in the entire giant universe."

Morely placed Oliver in Dahlia's arms, and the tears flowed down Dahlia's cheeks.

Morely put her arm around her. "Are you okay, sweetie?"

"He's just the best thing I've ever seen!" Her tiny teary voice made my own tears fall. "He's even cuter than I told myself he'd be."

Ryo grinned and looked over at me. "Hey Bryn, Dahlia is basically little you."

We all laughed, and I continued to watch my sister's perfect little family. After about an hour, Ryo took Dahlia out to get dinner. I brought my chair next to my sister's bed.

She stared at Oliver with her eyes full of exhausted love. "Do you want to hold him?"

"I'd love to." I got myself into bed next to her.

She handed my nephew to me. "We're naming him Oliver Zachariah. After Lachlan and my father."

"I love that!" I said.

Morely had let me read the letter from her father. I would forever be grateful to the man who kept my sister from going through purification. I knew the pain of his death, and it gave me a different level of understanding about what his sacrifice cost him.

I held little Oliver's hand with my finger. "He's so beautiful. I do see Ryo all over the place in his face."

Morely nodded. "He's his father's son for sure."

"I can't wait for him to talk. All the chivalrous humor he will say."

Morely laughed. "Bryn, would you give me a present?"

I looked at her surprised because Morely hated presents. She especially wouldn't ever ask for one. "I'd love to. Name it, and it's yours."

"Will you welcome Oliver into the world with a song?"

I thought about which song to pick. I glanced out the window and saw the blackbirds filling the sky, and that's what I sang, "Blackbird".

The day had started with me grieving my broken wings, but Oliver reminded me that I would still have life moments that made me soar.

The Witness

Bryn

We had an on-staff physical therapist, and I booked my appointments with them to prevent me from having to travel several times a week. I finished my session, trying to ignore how little the exercises were working. I was still bound to the chair except for very short distances.

I started toward the exit when a woman and her little boy caught my eye. "Cynthia!" I hadn't seen her since I'd gotten back.

She ran over, carrying Callum on her hip. She set him down, and we embraced. "You look so much better! I'm so happy."

"How is Callum?" I smiled at him.

He jumped up and down. "I rode in a big truck!"

"I knew you would." I made a mental note to get some cars and trucks for him.

"How's Luna?"

"She's doing great. I'll have to bring her by for a play date really soon." I looked at Cynthia's growing belly. "How's your other little one?"

"The doctor said everything looks great. We're here for Callum's PT session. Lachlan set us up with a support group at Boston children's hospital."

"A support group?"

She smiled at Callum. "He has something called Achondroplasia dwarfism. There are other kids with it who also come to the group."

"I've made lots of friends," Callum added.

"I'm so happy for both of you. Do you have everything you need here? Is there anything I can do for either of you?"

"Bryn, this is a dream. I never imagined how amazing life could be. Your generosity is unbelievable. Thank you so much."

I was bursting with happiness. "You're welcome for all of it. I'm grateful you believed in me and were brave enough to see all of it through. What are your plans for the future?"

She reached into her pocket. "Lachlan gave me the keys to one of the apartments today. It's beautifully furnished and everything."

We talked a bit longer until they had to get to their session. Callum's fate had turned from grim into one of friends, trucks, and happiness. Seeing Cynthia made me realize I wanted to know how Lilly was doing. I went to see my receptionist, and she gave me Lilly's room number. I knocked on her door and on the second knock she opened.

Her eyes widened, and she threw her arms around me. "Bryn! I've wanted to come to visit you but wanted you to get settled first."

I smiled at her belly, remembering how I thought she'd lose the baby the last time I saw her. "How's your little one?"

"They're doing great. It's twins."

"Twins? Congratulations!"

"Thank you!" She moved over to her mini-fridge. "Can I get you tea or anything?"

"No, I'm fine."

She sat on the edge of her bed. "It's a bit overwhelming."

"We have staff who can help you when the babies are born, even at night. All you have to do is ask. I'm going to ask you, and you tell me the truth about how much help you want."

"Thank you! That would be amazing."

"I'll bring by a catalog for you to select things for your babies. Also, how would you like to move into an apartment before they are born?"

"I'd love that! I appreciate this room very much but..." She hesitated.

"But, you need a home with room for your babies."

She nodded. "You've made all of this so much easier. I don't know what I would have done without you."

"I'm glad you had the courage to leave."

I told Lilly goodbye and made more notes of things I needed to do. There were three more cave people I had to know about, and I knew where one was. Lachlan had told me Atticus did morning activities with the children. I found him in the makeshift classroom with eleven kids sitting on a colorful rug. He changed his voice for each character. I stood and watched until he finished with the children.

As the kids filed out, he spotted me and grinned. "Bryn! How are you?"

"I'm great. I wanted to see how you and Deborah were."

"We're awesome. I got my GED last month and am getting my teaching degree online. After I'm done, I'd like to apply to be the teacher here. I'll get to teach things other than nonsense."

"That'll feel liberating."

"It already does." He started picking up books and putting them away. "Deborah has missed you. We wanted to come to see you but thought we'd wait until you got settled."

"It seems everyone has had the same thought. I appreciate everyone being thoughtful. For future reference, there will never be a time I don't want to see any of you. How is Deborah?"

"She's doing great. She's finishing her GED classes and isn't sure what she wants to do after that. We're getting married."

"I couldn't be happier for both of you."

"Thank you, Bryn. Without your courage to steal that map and make a plan to get us all out of there, I'd have lost her."

"All of you helping me is the only way it worked. Do you know what happened with Jack?"

"Yeah, his family came to pick him up. He has a sister, brother, and a puppy. It was the best reunion I've ever seen."

My phone rang, and I excused myself to the hall. I pulled it from a pocket in the side of my wheelchair. Ryo had attached the storage, so I'd quit leaving my phone behind. He figured if it was in my chair, I'd always have it. The only issue now was that I constantly forgot to charge it. Lachlan often remembered for me and put it back in the pocket each morning.

"Hello, Bryn West?" The voice on the other end greeted my hello.

"This is her."

"It's Detective Miller. I'm not sure if you remember me."

"I remember you."

"It's time for Brigid Feldman's trial. You're going to be getting a subpoena to testify, but I wanted to give you a heads up before it arrives."

"Thank you. I appreciate that." I hung up and told myself to calm. I knew this would probably happen, but now that it was here, I didn't know how I felt.

"Are you ready for this?" Lachlan squeezed my hand.

"I hope so."

He wheeled me toward the courtroom, and Ryo held the door open. They had subpoenaed both Morely and me to testify in court. My mom and dad had the kids back at the hotel. My bright pink wheelchair would be a giant neon sign that showed what Brigid Feldman had done to me. They brought her in handcuffed, wearing a pantsuit with her hair in a bun. She didn't make eye contact with me as I was brought to the front. My father was a trial lawyer and had prepared me for what to expect.

They swore me in and spent a lengthy amount of time asking me questions. The prosecution went first, followed by the defense.

Brigid's lawyer grilled me. "Did you see the defendant give you the poison?"

"No, she gave it to the man I was living with and told him it was vitamins for me."

He threw question after question at me, trying to discredit my testimony. I knew he was only doing his job, but it wore me down.

By the time they let me off the stand, I wanted to pass out. Lachlan took me out of my chair, so I could rest against him. "You're the most amazing person I know," he whispered and kissed my temple.

The judge hit his gavel on the podium and dismissed court for the day. We went back to the hotel. Winter blew a chill through the air, making it unwise to venture outside much. Morely and Ryo decided to call it a night. With a two-month-old, they had to get sleep where they could. We ate dinner with my parents, and on the way back to our room, I saw a poster for an indoor music festival.

Lachlan caught me looking at it. "Do you want to go?"

"Tonight? It's the last night for it."

"Unless you're too tired."

"No, I'm wide awake. I need to unwind."

We drove to the festival, and Lachlan placed Luna on my lap as we entered a massive room. Booths pertaining to all things music lined seven different rows.

My mom pointed at an area where toddlers were playing with plastic instruments. "Can I take Luna?"

I nodded, and my mom and baby left for fun with Dad following behind them.

"Where do you want to go first?" Lachlan asked.

"We might as well go up the first row."

He pushed me forward, and on the third row, we came to a man strumming his guitar. He sat in a wheelchair like me, and I asked Lachlan to stop. He played a song I knew, so I started singing with him. He looked up and smiled at me. He started the second song, and I sang that as well. After the third, he finally stopped.

"Where did you learn to sing like that?"

"I just always have. As a little girl, the man who raised me played his guitar, and I could hear all the notes. All I did was match my voice to them."

"You matched your voice all on your own?"

"Yeah, each note sounds distinct to me."

His eyebrows shot up. "That's a rare talent."

"I think it was given to me by God because my sisters needed comfort."

"Makes sense why you have an angel's voice."

I looked up to see a crowd had gathered. The man and I sang a few more songs together. At the end, everyone clapped for us. "Let me get you my card." He grabbed some metal sticks, stuck his arms through loops, and held bars that stuck out of each one. He used them to stand, and that's when I noticed he had straps around both of his legs. He walked over to his bag and grabbed a business card. He noticed me staring. "Do you like them?"

"What are they?"

"Leg braces and arm crutches. They let me do more than sit in this chair."

"They're amazing!"

An amused grin spread across his face. "I don't think I ever met anyone so impressed."

"Where did you get them?"

He wrote down the name of the company where he got his. "What's your name, by the way? I swear you look familiar."

"I was a Youtube star once." I waved as Lachlan wheeled me away.

We met back up with my parents and left the festival. Tomorrow we'd be back in court. I pulled myself into bed, humming.

Lachlan held me, burying his face in my hair. "You're extra happy for the day we've had."

"I'm going to walk again."

"I don't have any doubt you will."

I thought about the man's equipment as I drifted to sleep. I was going to walk again.

We sat back in court, and I wondered when all of this would end.

The judge read his notes. "Would the prosecution please call your next witness."

"Yes, your honor, we would like to call Zachariah Bronze to the stand."

A man with greying hair and matching beard stood in the back of the courtroom. He used a cane to slowly limp to the front. I looked at Morely and worried about all the blood draining from her face.

All the Way

Bryn

Z achariah took the stand, and they swore him in.

The prosecutor stepped forward and started the questions. "Do you know the defendant?"

"Yes, that's Brigid Feldman," he said with clenched teeth.

"How do you know the defendant?"

"She was the healer for the community I'd lived in since birth."

The prosecutor asked a few more questions and got to the ones about the poison. "Were you aware Ms. Feldman was giving you poison?"

"Yes."

"What reason did you accept this poison?"

"The men in the community have great power. If I had not, they would have given it to my daughter."

"Did you have any ability to stop this?"

"No, if I had fought back, they would have killed my daughter and me."

The defense started their line of questioning. Ryo held tightly to a crying Morely. It would be her turn to testify tomorrow. She'd known that the cult had sentenced her to purification for our other sisters and me escaping. She hadn't known Zachariah was the reason the punishment wasn't carried out until she'd read the journal. She was to testify on what she knew about Brigid and purification. Court dismissed for the day, and Morely ran toward the exit. We followed her, and I spotted her running toward Zachariah.

She cupped her hands to her mouth. "Zachariah Bronze!"

He turned around and stared at her. "Olivia?"

I could see her heavy breathing from where I stood. She shook her head and finally got out. "It's Morely."

He hobbled forward and threw his arms around her. She returned his hug, and they both stood there shaking.

He held her face. "You look just like her. I can't believe this."

"I can't either."

We invited him to dinner after that. My parents met us at the restaurant with all the kids. Zachariah climbed out of the taxi as Ryo and Morely were getting their kids out of the car. I had Luna on my lap as we went inside to eat Italian. Morely cradled Oliver, and Ryo held Dahlia's hand as they walked up to Zachariah.

"These are my children. Dahlia, and this is Oliver Zachariah." Morely tilted Oliver so he could be seen better.

Zachariah looked like he'd won a million dollars. We sat at the table talking, and Morely gave him most of our story. Ryo told jokes, making all of us laugh, which earned him nods from Zachariah.

Morely pushed her salad around with a fork, looking concerned. "Did you ever find my mother?"

Zachariah's eyes fell into sadness. "No, I'm sorry. I've never stopped looking. I know she grew up in a city called Stockton,

California. I went there looking for her, but there were too many Garcias for me to get far."

"I have an aunt in California. I found her through heritage DNA testing. She didn't know who my parents could be because she has fifteen siblings, and all their kids have lots of kids. With everything going on in my life, I haven't spoken to her in months. Maybe now that I have a name, she can help."

We all got up to leave, and once outside, Zachariah stopped us all. He looked at Ryo, Lachlan, and me. "Can I hug the three of you?" We all nodded, and he started with Ryo. "Thank you for being a soul of laughter and kindness for my daughter." He hugged Lachlan. "Thank you for being a soul of mercy and delivering good wherever you go." He smiled at me and bent down to hug me. "You and I know each other's pain. Thank you for being the brave soul I prayed for."

We got ready to get in our cars when Morely asked one last thing. "How did you survive?"

"Someone, all of you know, helped me. Rachel Slater visited me and said her husband was taken by the corrupt world. She'd decided the Above One wanted her to be the gatekeeper in his absence. She felt the Above One told her to set me free. At first, I didn't want to go because I thought they'd punish you, but she said she'd tell them she'd found me dead and had taken me on a cart to the furnace for a proper release. Those undergoing purification weren't given services, so no one would have thought twice about it. She led me out of an exit I hadn't known about and gave me a phone. She told me to keep pushing 911 and a green button until I reached someone. She gave me a bag with silver pills, water, and food. I was so sick, and it took me two days before the phone finally worked. I was taken to a hospital and spared. When I finally gained enough strength to go back for you, Morely, the caverns were emptied. I didn't know where they'd taken you."

Morely and Zachariah exchanged information, and Lachlan placed me in the car. I watched the scenery zoom by, realizing it was time to pay Rachel Slater another visit.

We sat through days of testimony and evidence. Brigid didn't testify on her own behalf but rather pleaded the fifth. Detective Miller took to the stand. He'd located Brigid's journal. A handwriting expert had determined it was in her writing, and fingerprints also concurred. The prosecution asked Miller to read a passage.

"Bryn Moretti is evil to the highest degree. I despise her kind, who thinks they have a right to lead others astray. I saw her smug face on the television. She spoke of how she helped others leave our ways. I knew we had to claim her and bring her back in to experience hell and punishment. My desire to see her punished has paid off. The elders agreed because the oracle has lost her mind some time ago. I believe dementia may be to blame. She thought Bryn's baby was her replacement. I have chosen the most painful form of death for Bryn, and even if she somehow finds rescue, the damage is too great. Not even her precious medicines will spare her from the poison. May her torment never cease."

With each word he read, the more I crumbled. Lachlan took me from my chair, and I cried silently with my head in his lap. His arms stayed tightly around me as if they were a shield to everything being said. I'd made peace with Brigid because I thought she was blinded by faith like Rachel. I thought maybe they'd tortured her, but she held only cruelty. She'd done this to me to make me suffer.

She started the chain of events that led to all that had happened with my second kidnapping.

Miller was asked to read more passages. When they detailed more of what Brigid had done to me, Lachlan picked me up and walked out of the courtroom. He always knew when to protect me.

The jurors rose. "We, the jury, find the defendant guilty." They went on to list all the charges, and they had found her guilty of all of them, including two counts of attempted murder for Zachariah and me. In the end, Brigid's own words had sunk her.

The time came for victim impact statements. Both Lachlan and I were allowed to give them.Lachlan went first. "A week after the most joyous day of my life, I found myself in the deepest sorrow. My wife and newborn daughter were stolen from me. When I got them back, I found my wife on death's door. A poison had destroyed her liver to the extent she needed a new one. I gave her half of mine. If you meet my wife, something becomes clear quickly, and that is her love for life. She loves to dance in the rain, climb mountains, and run across the beach, feeling the ocean against her legs. Brigid Feldman decided to poison my wife, and in doing that, she made it, so my wife has to fight every day to do the things she loves. I was recently told I am a man of mercy, and I would like to think that true. In this case, mercy should not belong to Brigid Feldman. Not only did she show none, but if she is granted mercy and released back into society, she will destroy everyone around her."

I went next. "I woke up this morning to start my routine and realized my wheelchair was across the room because my husband carried me to bed the night before. He'd left to get us both breakfast, and I wanted to see the sunrise from the window. I tried to walk to my chair but couldn't make it. I fell halfway. This is what my life has become. It's become a life of halfway. I can halfway do everything for myself before I need help. I've always liked giving help not receiving it, and this new way of life is constant depression and anxiety. My days are full of struggle to function, and my nights are full of nightmares. I have three different medications I have to take for the rest of my life because of the poison. I would normally grant mercy to someone who hurt me, but I fear for anyone else who might meet a free Brigid Feldman. I plead for mercy for those she will harm if she is released before the end of her life."

The judge deliberated after the last of the impact statements. We were called back into the courtroom, and the judge delivered the sentence. "Brigid Feldman, overwhelming evidence has shown the torture you unleashed on your victims. You showed no mercy to those you brought great harm. For this reason, I am sentencing you to three life sentences to be served consecutively."

The judge continued speaking, but I wheeled myself out of the courtroom, needing air. A lady opened the courtroom door for me, and I peered down all the steps. Pigeons pecked the concrete at the bottom, and a bicyclist pedaled past. In the distance, I saw a street vendor handing people plates of something. The clear sky gave room for the sun to shine on me. I'd gotten justice, but I couldn't walk down these steps. I heard a door open behind me, and I looked up to see Zachariah with his cane.

He put his hand on my shoulder. "It gets better eventually."

"The neuropathy?"

"No, the accepting of it and the ability to do things all the way."

I wiped a tear. "I want to dance."

"Spend every day getting stronger, and someday you'll dance."

"How is she doing?" I asked the receptionist.

"Really well. She's in the garden today."

I'd come to see Rachel Slater for the first time since my dad had helped me get her sentence overturned. We got her into one of the best mental health facilities in the country. She'd most likely spend the rest of her life there. While she'd probably never be well enough to live independently, it was a much better life than prison. They had regular activities she could be a part of, and the rooms were top of the line in comfort. She'd get regular therapy to help her with her trauma.

An orderly led me down the white hall with blue-tiled floor. Nothing hung on the walls, and we passed several cream metal doors. He brought me outside where we found Rachel sitting on a bench, staring at two monarch butterflies fluttering around red tulips. A little stone path wrapped around to a shallow pond with a stone water feature with an angel squirting water. A willow tree rose behind her, providing shade. Every color of flower brightened the green grass that dripped dew. It reminded me of Aurora's garden back in Denver. I moved in front of Rachel, and she looked up slowly until she found me smiling at her.

Recognition flashed in her eyes. "Little bird?"

"Yes, Mama, it's me."

She grabbed my hands and stopped. She examined them carefully. "I hurt you."

"Yes, a long time ago."

"I was scared."

I nodded. "I know."

"James said if we found no correction for you, cleansing was all that could be done." Her eyes overflowed with tears. "I thought it was only water. I didn't know he'd cursed it to hurt you. I thought your hands would be washed, and he'd leave it at that."

I took her hand in both of mine. "I have forgiven you of everything."

She smiled, but it fell. She looked down at a patch of blue flowers growing next to the bench. "Why is the corrupt world so beautiful?" Her eyes pleaded with me to dispel her confusion.

"Because the Above One healed it."

Her eyes widened. "He did?"

"Yes, he did."

Her smile returned. "I'm glad. Maybe we will all find happiness now."

"I think we will."

I Get to Love You

Bryn

I sat on the edge of my bed, taking in the blue jay sitting in the tree outside my window. I used the grabber by my bed and opened my dresser drawer for a pair of socks. I'd gotten great at using it over the last few months. Brigid's trial had ended four months ago, and today was a big day. Luna toddled into the room with Lachlan hovering close behind her. She wouldn't fall on his watch.

She held her chubby baby arms up to me, and I picked her up. She touched my face, and I gave her forehead a kiss. "You're becoming an amazing walker."

"No falls today either," Lachlan added.

"How can she fall with your arms inches from her body at all times."

"She must be protected. That's my job."

"Sometimes, we have to learn to fall to know how to pick ourselves up."

He shook his head. He might let her go when she turned thirty. He went to the closet and brought me the white sneakers I'd picked for today. They weren't as dressy as they should be for the occasion, but they would have to do. I needed excellent traction for my leg braces to keep me upright.

Our doorbell rang, and Lachlan took Luna with him. I placed the braces under each leg and yanked the straps tight all the way around my legs. My arm crutches worked well to get me to standing. I made it to my chair and sat down, sticking the crutches behind me in the compartment Ryo had rigged.

Lachlan returned with my dress, which was a dusty blue. The lace sleeves ended halfway to my elbows, and the neckline dipped to a V but covered well. The skirt flowed to right above my heels, and I hoped it would cover the shoes. Lachlan helped me put it on and smoothed it out as I sat to prevent wrinkling. Someone knocked on the bedroom door, and Lachlan let in my mom.

She had a bag over her shoulders and set it on the bed. "Are you ready for your hair?" She started brushing and braiding it. I watched in the mirror as she put it into an elaborate bun and pinned it well. She sprayed it thoroughly until I thought I'd drown in the stuff.

She pulled out her fancy bag with roses painted all over the white background. "Makeup?"

"Yes, please."

She started, and I kept my eyes closed as she worked. My mother had grown up as a socialite and knew how to quickly do makeup well. Her mother had expected her to have everything perfect at a moment's notice.

She stood back and looked at me. "My baby is still the prettiest girl to exist." She kissed my head.

"Thank you, Mom. You look amazing yourself. "

She had her own hair pinned and wore a pretty long-sleeved maroon dress. My mother still looked vibrant and gorgeous in her fifties. I had a feeling she'd look the same at eighty. She felt timeless to me. She wheeled me out to where Lachlan had Luna in her fluffy white dress. He tenderly brushed her hair like she might go bald if he didn't take the utmost care. He put a little white bow on the side and inspected it. He turned around to grab her shoes, and she put her white basket on her head, destroying his effort.

He turned around. "Hey, silly girl." He tickled her, and she giggled. "Let's try this again," he said.

He took the basket off her head and put it on the table behind him. He brushed her hair and replaced the bow. Luna still had the thickest hair. It had lightened to match my brown and ran in ringlets nearly to her shoulders. Her eyes still matched her daddy's stunning blue ones, and I had hope that she'd keep them. I loved looking into hers and seeing a part of her that was Lachlan.

She tried to stand in her puffy dress and wobbled. Luna grabbed Lachlan's finger, and he helped her to me. I placed her in my lap, and we strolled through the tunnel. Jada's house was abuzz with everyone running around, putting the final touches on decorations. Caters were moving trays of food where they needed to go.

Lachlan went to find the other guys, and I set out to find Morely. Oliver rested on his tummy, reaching for a light-up mirror toy. His tiny tux and black dress shoes were almost too much cuteness. Dahlia and Adely spotted me and twirled in their dresses that matched Luna's. Luna squirmed, and I helped her to the ground. She tried to copy the big girls' twirls but landed on her butt. It was a good thing Lachlan wasn't here to fuss over her minor injuries. Adely helped Luna to her feet, and slowly the three girls twirled in a circle.

A woman was pinning my sister's hair, and I took in her lace flowing dress. Her sleeves were around the same length mine were, but the V of her neckline dipped slightly lower. The white dress curved gently around her body and suited her perfectly.

She spotted me in the mirror. "Come here, sister."

I turned my chair to face her, and we grabbed hands. "You're getting married today!" I squealed.

"I'm so happy. I can't believe my life." She blinked quickly. "I have to keep these tears in until the end." She gentle dabbed her eyes.

"Joyful tears are very hard to keep in."

"Yes, for you, they definitely are. You are the most joyful crier I have ever known," she said.

"Darling!" Ryo shouted from somewhere behind us.

Morely ducked. "What is he doing here?"

"I'll go chase him out." I found Ryo with his back to the wall outside the room. "What are you doing? You want gobs of bad luck to rain down on your marriage."

He shrugged. "Whatever will be will be. I needed to see you."

"Me? Why?"

"I wanted to make sure the leg braces felt right today or if I needed to adjust them. I know this is a big deal for you."

"You just don't want me to trip on your wedding day."

He raised an eyebrow. "Of course, I don't want you to trip on my wedding day. I prefer you trip on no days."

"My braces are fine." I patted his spiked hair. "Red tips for love?"

"Sure. We'll go with that. That'll be good for later when I see Morely.

"You go get ready to marry my sister and let me worry about my legs. Don't look all intense when I walk either. Lachlan will have me, and you know it."

"He might be too distracted with your beauty to pay attention to your footwork."

I gave him a little shove. "Go!"

"Fine. Fine. I'm cheering for you." He started to leave.

"Ryo?"

He turned. "Yeah?"

"Thank you for always being my best friend."

"For as long as I breathe, then I might haunt you and do some fun things to freak you out."

"If you were to die before me, I hope that you would."

He grinned before disappearing into the auditorium.

Koa came running out from a side door. "Am I late? Did they start?" She spotted me and paused to catch her breath. "Phew! I thought for sure Morely was going to give me that look she always gave us when we did something she didn't approve of."

I straightened her dress that her running had disheveled. "I remember that look."

"It was a scary look," Capri said, joining us in line.

"You guys realize I can hear you?" Morely shouted.

"We love you!" Koa shouted back.

I looked down at her shoes. "Sneakers again."

"I have to be fair. If Capri can't get me in heels, neither can Morely. You're one to talk." She nodded toward my shoes."

"I have a good reason. I need traction to walk."

"And I need comfortable feet to make it through the fluff."

Dahlia came out, pulling a white decorated wagon with Oliver and Luna in it. Adely trailed closely behind them.

"I think I'm going to die from adorable overload." Koa helped Dahlia make it to the front of the line.

"Maybe you'll have a couple of your own someday," I said innocently.

"Bahahaha! Not happening. I'll enjoy all my nieces and nephews when I come to visit. Then I get to go home and sleep in until noon if I want."

The music began to play, and Lachlan hurried over to me, handing me my arm crutches. I stood, and we linked arms. He gave me an intense look. "How is it possible you stun me every time I look at you?"

"You must stun quite easily."

He chuckled. "No, your beauty surpasses everything I've ever seen."

"How can you guys still look at each other so googly-eyed. It's not even your wedding." Koa turned around and hurried off after Dahlia, who was rapidly pulling the wagon.

"Maybe you should be paying attention to your job and not us," I said.

Koa waved her arms at my words and caught up to the wagon. Zachariah came out in a tux with his grey hair slicked back, and his beard neatly trimmed. He hooked arms with Morely.

Lachlan handed me a tissue. "I stocked up because I knew you'd need them."

I gently dabbed my face. "I'm glad my mom bought the best makeup. It may never wash off, but at least the tears won't smear it."

We moved forward, and I took steps as I'd practiced for the last month. I could have just had someone push me, but I wanted to walk so badly for my sister. I tried to hurry, and Lachlan whispered in my ear. "Take your time. No one minds. Especially not Morely and Ryo." I slowed down to a manageable pace. It took a lot of effort, but I'd accomplished my goal of making it to the front. Lachlan helped me into a chair and took his spot next to Ryo and Thane.

Morely started up the aisle, and my favorite was always watching the groom. Ryo could barely stand in place as Morely walked to him. It was like he wanted to run to her and kiss her on the spot. She made it to the front, they clasped hands, and both their faces lit up like the sun. Zachariah took in the scene of his daughter happy before turning to me and giving me a thumbs up. I grinned back, and he took his seat next to my parents.

Ryo started off the vows. "Morely Hope, you are my one and only. I get to love you until the end of our days. I plan to wake up every morning with that feeling you put in my chest when I look at you. I plan to still feel that happiness when we're ninety and beyond. For the intensity of my love will never fade with any action, time, or event. I promise to bring you flowers every week so every time you look at the table, you can see I thought of you on a day I wasn't obligated. I promise to let no harm befall you, and my arms will destroy the sad and scary things life brings to us. I promise your life will always be full of laughter and kindness. I promise to be faithful and cherish you with every ounce of my life. I promise every bit of these words until death do us part."

Morely had given up on stopping her tears as she started her vows. "Ryo Bae Paik, you are my hero, my laughter, my all things good. I promise to make our home a place you love to come home to. A place you will find sanctuary from all the things life will throw at you. I promise to support your goals not out of obligation as your wife, but because I will always believe in you. No matter how crazy the idea seems, I will always believe you can make it happen.

I promise my arms will cause your sorrow and fear to fade. For as long as we hold to each other, we will survive any night. I will forever feel like the most blessed girl because I get to love you, and that makes everything right. I promise to be faithful and cherish you with every ounce of my life. I promise every bit of these things until death do us part."

The preacher had them do the rings. When that concluded, he turned toward me. "The bride's sister Bryn West is going to sing."

I used my arm crutches to stand, and I sang, "I Get To Love You" by Ruelle. The song ended, and the preacher announced the kiss. Ryo grabbed Morely and hugged her before spinning her around and dipping her back into a passionate kiss. When they came up for air, Morely's cheeks were pink, and she had the largest smile I'd ever seen on her face. They ran down the aisle. Before stepping out of the room, Ryo lifted her in the air and kissed her again. "An extra for luck," he said as he intertwined their fingers and exited.

The reception was a giant celebration, and I sat in my chair watching most of it. I soaked in Lachlan dancing with Luna in his arms and Ryo dancing with Dahlia and Morely at the same time. My parents took to the dance floor, still full of love in their eyes for each other. They were proof that a marriage could last through a lifetime of difficulties.

A carriage arrived for Ryo and Morely. Ryo opened the door and bowed. "Your carriage awaits, my lady."

Morely held up her finger and hugged me. "I'm so proud of you, my sweet, sweet sister. Your strength trumps all others."

I squeezed her. "I love you and am so happy for you."

She disappeared into the carriage with Ryo, and horses took them away. My parents would have Dahlia and Oliver for the two weeks they'd be gone. Zachariah said he'd come over a lot to help.

I helped clean up the best I could until Lachlan found me with a sleeping Luna cradled in his arms. He placed her on my lap and pushed me back to our house. He got Luna in her crib and dropped to his knees behind me, undoing my hair. He kissed my neck. "This is my favorite part of weddings" He kissed again, causing shivers down my spine.

I closed my eyes, absorbing all of his touches. "What part is that?"

"The part I get to remove your dress." He picked me up and ran me into the room. He softly flopped me on the bed, and our mouths met as he pushed my dress off my shoulders. In the euphoric high of a joyful night, Lachlan closed it by bringing all of me alive.

Epilogue- Endlessly Proven

♥

Lachlan- Four years later

I watched Bryn's determined eyes and set jaw. "I could just carry you the rest of the way."

She sent me a glare. "Not a chance."

"I was joking. Kind of."

She ignored me and continued her hike up the trail. She gripped her arm crutches as a precaution, but she'd left her leg braces in the wagon her parents had pulled up before us. It took another twenty minutes, but we made it to our ledge overlooking Glacier National Park. Our mountain goats still climbed, and our buffalo still grazed. An eagle soared, matching our spirits.

"I told you I could do it," she said proudly.

I gave her a quick peck. "I never doubted you."

She shot me a skeptical look. "Yes, the fifty times you asked if you could carry me said otherwise."

I touched her stomach. "I was worried the baby would get tired."

"The exercise is good for both us. The doctor said so."

"I'm a doctor too."

She smiled, amused. "You are, and I'm very proud."

"Daddy! Mommy! You took forever!" Luna ran out of the tent and straight for my arms. I tossed her in the air, and she giggled.

Anna came out of the tent with two-year-old Orion on her hip. "Mommy!" He reached for Bryn, and she plopped into her waiting chair. He crawled onto her lap, and she wheeled him over to where Ryo was starting the fire.

"Luna, let's play tag!" Dahlia yelled.

Luna wiggled out of my arms to chase after Dahlia and Oliver. "Stay away from the ledge!" I called to them."

I smiled at my family grateful for the amazing life we had now. Because of the transplant, Bryn had to wait two years to have another baby. Once we started trying, she'd gotten pregnant with Orion almost immediately, which quelled her fears that the poison had stolen future children. He was wild to Luna's calm. Bryn said she'd expected it because her mother had warned her. Our third would be our last and exactly what we'd planned.

Over the last four years, Bryn had strengthened her legs. She'd never walk normally again, but she'd stop letting it change her life long ago. She'd found a way to do everything she loved in a way that continued to awe me. Bryn defined resilience.

She kept our children the focus of her life while running Jada's house full time.Hundreds of women and children had found safety within its walls. Each one had found healing physically, emotionally, and mentally thanks to the counselors and staff who gave their time to carry out my wife's vision.

The sun began to slip in the west, and the sky turned orange and pink. All of us sat around the campfire, telling stories and singing songs. When the first stars began to show, Luna pointed at the sky. "Daddy, a star fell."

"Quick, make a wish. Don't tell me, or it won't come true."

She closed her eyes tightly. "I wished for the bestest thing, Daddy."

Bryn sang to a sleepy Orion as green sputtered on the horizon. She and I caught each other's eyes and passed a look that only held meaning to us. She handed Orion to Anna, and I whispered in Luna's ear to go listen to the story Uncle Ryo was telling with dramatic hand movements and strange voices.

I picked up Bryn and carried her to where trees blocked us from the view of the others. I held her against my chest as the lights became vibrant and took over the park. The swirls and leaps of magical lights brought the tears I wiped from my wife's face. I played "Outnumbered" on my phone, and I helped Bryn to her feet. With her safe and steady in my arms, we swayed and danced.

"I'll love you until the end of time, firefly."

"Until the Universe turns to dust, I will love you more than the sky."

Never were any truer words spoken than they were on that night. Bryn and I had defeated the tallest mountains and the deepest valleys, always finding our strength from each other. Stars fell around us as a meteor shower added to the Northern lights. All of nature rejoiced because we had endlessly proven that love vanquishes darkness.

Bonus: The Window

♥

My firefly with crumpled wings sits in the window with sunlight cascading down her face. I carried her to the glass that views crashing waves, bringing treasures to the shoreline. A small collection of shells and starfish she can no longer inspect with easy movement.

Her hand rests on her belly, where our third child sleeps. His strong kicks live up to his name Orion. A constellation gazed on in a tiny cabin where magic was made. That magic lives with angels now. My son's presence makes his mother's face glow more than the sun already is. The smile on her lips carries joy from seeing the sky. A joy she never takes for granted.

I have loved her from the moment she wore pink in the moonlight and twirled in my arms for the first time. We watched falling stars on rooftops and kissed in the rain. I have loved her since all those moments. Those moment took my feet a thousand miles to reach her because her heart called to mine across an unfathomable distance.

Her heart has never stopped calling to mine since. Even as she sits in the window, most of me longs to be next to her, but my eyes choose to watch her instead. I watch her endlessly, wanting to help the minute she struggles, but I know she has to do most of it herself. She must learn to fly on her own—a different type of flight than any she's had before.

As she watches out the window, I see no evidence of all her falls that happen daily, leaving bruises behind. I see no sign of her battle to make it to breakfast each morning. I see no sign of defeat from the days she can use only her chair.

What I see on my girl's face is a love for the beautiful things that make up the world. She finds them in the darkness. She always has. She pulled the smallest thing from an ugly cave and turned it into something that brought light and hope. Something that held her dreams for another day. Another day of survival until that survival turned into thriving. Thriving turned into soaring wings.

My firefly sits in the window with crumpled wings, but she holds no despair. She sees wonder that fills her with gratitude for a window that lets in the sun.

Bonus Short Story: Unexpected Roots

❤

I typed in the last patient report of the day and glanced at the clock. Anxiousness for home was prominent in my mind since Nash's birth a little over a month ago. I'd taken six weeks off but always wished I'd had more. My practice needed my return. I loved being a doctor, but time away from my family was something that bothered me.

I waved at Marty, my nurse, on the way out. "I'll see you tomorrow. Tell Dave hi for me."

"Sure thing. He says you need to come over for the Super Bowl in January."

"Count me in," I said.

"Bring the wife and babes if you want."

"I'll see if the wife is up to it. Nash has been keeping her up pretty regular."

Marty sighed. "I remember that stage. I miss and don't miss it at the same time."

I put on my coat and hat. "I hear you."

I went through the waiting room to walk Nicole to her car. I didn't like my receptionist traveling through our long parking lot alone at night. Burned out bulbs toward where she parked her vehicle made it especially dangerous. The landlord had yet to listen to my requests, and I was about to find a tall ladder and do it myself.

Nicole spotted me and nodded toward the exit. "He's been waiting a while. Said he won't leave until he gets to talk to you."

I turned around to see a man with a black stocking cap over his head and a brown trench coat. He appeared middle-aged with a greying beard.

I approached him. "Can I help you, sir?"

He set the magazine beside him. "Are you, Dr. West? Lachlan West." He spoke with a heavy Irish accent, which was unusual for the area. I was used to the Boston one.

"Yeah, that's me."

"I'm your father."

I let out a short laugh. "I don't have a father. My mom was a drug addict who couldn't tell me who my father was. She didn't have a clue."

"Lizzy didn't tell me about you until a week ago. She gave you my father's first name and her last name. You're a Murphy."

"I'm sorry. I have to walk my receptionist out and get home to my family." I started toward the door where Nicole waited for me.

"Please. This is a doctor's office. You have those paternity kits, don't ya?"

"Sir, we need to lock up."

He stepped out the door. "*Please*. I want to get to know you."

"I'm sorry. I really must be going."

His face fell, and he brought out a small card from his pocket. "This is my contact info. Please take it in case you change your mind."

I took the card, hoping it would make him leave, which he did. I told Nicole goodnight and climbed into my car. Taking a brief look at the card showed me his name was Declan Murphy. His name and phone number were all it revealed. Driving home, my mind stayed deep in thought. Was it possible he could be right? The guard at the gate let me in, and I drove the road along the beach.

Inside my house, Bryn rocked Nash, looking like she could collapse any second. "You're home. I'm so happy you're home. Kiss me!" Bryn never failed to greet me with enthusiasm.

I gave her a kiss and rubbed the head of my baby son. "How is he?"

"Hungry. Endlessly hungry."

"Mommy looks tired." I gave her another kiss.

"I'm so tired but happy tired."

I took the baby from her. "I'll get him settled. You need any help?"

"Maybe. I took my braces off for the night, and I'm too tired to put them back on."

I changed my son and got him to sleep. I returned to find Bryn had nodded off. I scooped her up.

She groaned. "What's happening?"

"I'm carrying you to bed because you fell asleep on the couch."

"I wasn't sleeping. Only resting."

"You were snoring a bit."

Her eyes opened. "I don't snore."

I grinned and carried her to the bathroom and set her in front of her bars. She gripped them as I handed her the things she needed for her nightly routine. She stumbled a bit, and I caught her, carrying her to bed.

She became a starfish on the bed. "Help me out of my clothes."

"Gladly." I grinned and got her pajamas.

I showered and followed my routine before shutting out the lights.

Bryn snuggled into my chest. "Showered Lachlan smells amazing."

"You smell me every night."

"And it never gets less amazing."

I laughed and kissed her head. "Something strange happened tonight." I told her about the man.

Her eyes snapped open. "What if he's telling the truth? What if he's your father?"

"It doesn't make any sense. Why would my mom tell him now after all this time?"

"I'm not sure, but it sounds like you didn't give him much time to explain."

I ran my fingers over her back. "You think I should hear him out?"

"Yeah, I do. I think you should at least get the paternity test. If he's lying, you'll know then. If he's not, this could mean great things. Luna, Orion, and Nash can meet their grandpa. This would be amazing!"

One would have thought Bryn was stacking her hopes way too high, but she was just being herself. Most things made Bryn excited.

I kissed her, drawing it out, and then brought her close. "Okay. I'll give him a call and do the test."

"This is going to be great." She yawned. "So great." Her breathing steadied, and I knew she'd already fallen asleep.

**

Sipping soda in a diner, I stared at the report, not believing that Declan Murphy was, in fact, my father. Bryn would be ecstatic and embrace him without a second thought. Bryn did that with everyone. If there was any way that she could get away with calling someone family, she would do it. Unease, excitement, and dread all battled for spots in my emotions.

He slid across from me in the booth. "This is a great day. I knew as soon as I saw your eyes that you were mine. Murphy eyes are a strong trait. I have a son."

I nodded. "Yeah, I'm still trying to take all of it in. I don't understand why my mother would have only told you about me recently."

"I came into her town and thought I'd look her up. A mutual friend we had put me in contact with her. I called her for dinner, and we went out. Then at the end, she started bugging me for money. I could tell she wasn't sober. When I offered to pay a bill for her instead of giving her cash, she got agitated. She said she raised my son and should get past child support."

I howled in laughter. "That's what she told you?"

His eye widened. "Yeah, I think I'm missing the joke."

"She told you she raised me? More like the closets raised me. Sides of the road, parks, all the places she left me raised me. Group and foster homes. All while she kept permanently branding me. I rolled up my sleeves to show some of my cigarette burns."

His eyes grew even larger. "She didn't tell me any of that. I wished I'd known. I'd have taken you home with me. She never told me about you, Lachlan. I swear it."

"I believe you. Mainly because the one time I asked about my father, she launched one of those old books that had people's phone numbers at me. We were in a hotel, and they keep them in drawers under the phone. After it hit me in the head, she told me to open it and take my pick of names because my guess was as good as hers."

His eyes watered. "I'm sorry, my boy. I'm so sorry."

At that moment, the brokenness in his gaze told me everything I needed to know. He hadn't known about me, and he was a man who saw the horror behind my mother's actions.

***

O Little Town of Bethlehem played quietly in the background as the glow of the Christmas tree lit up the beautiful face of my wife. She finished up Luna's braids and tied them off with red ribbons. Orion smashed his trucks together on the floor, and Nash babbled happily in his bouncy chair. The doorbell rang, and Bryn grinned at me so big my nerves dissipated.

I answered the door and let Declan in. "I'd like you to meet my family. These are my children. Luna, Orion, and Nash." I pointed to each of them as I said their names. "And this is the love of my life and soul mate, Bryn."

Bryn grabbed her arm crutches and pulled herself up. "We are so happy to have you here. This is such a happy day for our family. I hope you feel welcomed and loved."

"Well, I was kind of nervous, but you took care of all that with your words."

I held Orion and Luna's hands, leading them to the table, and my father joined us. I went back and brought Nash's bouncy chair in and set him close to us. We ate dinner together and talked. I watched my father smile, and the more I watched him, the more I saw the Murphy eyes. Bryn claimed our children had my eyes, but I never saw it until right then. She was right. In the eyes of that man, I could see my children.

All of my life, I'd found connections and loved people who were not my blood. My best friend Ryo always said, "blood isn't always family, and family isn't always blood." That had been my life motto. My children were the first biological family I'd ever truly had and loved. But sitting across from me at our Christmas table was a man of my roots. We shared the same family blood, and for the first time, I felt like I had a past I wanted to learn about.

Sneak Peek at The Melody of Indigo

♥

Prologue: Concert Hall

Olivia

The day I turned six, I discovered my rare gift. I gripped my mother's hand tightly as we weaved through the crowd. The man in the nice suit tipped his top hat and pointed at our seats. I kicked my energized legs and squirmed in my chair.

"When are they going to play, Mama?" I stood up and put my hands on the seat in front of me. The lady occupying the spot turned around to glare at me. I cringed and retreated to my mama.

The orchestra filed onto the stage. I watched cello players position their instruments at their knees, and I wanted to be them. I wanted to be them so badly that I studied each movement they made as they readied for the concert.

The first note struck the concert hall, and green burst into life. Red, yellow, and orange followed. Vivid fireworks that only my eyes could see glided all around the room. I lifted my hands out as though each note could be captured and treasured in my hand.

I squeezed past audience members and rushed to the bottom of the stairs. I needed to submerge myself fully in the wonder of shades and tones that coordinated with the music played by the instruments.

I ascended the stairs that led to the stage, tripping on the fourth one up. I knocked my chin on the step but picked myself up in a desperate attempt to reach my destination. I twirled next to the conductor, letting my body synchronize with the melody of indigo.

Chapter One: The Meadow

Olivia

My bow moved across my cello in long swift movements as I played "The Swan". I closed my eyes to focus on the music, but I knew all the colors I'd see if I looked. Each note had its own distinct shade. B was the prettiest note because it exploded bright indigo everywhere and appeared the most vivid.

I brought the song to a close and opened my eyes to see Carson watching me with his famous half-grin.

He pushed off from the wall he'd used for support. "You amaze me every time you move that bow across those strings. You bring the entire song to life. You're going to slay this Julliard interview."

I zipped my cello in its case. "You have so much faith in me only because you've never heard other Julliard bound people play."

"There's no way they can be better than you. You could play in the heavenly orchestra."

I laughed. "My best friend is delusional."

"Your doubt in my perceptions will be rectified when you get your acceptance letter. I'll get to say told you so all over the place."

I grabbed the handle on my cello case, rested it on my hip, and headed to the door. "I'll take your told you so if it means my greatest dream has come true."

Sadia caught up to us, almost tripping over the janitor's bucket in the process. "What time are we leaving Saturday?"

Carson took my cello from me and carried it the way I'd shown him in the past. "I think we should leave early. Five, maybe."

Sadia groaned. "Five?"

"We have nearly three thousand miles to drive. That's about forty-two hours."

She groaned. "Remind me again why we aren't flying?"

"Because it's a road trip. We have to make more memories than being cramped in a plane for hours."

We climbed into Carson's truck, and I leaned against the window until he turned on the radio. He flipped from his usual country station to the classical one for me. My gaze moved from the outside world to the air around his speakers. I watched the colors dance in perfect rhythm. The fact that no one around me could ever see them didn't seem fair.

We dropped Sadia off first, and I watched her run into the house. She stumbled over her entryway but quickly recovered. Her mind always wanted to move faster than her feet. I returned to watching my lights show. Carson kept grinning. He found my gift amusing, or rather he found me staring at the air in wonder amusing.

"Do you want to go to the meadow?" he asked.

I sat up straight. "I'd love to. Do you have time?"

"Wouldn't have suggested it if I didn't."

"Sometimes, you sacrifice too much time for me."

"That's not even possible." He drove us to the meadow, which was one of the few places in our city not consumed by capitalist ventures.

Mrs. Matthews owned it and had let me play my cello in it since I was a small child. She'd held stubbornly to the plot of land. I asked her about it once, and she said if she sold it, she wouldn't have easy access to beautiful music anymore. We parked in her driveway. I grabbed my cello, and Carson carried my folding chair. He set it up for me, and I got my cello into position.

He plopped down among the wildflowers. "Can I make a request?"

"I like it when you do. That way, I know you're pleased with the selection that you have to put up with hearing."

"There's nothing 'put up with' about your music. It's a phenomenal experience."

I rolled my eyes with a smile. "Too much of a sheltered life you have lived."

"Play 'Orange Blossom Special'. I like how into it you get. Especially the train part. What color is the train part?"

"It's multiple colors. The whole song is the train part."

He played with a long blade of yellow grass. "I meant the part that sounds like a whistle. I wish they made special glasses that transferred your vision to mine. I'd love to see your fireworks."

"I wish you could too. I wish I could see buildings the way you do. All the shapes look the same to me."

Carson and I became best friends because of our wonder in things other people couldn't see. I met him in fourth grade when I caught him staring at the side of the school. He found awe in the way buildings were designed. He could look at any building and tell how to reconstruct it in a model. The older he got, the more complicated he made his designs. Building models covered his basement.

I closed my eyes and played my heart out for Carson. After this summer, if all went well for our dreams, thousands of miles would separate us. He'd study architecture at Berkley, and I'd play my cello in the halls of Julliard.

Carson asked me to play three more songs, and I gave in until the sun dipped too low on the horizon. We packed up, and Mrs. Matthews caught us.

She stood at her front door, watching us load the truck. "I have cookies if you kids want some. They're payment for that magnificent concert."

We ate cookies with Mrs. Matthews before heading back to my house to study.

**

I looked over all my bags and zipped up the last one. I hated the feeling that I forgot something, but I had it every time I took a trip. Carson and Sadia would arrive soon, and we'd leave for New York. I located my mom in the kitchen. She handed me a plate of Huevos Rancheros and freshly made sopapillas.

I kissed her cheek. "Thank you, but isn't that a little heavy for four in the morning?"

"I needed to see you off in a way you knew I'm proud of you. Go eat!" She shooed me to the table.

"Carson had planned on stopping for donuts, but this is so much better." I gobbed honey on the still-warm sopapilla, and about died as it melted in my mouth. "I always know you're proud of me. You've always supported me since I was little and first wanted to play. I don't know if I've ever thanked you enough for my cello."

My dad had died when I was two, and my mom worked multiple jobs to support us. When I turned seven, I told her I wanted to play the cello, and she worked extra shifts and saved for a year to get me one. She saved another year to afford the lessons. I wouldn't have had the possibility of Julliard without her.

"Your happiness is gratitude enough. You'll call me every night on this trip?"

"Yes, I can't have my mama worrying. Thank you for letting me do this. I know you're nervous about it."

She sat down with her coffee mug and took my hand. "I am worried about this, but a mother has to let go sometimes and let her child live. You're eighteen, and your choices are yours. I pray I've raised you well enough that you make wise ones. Even if you don't make wise choices, I hope you know you can always come home and tell me your mistakes. Nothing will make me not accept you home."

"You're the best mother. Lots of people say that, but with mine, it is so true. Nothing has ever been truer."

"My sweet girl, no one has ever had a better daughter."

Carson waltzed in wearing his fedora, Bermuda shirt with bright orange tropical flowers, and khaki shorts. "Who's ready for a road trip?" He looked over my nearly empty plate. "That looks so much better than donuts."

"A thousand times better," I said.

Mom nodded toward the kitchen. "I already have a plate waiting for you."

Carson fist-bumped her like usual. "You are the coolest mom, Mrs. Garcia."

"I try to raise my coolness every day."

He grabbed six sopapillas. "You definitely succeed."

I rinsed off my plate and looked out the window at his truck. "Where's Sadia?"

He took out his phone. "Oh! I should text her and tell her breakfast is here instead."

Sadia came in just as happy to indulge in my mother's cooking. When we finished, my mother saw us to the door.

Carson gave her a bear hug, lifting her off the ground. "Thank you for breakfast. I promise to take care of your baby."

"I have complete faith in you, Carson. You kids make wise choices as your mothers have raised you to do." Mom turned to me and hugged me tightly. "I love you. You have fun and no nerves. Julliard won't see you coming. You have a unique gift that the world needs to experience. Never forget that."

I squeezed her tighter. "I won't because the greatest mom in the world never let me forget my worth. I love you too."

We stepped out the door, and an odd sensation ran up my spine. I shook it off, not willing to consider one road trip would change that much.

Carson nudged my arm. "Are you alright?"

"I'm fine."

He loaded my bags and cello while Sadia climbed to the back row, and I claimed shotgun. Sadia wanted plenty of room to sleep the driving away. I wanted to be close to Carson for the little time we had left together. He started the car and flipped the station from country to classical.

He reached over and squeezed my hand. "Are you ready for this?"

"Completely ready! Let's do this thing."

"You got it!" He pulled away from my house.

I watched as my childhood home disappeared with my mother safe inside. I refused to let this feeling ruin my trip. I concentrated on the colors, allowing them to soothe me the way they always did.

Follow the author

To learn more about or follow Andi J. Feron, use the link or QR code below.

https://linktr.ee/andijferon

www.ingramcontent.com/pod-product-compliance
Lightning Source LLC
Chambersburg PA
CBHW020944260626
47169CB00006B/1811